The Takeover

Muriel Spark

Penguin Books

Penguin Books Ltd, Harmondsworth,
Middlesex, England
Penguin Books, 625 Madison Avenue,
New York, New York 10022, U.S.A.
Penguin Books Australia Ltd, Ringwood,
Victoria, Australia
Penguin Books Canada Ltd, 2801 John Street,
Markham, Ontario, Canada L3R 1B4
Penguin Books (N.Z.) Ltd, 182–190 Wairau Road,
Auckland 10, New Zealand

First published in Great Britain by Macmillan 1976
First published in the United States of America
by The Viking Press 1976
Published in Penguin Books 1978
Copyright © Verwaltungs AG, 1976
All rights reserved

Made and printed in Great Britain by
Hunt Barnard Printing Ltd, Aylesbury
Set in Linotype Pilgrim

Chapter One

At Nemi, that previous summer, there were three new houses of importance to the surrounding district. One of them was new in the strict sense; it had been built from the very foundations on cleared land where no other house had stood, and had been planned, plotted, discussed with an incomprehensible lawyer, and constructed, over a period of three years and two months ('and seven days, three hours and twenty minutes,' the present occupant would add. 'Three years, two months, seven days, three hours and twenty minutes from the moment of Maggie giving the go-ahead to the moment we moved in. I timed it. God, how I timed it!')

The other two houses were reconstructions of buildings already standing or half-standing; both had foundations of Roman antiquity, and of earlier origin if you should dig down far enough, it was said. Maggie Radcliffe had bought these two, and the land on which she had put up the third house.

One was intended eventually for her son, Michael; that was the farm-house. He was to live in it when he got married.

Maggie herself was never there that previous summer, was reputed to be there, was never seen, had been, had gone, was coming soon, had just departed for Lausanne, for London.

Hubert Mallindaine, in the new-built house, had news of Maggie; had seen, had just missed, Maggie; had had a long discussion with Maggie; was always equipped to discuss knowledgeably the ins and outs of Maggie's life. He had been for years Maggie's friend number one and her central information agent.

The third house had been a large villa in bad repair. It was now in good repair, sitting in handsome grounds, with a tennis court, a swimming-pool, the old lily-pond made wholesome and the lawns newly greened. Maggie could do everything. But it had taken years and years. The Italian sense of time and Maggie's

lack of concentration due to her family troubles and involve-
ments had held things up. But the villa, too, was ready that
previous summer. In an access of financial morality, although it
was quite unnecessary, Maggie had decided to let this house for
a monthly rent to a rich businessman. She didn't need the money,
but it put Maggie in a regular sort of position. Her present
husband, Ralph Radcliffe, who also had money and never
thought of anything else, had less justification to resent the
whole idea when he could be reminded that Maggie was drawing
a rent from one of the houses. This was the summer when it was
said Maggie's marriage was going on the rocks.

Hubert Mallindaine's terrace had a view of the lake and the
Alban hills folding beyond.

Hubert needed the best view : he had so encamped himself
in his legend that Maggie had not questioned that he was entitled
to the view. His secretaries from their bedrooms also had
splendid views.

There were four secretaries that summer : Damian Runciwell,
Kurt Hakens, Lauro Moretti, Ian Mackay. Only one, Damian,
did the secretarial work.

'We can't stay here all summer, darling.'

'Darling, why not? I hate to travel.'

'Take off those earrings before you open the door to the
butcher.'

'Darling, why?'

'Did you remember the garlic?'

'My dear Kurt-o, we do not need garlic today.'

'Ian, we do . . . The salad.'

'Dearie, we have a clove of garlic for the salad. More garlic we
do not need today.'

'Oh, get out of my kitchen. Go on. You make me nervous.'

'My boredom,' said Hubert Mallindaine, the master of the
house, 'makes you all look so tawdry.' He was addressing the
others at the lunch table. 'Forgive me that I feel that way.'

'Feel what you like,' said one of them, 'but you shouldn't
say it.'

'The mushrooms are soggy. They have been done in oil. Too

much oil, too. They should have been done in butter and oil. Very little butter, very little oil.'

There was a heatwave so fierce you would have thought someone had turned it on somewhere by means of a tap, and had turned it too high, and then gone away for the summer.

Hubert lay on the sofa in his study and deplored Maggie's comparative lack of chivalry. It was siesta time and his room had been made dark. Hubert decided to talk to Maggie about air-conditioning. But this decision annoyed him. One should not find oneself in the position, he thought, of having to ask, having to wait for the opportunity to talk on practical matters with a woman of no routine. She might progress into the neighbourhood, looking gorgeous, at any moment, without advance notice. She had no sense of chivalry. A protectress of chivalry would not have left him dependent on her personal bounty for little things; Maggie should have made a settlement. Even the house, he thought, as he lay on the sofa at the onslaught of that previous summer, is not in one's own name but in Maggie's. One has no claim to anything. Something might happen to Maggie and one would have no claim. She could be killed in an air crash. Hubert, staring at the ceiling, pulled a hair from his beard, and the twinge of pain confirmed and curiously consoled the thought. It was unlikely that anything would happen to Maggie. She was indestructible.

Chapter Two

'Miss Thin,' Hubert said, 'I wish you would not try to use your intelligence because you have so little of it. Just do as I say. Put them in date order.'

'I thought you would want to keep the personal separate from the professional,' said Pauline Thin belligerently. 'That would be the logical way.'

'There is no distinction between the two so far as I'm concerned,' Hubert said, looking, with a horror that had no connection whatsoever with Pauline Thin, at the great trunkfuls of old letters still to be gone through. Masses of old, old letters are very upsetting to contemplate, each one containing a world of past trivialities or passions forever pending. The surprise of words once overlooked and meanings newly realized, the record of debts unpaid or overpaid, of boredom unrequited or sweetness forever lost, came rising up to Hubert from the open boxes.

'Put them in chronological order,' Hubert said, 'a bundle for each year, then break each bundle up into months. That's all you have to do. Don't read them through and through, it's a waste of your working hours.'

'Mine not to reason why,' Pauline Thin answered, pulling towards her a pile of letters which she had set on the table.

'Yours *is* to reason why,' Hubert said. 'You can reason as much as you like if you know how to do it. You're free and I'm free to reason about anything. Only keep it to yourself. Don't waste my time. Don't ask me for the reasons. Just put them in order of dates.'

Hubert walked to the door and went out to the shady verandah overlooking the lake. It was a warm day for March. Spring was ready. He thought maybe he had better try to get on well with the girl and start calling her Pauline. She already called him Hubert without the asking. His nerves were edgy since, at the beginning of the year, a sequence of financial misfortunes had begun to fall upon him, unexpectedly, shock after shock. Hubert thought of these setbacks as 'curious' and 'unexpected' although, he would presently be brought to reflect, they had not been actually unforeseeable and were linked by no stronger force of coincidence than Maggie's second divorce and a new marriage to an Italian nobleman, probably jealous, and to the deterioration of money in general, and the collapse of a shady company in Switzerland where Hubert had put some of his personal money in the hope of making a fortune. He didn't know quite what to do. But he had one resource. Its precise application was still forming in his mind and wandering lonely as a cloud, and meantime he was short of funds.

The very panorama of Nemi, the lake, the most lush vegetation on earth, the scene which had stirred the imagination of Sir James Frazer at the beginning of his massive testament to comparative religion, *The Golden Bough*, all this magical influence and scene which had never before failed in their effects, all the years he had known the place and in the months he had lived there, suddenly was too expensive. I can't afford the view, thought Hubert and turned back into the room.

The sight of Pauline stacking the papers gave him a slight euphoric turn. There, among the letters and documents of his life, he had that one secret resource and he had decided to exploit it. Maggie could never take Nemi away from him because, spiritually if not actually, the territory of Nemi was his.

Actually, of course, not even the house was his. Maggie was . . . Maggie had been . . . Maggie, Maggie . . .

Pauline Thin was reading one of the letters. Sometimes when a letter was undated it was necessary for her to read it for a clue as to its appropriate place in the various piles of correspondence set out on the table. But Pauline was reading with a happy sort of interest and Hubert was not sure that he could afford Pauline Thin's happiness in her work, seeing she was theoretically paid by the hour. He was not sure, because on the one hand she was paid very little by the hour, and, further, she was greatly to be trusted and he relied on her now more than ever; he was not sure, on the other hand, if he could afford her at all, because, moreover, he owed her a lot of hours' pay, the debt increasing every hour in proportion as the likelihood decreased of his ever discharging it.

Hubert glanced back again at Pauline with her tiny face and her curly hair and felt the absence, now, of Ian, the boy from Inverness, and Damian, the Armenian boy with the curious surname of Runciwell who, as secretary, had been the best secretary, and he missed the other two with their petulance and their demands, their talents for cooking or interior design, their earrings and their neck-chains and their tight blue jeans and twin-apple behinds, fruit of the same tree. He felt their absence without specified regret; it was their kind he missed. Their departure was a fact which still paralysed him, belonging to a time so recent and yet so definitely last summer, in the past.

The morning news had announced the death of Noël Coward, calling it 'the passing of an era'. Everything since Maggie's sudden divorce and equally sudden Italian marriage last year had been to Hubert the passing of an era. Eras pass, thought Hubert. They pass every day. He felt dejected. He cheered up. Then he felt dejected again.

He glanced back at Miss Thin. She had finished reading the apparently absorbing letter and was bending with her back to him over the table stacking the piles of documents neatly. She was broad in the behind, too large. Where is the poetry of my life? Hubert thought. He retained an inkling that the poetry was still there and would return. Wordsworth defined poetry as 'emotion recollected in tranquillity'. Hubert took a tranquillizer, quite a mild one called Mitigil, and knew he would feel better in about ten minutes. To make sure, he took another. In the meantime a familiar white car turned into the drive and stopped before it reached the door. 'Oh God, it's him,' Hubert said and turning to Pauline Thin he called out, 'Miss Thin, this is a tiresome person. Please hang around and keep on bothering me with letters to sign. Remind me emphatically that I have a dinner date this evening. I'll give him one drink. This man's a pathological pest.'

The girl came out to see who had arrived. A medium-sized thin man in a clerical suit had got out of the car, had slammed the door and was walking towards them, smiling and waving.

'He's a Jesuit,' said Hubert, 'from Milwaukee.'

'I've seen him before,' Pauline said. 'He pesters everyone.'

'I know,' Hubert said, feeling friendly towards Miss Thin. He stepped forward a little way to meet the priest.

'Oh, Hubert, this is wonderful to find you in,' said the priest in a voice that twanged like a one-stringed guitar. 'I just drove from Rome as I wanted to talk to you.'

'How are you?' said Hubert politely. 'I'm afraid I'm going to be a bit pressed for time. If you'd have phoned me I could have made a date for you to come to dinner.'

'Oh, oh, are you going out . . . ?'

'About sevenish,' said Hubert putting on a weak smile. It was then sixish. 'I have to go and change soon' – Hubert indicated his old clothes – 'out of these things. Have you met Pauline Thin? – Pauline, this is Father Cuthbert Plaice.'

'Why, I think I know you, Pauline,' said the priest, shaking her hand and, it seemed, trying to locate her in his social register.

'I worked for Bobby Lester in Rome,' Pauline said.

'Why, of course! Yes. Well, now you're here?'

'Yes, I'm here.'

'Hubert, I've got a Jesuit friend down there in the car,' said the priest, 'that I want you to meet. I thought you would like to meet him, he's been studying the ancient ecological cults and in fact he's taken some tape recordings of modern nature-cultists which you have to hear. There are the conscious and the unconscious. It's fascinating. I thought we could have dinner together but anyway I'll just go call him and we can have a drink. I just wanted to tell you before you meet him, you see, that he's on your wave-length.' The priest made away towards the car stretching one arm behind him as if Hubert were straining away from him at the end of an invisible cord.

'Bloody pest,' said Hubert to Pauline. 'Why should I give them my drinks? He knows — I've told him — that I can't afford those lavish entertainments any more. And dinner — he wanted to stay with his friend for dinner. He marches in, and one's house isn't one's own. Priests can be very rough people, you know. Such a bore.'

'This one's an awful bore,' said Pauline. 'Bobby Lester couldn't stand him.'

Father Cuthbert was returning with a younger Jesuit of the same size to whom he was talking eagerly.

'Hubert,' he said, when he had reached the verandah, 'I want you to meet Father Gerard Harvey. Gerard has been doing studies of ecological paganism and I've told him all about you. Oh, this is Pauline Thin. She's working for Hubert. I knew Pauline before. She — '

'Come in and have a drink,' said Hubert.

'We can sit right here on the terrace. I want Gerard to see the view. What marvellous weather! That's the thing about Italy. You can sit outside in March, and — '

Hubert left them sitting on the terrace and went inside to fetch the drinks. Pauline followed him. 'Do you want me to stay with them?' she said.

'Yes, make a nuisance of yourself. Hang around looking silly so that they can't speak freely. Remember I'm supposed to get ready for dinner in about half an hour's time. These people need to be house-trained.'

Pauline went out on the terrace and sat down with the two men.

'Have you been in Italy long?' she said to the younger man.

'I've been here six months.'

She looked at her watch. 'Hubert has to go and change very soon,' she said. 'He's got a long drive ahead to arrive for eight. He has some letters to sign first.'

'Oh, where's he going?' said Father Cuthbert.

'You shouldn't ask,' she said.

'Well, now, that's not the way to talk,' said Cuthbert, looking very amazed.

'I guess she isn't a Catholic,' said Gerard soothingly.

'I'm a Catholic,' said Pauline. 'But that's got nothing to do with it. One doesn't tell people all one's business and all one's employer's business.'

Hubert appeared with a tray of drinks. The whisky bottle was one third full and the gin was slightly less. There was a box of ice and a bottle of mineral water.

'It's terrorism,' said Pauline.

'What's this?' Hubert said, setting down the tray.

'Priests,' said Pauline. 'They're terrorists. They hold you to ransom.'

The Jesuits looked at each other with delight. This was the sort of thing they felt at home with, priests being their favourite subject.

'Times have changed,' Hubert said to Pauline, 'since you were at school at the Sacred Heart, I'm afraid.'

'It isn't so long ago,' Pauline said, 'since I was at school. My last years, I went to Cheltenham.'

Father Gerard said, 'What goes on at Cheltenham?'

'Ladies' College,' said Hubert. 'If you look closely, it's written all over her face.'

'What do you have against us?' Father Cuthbert said, shifting about with excitement in his chair as if he were sexually as much as pastorally roused.

'It seems to me,' Hubert said, turning with gentle treachery towards Pauline, 'a bit inhospitable to carry on this conversation.' His Mitigil had started to work. He had put ice in the glasses. 'What will you drink?' he said to the guests.

'Whisky,' said both priests at once. Hubert looked sadly at his whisky bottle, lifted it and poured.

'Hubert,' said Pauline, 'that's all the whisky we have.'

'Yes,' said Hubert. 'I'm having gin. What about you, Miss Thin?'

'Plain tonic,' said Pauline.

The younger priest sipped his drink and looked out over the still lake in its deep crater and the thick wildwood of Nemi's fertile soil. 'Terrific ecology!' he said.

'You mean the view?' Pauline said.

Hubert sat in a chair with his back to the grand panorama and he sighed. 'I have to give it up,' he said. 'There's nothing for it. The house isn't mine and Maggie's changed so much since her new marriage. They're insisting on charging me rent. A high rent. I have to go.'

'Remember your dinner date,' Pauline said, 'and Hubert, would you sign some letters, please?'

'Dinner date . . . ?' said Hubert. Since Maggie's marriage following on her son Michael's marriage, and since the trouble with his money in Switzerland, he had been asked out less and less. He looked into his little drop of gin, while Father Cuthbert seized on the doubt about dinner. 'You're going to go out for dinner?'

'We've already told you so,' said Pauline.

'Oh, I didn't know if you meant it,' said the priest.

Hubert, remembering, said, 'Oh, yes, I am. I have to go and change very soon, I'm afraid. They eat early, these people.'

'What people?' said Father Cuthbert. 'Do I know them? Could we come along?'

His companion the ecologist began to show embarrassment. He said, 'No, no, Cuthbert. We can go back to Rome. Really, we mustn't intrude like this. Unexpectedly. We have to . . . ' He rose and looked nervously towards the car where it was parked half-way down the drive.

'Why don't you go and see Michael?' Hubert said, meaning Maggie's son, whose house was near by.

Father Cuthbert looked eager. 'Do you know if he's home?'

'I'm sure he is,' said Hubert. 'They're both in Nemi just now. He got married himself recently. Marriage does seem to be a luxury set apart for the rich. I'm sure they'll be delighted to see you.'

While Hubert explained to the excited priest how to get there by car, his friend, Father Gerard, looked around him and across the lake. 'The environment,' he said. 'This is a wonderful environmental location.'

'It's your duty to visit Michael and Mary, really,' Pauline egged them on. 'They have sumptuous dinners. They had a shock when Maggie got divorced and married again, you know. It's been an upset for the Radcliffes. Her new husband's a pig.'

'Don't they see his father?'

'Oh, I dare say,' Hubert said. 'Radcliffe was Maggie's second husband, of course. The new one's the third. But it was so sudden. The family's all right financially of course. But I must say it's left me in a mess, personally speaking.'

When the priests had left, Hubert went with Pauline into the kitchen. He opened a tin of tuna fish while she made a potato salad. They then sat down to eat at the kitchen table, silently, reflectively.

It seemed as if Hubert had forgotten the priests. Pauline, as if anxious that he should not forget a subject that had served to bring them closer, assiduously said, 'Those priests . . .'

At first he didn't respond to the tiny needle. He merely said dreamily, 'It's not too much to wonder if they're not a bit too much,' and took in a mouthful of food.

'But so pressing, so insufferably pushy,' Pauline said, at which Hubert was roused into agreement, chummily communicating it : 'It's an extraordinary fact,' he said, 'that just at the precise moment when you're at your wits' end it's always the last people in the world you want to see who turn up, full of themselves, demanding total attention. It's always the exceptionally tiresome who barge in at the exceptionally difficult moment. Would you believe there was a time when a Jesuit was a gentleman, if you'll forgive the old-fashioned expression?'

Pauline passed him the potato salad. It had onion, too, in it, and mayonnaise. 'Forget them, Hubert,' she said, plainly intending him not to do so.

But Hubert smiled. 'Miss Thin,' he said as he took the salad bowl from her hand, 'I have inside me a laughter demon without which I would die.'

Chapter Three

'Demons frequented these woods, protectors of the gods. Nymphs and dryads inhabited the place. Have you seen the remains of Diana's temple down there? It's terribly overgrown and the excavations are all filled in, but there's a great deal more to see than you might think.'

'No, I haven't seen it,' said Mary, curling her long legs as she sat, yoga-style, on a cushion on the pavement of the terrace. She was a young long-haired blonde girl from California, newly married to Michael Radcliffe. The priests were entertaining her enormously. She didn't want them to leave and pressed them to stay on for a late dinner. Michael had gone to Rome and wouldn't be back till nine. 'He said nine, which most probably will be ten,' she said.

'Pius the Second,' said Father Gerard, 'said that Nemi was the home of nymphs and dryads, when he passed through this area.'

'Really?'

An Italian manservant, young and dark-skinned in a white coat with shining buttons and elaborate epaulettes, brought in a tray of canapés and nuts which he placed on the terrace table beside the bottles. He looked with recognition at Father Cuthbert who, without looking at the manservant, took a handful of nuts, as also did Father Gerard. The ice clinked in the glasses, and they helped themselves to the drinks when their glasses were empty, refilling Mary's glass too. They were Americans together, abroad, with the unwatchful attitude of co-nationals who share some common experiences, however few.

'I majored in social science,' said Mary who had been to college in California.

'Did you come to Italy before?' said Father Gerard.

'No, never. I met Michael in Paris. Then we settled here. I love it.'

'How's your Italian?' said the other priest, beaming with idle pleasure – as who would not after two months' continuous residence in the priests' bleak house in Rome, anonymous and detached in its laws of life?

'Oh, my Italian's coming along. I took a crash course. I guess I'll get more fluent. How about yours?'

'Gerard's is pretty good,' said Father Cuthbert. 'He doesn't get enough practice. There are Italians at the Residence of course, but we only talk to the Americans. You know the way it gets. Or maybe the French –'

'Cuthbert speaks almost perfect Italian,' said Father Gerard. 'He's a great help when I'm talking to the locals around the country about their legends and beliefs.'

'Gerard,' said Father Cuthbert, 'is doing a study on pagan ecology.'

'Really? I thought the Italians were mostly all Catholics.'

'On the surface, yes, but underneath there's a large area of pagan remainder to be explored. And absorbed into Christianity. A very rich seam.'

'Well,' said the girl, 'I don't know if you've talked to Hubert Mallindaine about that . . . '

Hubert was a whole new subject, vibrating to be discussed. The priests began to speak in unison, questions and answers, then the girl broke in with laughing phrases and exclamation marks, until Father Cuthbert's voice, being the highest and most excitable, attained the first hearing. The manservant hovered at the terrace door, his eyes upon them, waiting to serve. Mary stretched her fine long suntanned legs and listened. 'We arrived this evening,' said Cuthbert, 'without letting him know in advance. Well, that's nothing new. As a matter of fact the last time I saw him, about six weeks ago, in Rome, he said, "Come to dinner any time. Sure, bring a friend, you're always welcome. There's no need to call me. I never go out. Just get into that car and come." That's what he said. Well. We arrived this evening – didn't we, Gerard?'

'We did,' said Gerard.

A person with a good ear might have questioned the accuracy of Cuthbert's report on the grounds that Hubert, not being American, was not likely to have used a phrase like, 'Sure, bring a friend . . . ' But it did seem that the priest had been in the habit of dropping in on Hubert from time to time, whether welcome or not. Clearly he regarded it as his right to do so, anywhere.

'I was embarrassed for Gerard,' Cuthbert was saying, 'especially as this was his first visit, you know. He had an awful secretary, a girl who used to work for another friend of mine in Rome. A terribly – '

Here Gerard broke in, and so did Mary. When they had finished exclaiming over Pauline, Cuthbert continued, 'I think she's got a problem. Then she kept telling Hubert he had to go out to dinner, which I'm sure wasn't true because of the way it was said, you know.' He finished his drink and the manservant came out of the shadows to replenish it. This time Cuthbert recognized the man's face but couldn't at first place it.

The servant lifted the glass with a well-paid and expert air and smiled.

'I know you, don't I?' said Cuthbert to the man.

'It's Lauro,' said Mary. 'He was one of Hubert's secretaries last summer.'

'Why, Lauro, I didn't recognize you in that uniform! Why Lauro!' The priest seemed confused, realizing the man had understood their conversation.

Lauro answered in easy, accented English. 'You surprised to see me here? I lost my job with Hubert and I went to a bar on the Via Veneto then I came back to Nemi to work for Mary and Michael.'

'Lauro's on first-name terms with us,' Mary said. 'The Embassy crowd are shocked. But we don't care.'

Lauro smiled and slipped back to his doorway.

'Lauro could tell you everything you want to know about Hubert,' Mary said. Lauro's shadowed form stooped to adjust a rose in a vase. Cuthbert looked carefully at Mary as if to see quite what she had meant by her words, but she had evidently meant far less than she might have done.

'Oh, I like Hubert. Don't misunderstand me,' said Cuthbert, and he looked towards Gerard who gave it as his opinion that Hubert had seemed very likeable.

'Well, I used to like him too,' said Mary. 'And I still do. But when Maggie and her husband number three got kind of mad

2

at him we had to take her part; after all, she's Michael's mother. What can you do? There's been a bad feeling between the houses since Maggie got into this marriage. She wants Hubert to go. He says he won't and he can't pay rent. She's going to put him out. The furniture belongs to Maggie as well. But my, she's finding it difficult. The laws in this country . . . Hubert might get around them forever.'

They sat down to dinner soon after Mary's husband, Michael, arrived. They spoke of Hubert most of the time. Hubert was a subject sufficiently close to them to provide a day-to-day unfolding drama and yet it was sufficiently remote, by reason of their wealth, not to matter very much. Hubert himself, since the young couple had ceased to see him, had become someone else than the large-living and smart-spoken old friend they used to know when he was Maggie's favourite. Now that Maggie had turned against him he was, in their mythology, a parasite on society. 'He's not like the old Hubert at all,' Michael said. 'Something's changed him.'

'I dread one day maybe bumping into him in the village,' said Mary. 'I don't know what I'd say.'

First one Jesuit and then the other offered advice as to the coping with this eventuality. So dark, rather short but so somehow splendid, Lauro served the meal, assisted by a good-looking maid. The spring evening air from the terrace stood around them like another ubiquitous servant, tendering occasional wafts of a musky creeper's scent. The wine had been sent by Maggie's new husband from his own vineyards in the north.

'Hubert,' said Michael, 'of course considers he is a direct descendant of the goddess Diana of Nemi. He considers he's mystically and spiritually, if not actually, entitled to the place.'

'No kidding!' said Gerard.

'No kidding,' Mary said. 'That's what Hubert believes. It's a family tradition. All the Mallindaines have always believed it. Michael and I met an aunt of his in Paris. She was convinced of it. But I think her health had broken up.'

'She was old,' Michael said.

'Well,' said Gerard, 'I should look into this for my research.'

The other Jesuit said, 'I always thought, you know, the Diana mythology was just an interest of his. I didn't know it was in the family. We'll have to go see him again.'

One of the stories to be read from the ancient historians of Imperial Rome is that the Emperor Caligula enjoyed sex with the goddess Diana of Nemi. And indeed, two luxurious Roman ships, submerged for centuries in the lake and brought to land in recent times, have been attributed variously to the purpose of Imperial orgies on the lake of Nemi, and to service in the worship of Diana. These ships were brought to land in reconstructable condition only to be destroyed by some German soldiers during the Second World War; however, their remaining contents and fittings testified to the impression that something highly ritualistic took place on board, well into Christian times, although the worship of Diana at Nemi reaches back into the mythological childhood of the race. Hubert's ancestors . . .

But it is time, now, to take a closer look at Hubert on that spring evening, seeing that he had provided a full and wonderful stream of conversation for the party over there in the other house, where the frank spirits rose higher, Lauro glowed in the shadows and Mary, with her golden Californian colouring, her dark blue eyes and white teeth, was so far stimulated as to repeat for good measure a recent saying of Maggie's: 'The goddess Diana presents her compliments, and desires the company of her kinsman Mr Hubert Mallindaine at the Hunt Ball to be held at Nemi . . . '

Meanwhile, then, Hubert watched Pauline Thin wash up the plates. He carried their coffee through the sitting-room and out to the terrace. 'At my age,' Hubert said, 'I shouldn't drink coffee at night. But, Miss Thin, it doesn't always bear to think of what one should or shouldn't drink. There's a limit to everything.'

'I can see that,' said Pauline, looking out over the marvellous lake.

'Miss Thin,' said Hubert, 'I have decided. I will not leave this house.' Hubert had shaved off his beard shortly after hearing of Maggie's divorce last year in the December of 1972. Then, a week after he heard, in the following January, that she had married the northern Marquis, he had shaved off his moustache. Not that he felt these actions were in any way connected with Maggie's. It does, however, obscurely seem that in these two shavings he was expressing some reaction to her divorce and marriage, or, more probably, preparing himself for something, maybe an ordeal, requiring a clean-cut appearance.

He looked younger, now. Pauline Thin who had come to work for him this February, had never known him with his hairy maestro's face. She described him to her best friend in Italy, another English girl who was working in Rome, as 'dishy'.

Hubert was now forty-five. His generally good looks varied from day to day. Sometimes, when she went into Rome for shopping and stopped to lunch with her girlfriend, Pauline described him as 'a bit fagoty'. However that may be, Hubert undoubtedly had good looks, especially when anguished. By a system of panic-action whenever he started to be overweight, he had managed to keep his good line. The panic-system, which consisted of a total fast for a sufficient number of days, never more than twelve, to make him thoroughly skinny and underweight, allowed him then to put on weight comfortably with small indulgences in food and drink which otherwise he would never have enjoyed. Hubert had been told, much earlier in his life, that eventually this course would ruin his health but the event had never happened. Indeed, most of his active life was formed by panic-action and in the interludes he was content to dream or fret or for long periods simply enjoy sweet life. One such of these interludes was just coming to an end, which accounted for the especially good looks of his worried face. He was fairly dark-skinned with light blue eyes and sandy-grey hair. His features were separately nothing much, but his face and the way his head was set on his body were effective. Quite often, he was conscious of his physical assets, but more often he simply forgot them.

This house, with the best view of all Maggie's three houses in the neighbourhood, was furnished richly. After only a year's occupancy this new house still had newness penetrating its bones. Even the antiques, the many of them, were new. Maggie had brought back across the water from an apartment high in the air, on the east-sixties of Manhattan, large lifts of itinerant

European furniture and pictures. The drawing-room furniture was Louis XIV; there had been six fine chairs, at present only five; one was away in a clever little workshop on the Via di Santa Maria dell'Anima in Rome, being sedulously copied. Hubert was short of money and, almost certain that Maggie would at least succeed in removing the furniture from the house, he was taking reasonable precautions for his future. The new chair was almost finished, and it only remained for the upholstery on the original to be tenderly removed and fitted on to the fake before Pauline should be ordered to go into Rome and fetch the chair. She had been told only that it was being mended. The original would remain in Rome for a while at Hubert's disposal. Like money in the bank, Hubert thought of switching and rearranging, perhaps, a few more items, and maybe, if there was time, another chair. Maggie had put on the drawing-room floor a seventeenth-century rug; Isfahan. Hubert brooded upon it : not at all possible to copy with excellence. He didn't use the drawing-room much these days; the heart had gone out of it.

Maggie's withdrawal from Hubert had taken place quite slowly. It was only to him that it seemed abrupt. To him it was the heedless by-product of a too-rich woman's whim or the effect of her new husband's influence, the new husband also being rich. But Hubert's memory was careless. As we have seen, as far back as the previous summer he was privately lamenting Maggie's lack of chivalry. His protectress had already started, even before that, to recede. She had let him occupy the new house, as one silently honouring a bad bargain; the house had been ordered to his taste more than three years before it was ready. But it was during those three years and more while the house was being made that she had gradually stopped confiding in him and even before that, perhaps, the disaffection and bore-dom of the relationship had set in for Maggie.

Hubert had been uneasy about his position, really, for many years more than he now admitted when he thought or spoke of Maggie. 'Like any other spoilt moneybags she used me when she needed me and then suddenly told me to go, to clear out of her house and her life. All my projects were based on her promises. We had an understanding . . . ' So he dramatized it in a nutshell, first to himself, then, later, to Pauline Thin.

Pauline assumed there had been a love affair till one night, when he was confiding in her for the sheer lack of anyone else to talk to about himself, he remarked, 'I never touched a woman. I love women but I never went near one. It would break the spell. There's a magic . . . women are magic. I can't live without women around me. Sex is far, far away out of the question in my mind where women are concerned.'

Which bewildered Pauline. Quickly rearranging her ideas, and in the spirit of the missionaries of old who held that conversion was only a matter of revealing the true doctrine, she ended with the conviction that he had not yet met a truly appetizing, faithful woman and decided more than ever to stick by Hubert in these reduced days of his.

Chapter Four

> 'Lo, Nemi! navell'd in the woody hills
> So far, that the uprooting wind which tears
> The oak from his foundation, and which spills
> The ocean o'er its boundary, and bears
> Its foam against the skies, reluctant spares
> The oval mirror of thy glassy lake;
> And calm as cherish'd hate, its surface wears
> A deep cold settled aspect nought can shake,
> All coil'd into itself and round, as sleeps the snake.'

'It's a perfect description,' said Nancy Cowan, the English tutor. 'Can you imagine what Byron meant by "calm as cherished hate"? – It's mysterious, isn't it? – Yet perfectly applicable. One can see that in the past, the historic long-ago, there was some evil hidden under the surface of the lake. Many evils, probably. Pagan customs were cruel. "Cherished hate" is a great evil, anyway.'

Her pupils pondered, perhaps being nice enough to feel they had missed the point. Letizia, a girl of eighteen, was not quite sure what the phrase meant. 'Hatred,' explained the tutor, 'which has been kept hidden, secret, never expressing itself behind its impassive face. That's why the poet wrote "calm as cherished hate".'

'It's very good,' said Pietro. He was twenty. Both Letizia and Pietro were cramming for entrance exams to American colleges.

The villa at Nemi where they sat in early summer with the English teacher had no view at all of the lake. One could only glimpse the castle tower from one of the windows. It was the third of Maggie Radcliffe's houses, the newly-restored one, recently let to the family. Letizia, a passionate Italian nationalist with an ardour for folklore and the voluntary helping of youthful drug-addicts, resented very much the fact that her father rented the house from an American. She was against the foreign ownership of Italian property, held that the youth of Italy was being corrupted by foreigners, especially in the line of drugs, and asserted herself, with her light skin and hair, large-boned athletic shapelessness, and religious unbelief, to be a representative of the new young Italy. The father, who was divorced from the mother, was extremely rich. She was in no accepting frame of mind to study for an American university entrance, and had already almost converted Miss Cowan, the tutor, to her view. Her brother Pietro, dark-eyed, long-lashed, with a pale oval face, wanted very much to be in a film and then to direct a film, and whenever he was free he spent his time among the courtiers of famous film directors, skimming the speed-routes by day and by night in his Porsche, his St Christopher medal dangling on his chest, speeding the length of the boot of Italy and back to be with some group of young men who clustered round the film director wherever the film should be in the making. Italy is a place much given to holding court. Pietro, when he was not at one or another court, was happier at home now than he had been in recent years because of the presence of Nancy Cowan.

She was thirty-six, well-informed, rather thin, long-nosed, tender-hearted towards anyone within her immediate radius at any one time. She had come in answer to an advertisement in *The Times*, bringing her Englishness, her pale summer dresses, her sense of fair play, and many other foreign things with her. Letizia had been at first delighted to find that the English tutor was so easy to walk all over in intellectual matters; it was as if

Miss Cowan had anything you like instead of views of society or political stands. But at times she suspected that Nancy Cowan really didn't feel it worth while to give her own opinions; sometimes it almost seemed, in fact, as if Nancy was making herself agreeable to either the brother or the sister simply because they mattered very little to her. Letizia, when this feeling struck her, would force her own views the more strongly, and would sometimes speak her mind to the point of insult. Pietro thought Nancy's malleability to be very feminine, and with an intuitive artistic sense of economy, he set out to get his father's money's worth out of her in his studies. It seemed likely that their father was already sleeping with her. It would have been possible to find out for sure, but Pietro felt too young and sex-free to make the effort; it would have been unhealthy, indelicate, but Pietro one night when they were taking their coffee after dinner in the garden, from the way Nancy Cowan responded to the night-beauty, decided that his father had wooed and won her there. She was also better-looking in the moonlight, quite handsome as in a film; and then, again, the manner towards Nancy of the big fat whiney parlour maid, Clara, told Pietro something. He supposed it also told Letizia something, but he didn't expect Letizia to acknowledge any such unsevere facts about their father or their English tutor. It was thoroughly in keeping, though, that Papa was getting all full value out of Nancy Cowan, as was she from the job.

The brother and sister sat reading Byron with Nancy in the shady garden a few yards from the house. It was six in the afternoon. To humour Letizia, Nancy had bent her English lessons in the direction of local lore. A poor rescued drug-addict in the wreckage of his twenties was cleaning out the swimming-pool under the direction of a gardener and fat Clara. This simple operation made a terrific background noise since Clara's only tone for all occasions was one of lament, and the gardener, in trying to make a simple instruction penetrate the saved youth's brain, treated him as if he were hard of hearing. The youth, who had been brought in by Letizia from Rome that morning, would be given a meal and an old pair of Pietro's trousers for his services before he was taken back to the welfare centre. A few such garden chores got done in this way; only garden chores, since Letizia did not bring these strange people into the house for fear of what they might see and be tempted either to take away or send their friends to procure. To her father, Letizia's protégés were more or less what in the old days were gypsies. To the eyes of Nancy Cowan they were young drug-addicts just like the London variety. Letizia referred to them as 'our new social phenomena' and this, oddly enough, was the title they liked best; they seemed to respond to Letizia, to her statistics and her sociological language which apparently gave them a status in life, and it was rarely that any one of them attempted to take undue advantage of her or ask her for money. Mostly they demonstrated an allergy to Pietro with his Bulgari steel watch, his Gucci shoes and belt, his expensive haircut, and with his Porsche being endlessly cleaned by the house's young lodge-keeper in overalls.

Big Clara lumbered up from the pool to the house, clutching her heart. She was not yet fifty but she looked much older and yet behaved like a child of twelve which evidently she still felt herself to be. 'A headache,' she said in her babyish whine. 'It's too hot. You need a professional to clean out the pool. He'll never understand the chlorine. I've got a headache. He has no capacity. You need a man, a real man. He'll never learn.'

Letizia sprang up from her seat beside Nancy Cowan, full of what it took to cope with Clara in their native tongue. Letizia's young skin glowed in the late afternoon, her pale blue eyes had a fishy bulge. She swung around in her folklore skirt, her red platform clogs and smocked blouse, gesticulating with her healthy arms. As a specimen, Letizia at eighteen was rounded-off and complete; the finishing touches were already put, there was no room for further contention between character and contours, there was scope only, now, for wear and tear. She was much as she would be, she thought, much as she would think, and looked not much different from what she would look, at forty-eight.

The grumbling servant having been coped with, Letizia returned to her garden chair beside her brother and Nancy, with a grin full of healthy teeth.

Nancy Cowan held out her hand for the copy of Byron which Pietro had taken to look at.

'He must have come here in winter,' Pietro said, 'since he wrote about the wind tearing up the oak tree.'

Letizia leaned over Nancy Cowan to examine the lines. 'He says the wind spares the lake, which is true. Nemi is a very secluded spot. Was Byron at Nemi in winter, then?'

'Look, you'll have to get a Life of Byron . . .'

'I think Papa has a biography of Byron. Pietro, do you know?'

' . . . something you ought to know about, though. Byron's always – '

'He was a lame lord . . . ' Pietro had taken the book from Nancy and was reading aloud from the biographical foreword to the poems : ' . . . a spendthrift and a rake . . .'

'What is that – spendthrift . . . ?' Pietro reached for the dictionary. Nancy Cowan began explaining Byron while the air grew cooler, the light faded over the lawn and Letizia suddenly recollected a bit of Byron's history from her earlier schooldays.

Just then Letizia was called to the telephone and cursing in Italian went indoors to answer it.

Nancy caught Pietro looking closely at her, and turned her head to look back into his face.

'Would it embarrass you if I asked you a question?' he said.

'You've just asked me an embarrassing one,' she said to gain ground, and was never to know what Pietro's other embarrassing question might be, for Letizia returned by way of the kitchen door to say, 'Papa has asked our landlady to dinner. She phoned Papa at the office. Her name was Mrs Radcliffe but she got married again to an Italian. La Radcliffe wants to see us.'

'What's she like?' Nancy said.

'We've never seen her. She rents the house through an agent. She's a rich American, Madame Radcliffe, and now she's a Marchesa married to a nobleman from the north. I hate Papa for renting a house from an American in our own country. It should be round the other way. Why doesn't Papa buy a villa?'

'Italians own property in England,' said Nancy.

'That is different. They settled there for two, three generations. They was poor.' Letizia looked angry, unable to clarify her thoughts, if indeed her feelings existed in thought-form. She slightly lost her grip on correct English. 'There is many reasons,' she said. 'Here in Italy the foreigner takes everything.'

'Maybe you're right,' said Nancy. 'I really hadn't thought of it before.' She thought of it now, looking with purely formal anxiety into the distance.

'This was an old Italian villa, the foundations are ancient Roman,' said the girl calming down a little, 'then along came an American woman with the money. She restores the house. She's got other houses, all over Nemi, full of foreigners. We're the only Italians and we pay her rent. Papa pays a huge rent. We had to put in a downstairs sitting-room. Before there was no sitting-room downstairs. We had to make over one of the garages at Papa's expense. Papa likes the house so he pays and pays.'

The large maid came out with a tray of drinks and ice, wearing a baleful expression. Nancy smiled at her but this made Clara close her eyes as if in pain.

'You shouldn't criticize foreigners in Nancy's presence,' said Pietro. He was hoping to get a part in a foreign film just at that time and although it was unlikely that their English tutor had many friends among the thousands of foreigners in Italy, far less the Americans who were making the film, he felt there was nothing to lose by shutting his sister up a bit.

'But Papa pays her to help us with our English and we're talking English,' Letizia said. 'And tonight we have to talk English at dinner for our landlady.'

Their father's car could be heard coming up the drive, where-upon Nancy Cowan smiled.

A sixteenth-century refectory table with some antique chairs from Tuscany waited for the party in a green damask dining-room. Some special-looking green and gold china was arranged on shelves in four flood-lit alcoves. The candles were ready to be lit in the silver candlesticks, the table was set for six, which meant that the seats were twice as far apart as they need have been. Letizia looked sulkily over the table, said nothing one way or another to the waiting manservant, then left the room through folding doors which led to the drawing-room. The manservant slipped out of another door to report, apparently, no complaints.

In the drawing-room Letizia's father sat back on a sofa with his contented drink. Nancy Cowan sat by his side, tentatively and upright, near the edge of the seat. Letizia, coming in from the dining-room, said, 'We should have dined in the north room. The green dining-room is far too formal for six.'

The father, Dr Emilio Bernardini, elegantly thin with a pale skin and rather beautiful, very dark eyes behind a pair of scholarly spectacles, black-glossy hair and sharply defined eyebrows, had a look of the portraits of the Stuart monarchs. He was a business lawyer occupied between Rome, Milan and Zürich; in fact, a good part of his business was real estate, and the reason he had yet to sell his own family villa and had chosen to rent from Maggie Radcliffe the one in which he now sat was presumably known only to himself. Although it annoyed his daughter she was too well-fabricated within the business world of Italy to believe she could persuade the father to buy rather than rent. Whatever his reason, it was definitely in his own interest.

He replied in Italian, carelessly, that the dining-room was best for their landlady's visit. Pietro, in the meantime, was telling Nancy he admired her dress.

Nancy answered, in correct Italian, that it was a new one. She added, 'After my first long stay in Italy when I saw how Italians dressed, I felt I was underdressed in my London things, so I always get some clothes for the evening when I come to stay here.'

'Do you mean we're overdressed?' said the charming father of the family.

'In England, at this moment, for this occasion, we would be quite overdressed.'

The father contemplated his children and then herself with some happiness. 'I think we all look very elegant,' he said. 'I'm glad we overdo it. Not long ago we overdid it far more.'

A new young man was shown in, whom Letizia had hastily summoned to dinner to make a respectable number. He, at least, had not overdone it, but was wearing a dingy, grey cotton round-necked shirt and dark trousers, both very much too tight. He was small and plump, bulging with little rolls of flesh under the arms, above the belly, all over; it seemed he had never even started to care what he looked like; Letizia introduced him as Marino Vesperelli, adding, for her father's sake, that he was a Professor of Psychology. Dr Bernardini took him in good part, cast a hand to indicate a seat, rose to ask him what he would drink. At which Letizia took over, and the young man followed her to the wagon of bottles and ice at the far end of the room. Emilio Bernardini then murmured to Nancy, 'I hate to think of *him* breathing all over my daughter.'

'Maybe he's just a friend.'

'Where does she pick them up?'

'I expect this one works with her in her welfare work.'

'He needs a bit of welfare himself,' said the father.

However, as soon as the young psychologist had sat down with his drink Dr Bernardini tried to engage him in conversation as to his profession. The young man answered briefly and asked no return questions; plainly he felt that his odd-looking presence was sufficient social contribution to the evening; which, in its decided oddity, it rather was.

'There's a car arriving; it must be *her*,' said Pietro.

Maggie Radcliffe was so much in the long, long habit of making heads swim when she came into view that she still did so. She looked somewhere in her late forties but the precise age was irrelevant to the effect which was absolutely imperious in its demands for attention; and what was more, Maggie achieved it carelessly. She cared only, and closely, about what was going on around her. And so, as soon as she had given her hand to everyone in the room, she started to admire the Bernardinis' pictures whose authors she recognized, one by one. Still administering her entrance like drops of heart-medicine, she turned to the owner and reminded him how the Klimt over the mantelpiece had very nearly remained in the Austrian collection, thus establishing with him the higher market-place communion that exists between rich and rich.

Nancy Cowan stood waiting for the special guest to sit down. She pulled, through her dress, at the top of her panty-hose, setting herself to rights like a schoolgirl. She then moved her finger under her hair at the nape of her neck. Maggie sat down. The men sat down. Maggie, on being asked what she would drink, turned to the uncomely young psychologist and asked what he was drinking.

'Sherry on the rocks,' he said.

Maggie gave a soundless laugh, looking towards her host in merry collusion, and said she would have a vodka-tonic. She had overdressed very tastefully, with a mainly-white patterned dress brilliant against her shiny sun-tan. Her hair was silver-tipped, her eyes large and bright. She had a flood-lit look up to the teeth.

The air-conditioner was turned off before dinner seeing that the evening was cool. The windows of the dining-room were opened to the breeze of the Alban hills. They sat at the long refectory table, spaced out, murmuring pleasantly one to the other, waiting to be served. Emilio Bernardini at the top of the table had Maggie on his right, Nancy on his left. Letizia sat facing him with Pietro on her left and her boy-friend bundled in his chair on her right.

Wine, water, avocado, sauce. 'What do you think of your villa, Marchesa, now that we're in it?'

'You've made it charming, more delightful than I remembered having seen it before,' Maggie said.

'We made some alterations,' Letizia said. 'We had to get workmen. One of the garages is now a downstairs sitting-room. Otherwise, there wasn't – '

'I know,' said Maggie. 'My agent mentioned it.'

'The Marchesa must see it later,' said the father.

'Yes, I must,' said Maggie.

'If we're speaking English why do you say "Marchesa",' said Letizia, ' "Marchioness" is English.'

Pietro said, 'Because it sounds nicer.'

'Oh, yes, it does,' Maggie said and laid down her little spoon to drink some water. 'And "Signora" would be better. "Mrs" and "Miss" make you close your mouth for the ms but for "Signora" and "Signorina" you don't shut your mouth. "Mrs" and "Miss" form a sneer but "Signora" and "Signorina" are a hiss.'

Marino the psychologist leaned forward to catch Maggie's drift, puzzled. The others laughed while Letizia explained the point to Marino in rapid Italian undertones. He said, 'Why is a hiss better than a sneer?'

'It's better,' said the father as the glasses were filled with his good wine.

'Anyway,' said Maggie, 'Signora is perfectly all right for me as I'm now married to an Italian and Italy's a republic.'

'The Signora is of course the Marchesa di Tullio-Friole,' said Dr Bernardini with his cool good manners, at the same time drawing the line at any excess of a tiresome subject arising from Maggie's logic.

'Oh, Marchesa is so formal. It suits me only when I'm with my husband.'

'I was at school with his son, Pino,' said Dr Bernardini. 'I remember your husband very well. I stayed at the villa up in the Veneto, often. I've hunted there.'

'Then you must come again,' said Maggie. 'He's there now, seeing to the alterations to my bathroom.'

The candles flickered. Came the spinach soufflé, the crumbed veal and salad, the lemon ice and the fruit, while Maggie talked on about the two other houses she owned in the neighbourhood, her son's and Hubert Mallindaine's.

'Mr Mallindaine's is new,' said Letizia sharply, 'but your son's house is a sixteenth-century farm-house.'

Pietro said he had always admired the old farm-house. He seemed uneasy about his sister.

'It should be in Italian hands,' Letizia said. 'Our national patrimony.'

'It cost a fortune to put right,' Maggie said.

The father intercepted Letizia's foreseen reaction to say that he understood Maggie had restored the old house beautifully, and built the new house beautifully as well.

Pietro, it seemed, knew the young Radcliffes and had been to their house.

'Oh, those are the Americans you spoke of?' This was Letizia again, so much so that her boy-friend laughed.

'What's funny?' said Letizia, seeing that the others were laughing.

'Something,' said Maggie, 'about the way you said "Americans".'

'Letizia, don't be silly,' said the father.

Letizia said, 'Shall we have coffee outside, Papa?' Then, as she led the way through the french windows to the upper terrace, she said, 'I believe in Italy for the Italians.'

'Letizia!' said Emilio.

'You are so impolite,' said her brother.

'What about the English?' said Nancy. 'Are we unwanted here?'

'The English the same,' Letizia said as she waited for her guests to be seated.

The father was explaining to Maggie. 'It's only a toy gun she's playing with, or at least, a gun filled with blanks.'

Letizia said 'Oh!' protestingly.

Maggie said, 'Oh, I agree with her, really I do. I think the Americans soon won't be able to afford to stay in Italy. You know, since I married an Italian, I feel myself to be an Italian.'

The young psychologist said to the father, 'You talk of guns, Dr Bernardini. Playing with guns. That's interesting.'

'It's a sexual image,' Maggie said, and they all laughed except Letizia and her boy-friend.

Letizia sat down and the coffee was brought to the terrace table. Letizia started pouring while Nancy took round the cups. 'And the third house?' Letizia said.

'An Englishman,' Maggie said. 'As a matter of fact, Dr Bernardini, he's my problem. He's the problem I wanted to ask you about.'

'It's a beautiful house,' said the father. 'It must have a wonderful view.'

'It has the best view of all three houses,' Maggie said looking one by one at her rings. 'And what's more, the furniture is mine. Every piece. I've given him notice to quit.'

'But he belongs to Nemi,' said Letizia.

'Who belongs to Nemi?' said Pietro.

'The occupant. The Englishman. He has an ancestral claim.'

Emilio Bernardini called for the brandy and liqueurs.

'He has to quit,' Maggie said. 'My husband insists.' She turned to Emilio. 'You know,' she said, 'what Italians are like, of the old school. Very conservative. And really, I admire it.'

'In our country it's difficult to get rid of tenants,' Emilio said, not anxious to take the landlady's part against a tenant so near at hand. 'Very difficult indeed.'

'He pays no rent,' Maggie said. 'He has been a guest for a year and now his welcome is outworn.'

'I'm not sure we can help you,' Emilio said, as if reinforced by the rest of the company.

'I thought we might, perhaps, get up a neighbourhood petition,' said Maggie, prompt, too, with her 'we'. She added, 'My son and daughter-in-law, of course, will – '

'It would make a scandal,' Pietro said.

'But he himself is quite a scandalous person,' said Maggie. 'I'm sure you must have heard – '

'There is a secretary but no scandal. Miss Cowan knows her, don't you, Nancy?'

'Well, I wouldn't say I know her,' Nancy said. 'I believe I met her in Rome one time at the house of some English friends. She had a job in Rome.'

'Well,' said Maggie, 'before this secretary there were boys.'

'It's a Mediterranean custom and in Italy not a crime,' the host said. 'I sympathize with you, Marchesa, but a petition . . . ' – he spread his hands – ' . . . a petition to get a man out of his house because of boys . . . The scandal would fall on us, definitely, as Pietro says.'

'What does your lawyer say?' said the psychologist.

'Oh, he's working on it,' said Maggie, somewhat vaguely and without conveying much enthusiasm for her lawyer.

'But Mr Mallindaine has a claim to Nemi,' said Letizia. 'His ancestry goes back to ancient times. He can prove it.'

'You know him well?' Maggie said.

'No, I don't know him at all, but I heard – '

'Well, I,' said Maggie bending her head sorrowfully, 'know him well.' Since the subject of Hubert had been discussed, she seemed to have been unexpectedly put in the position of asking an unwelcome favour; her looks seemed to have lost their sensational quality.

In bed that night Emilio Bernardini said to Nancy, 'She's an animal.'

3

'She looked stunning when she came in.'

'Animals can look stupendous. I wonder what she really wanted to see me about. She rang me in the office this afternoon and said she'd like to see me. I asked her to dinner. I wonder if she just wanted to see what we'd done to her house.'

'I think she wanted you to help her to get the other tenant out.'

'He was probably her lover.'

'No. No, he wasn't. He likes boys.'

'He could take women too, I suppose.'

'No, they had a long relationship but there wasn't any sex in it,' Nancy said, lying beside him in the cool of the summer night, under the thin white sheet.

'I don't believe it. Who would believe it?'

Nancy cast aside her half of the sheet and stretched her body. Her underdeveloped skinniness and boniness was, if it was not regarded as a defect, her considerable speciality; so that without her clothes she was changed, in Emilio's view, from a nobody into a somebody. 'What are you thinking of?' she asked her lover.

'I'm admiring your non-figure,' said Emilio. 'You look so much as if you need a good dinner.'

'I had a good dinner,' she said. 'Maybe I don't look very lovable but I don't care.'

'How seldom one falls in love with the lovable!' he said. 'How seldom . . . Hardly ever.'

'How do you know when you're in love?' she said.

'The traffic in the city improves and the cost of living seems to be very low.'

Chapter Five

'A typical business-man, about forty-three, I should imagine rather conceited,' said Maggie, 'with a son who looks like a gigolo, a daughter, a kind of Girl Guide, I couldn't stand the girl; then there was a downtrodden English governess and the girl's boy-friend, awful little fellow from under some stone. The only good thing about them was their house, which isn't theirs, it's mine.'

'Oh, but I know Pietro and Michael likes him,' her daughter-in-law said.

'I admit the son was the best of the lot,' Maggie said, 'but it isn't saying much. Very bourgeois; of course they were terrified of lifting a finger to help me to get Hubert out.'

'I'll do everything I can to help you,' Mary said eagerly. She was terribly anxious to make a success of her marriage, as she would put it; her father was a success and her mother was a well-known success in advertising although she didn't by any means need the job; moreover, Mary's elder sister was busy making a success of her marriage. Mary had been successfully brought up, neither too much nor too little indulged. And so, still half under the general anaesthetic of her past years, Mary was not disposed to regard Maggie as critically as she would have done had Maggie not been her mother-in-law; it was part of making a success of her marriage. 'So long as I'm here on the spot, Maggie,' Mary said, 'I'll do my best.'

'I know I was foolish to let things get this way,' Maggie said. 'I realize that. It was just that when I was married to Ralph Radcliffe I got just so bored, I just took on a number of artists and intellectuals in a number of cities, and I just . . . Well, Hubert of course was really sort of someone, I really helped him to be what he was, but he's not all that a somebody. He's better known in Paris, of course, or rather was a few years back – after *Ce Soir Mon Frère*, that play, you know –'

'Oh yes! Did Hubert produce it?' Mary said.

'No, Hubert wrote it. Well, I took –'

'Was it a success?' Mary said.

'Well, in Paris it was. So I took Hubert on more and more. He was doing this play. And after a couple of years he was doing another. I helped him a lot with funds and so on, the rent. Sometimes he'd give me a bit of advice about pictures, when we went to the galleries, New York and Paris. Then, well, there was advice and counsel about so much furniture and rugs. He has taste and knowledge, but of course that's not everything. Then you know he kind of took over my life; even when I was away I felt dependent, I felt trapped, and I couldn't rely on Michael's father as a husband, not at all; no, Ralph Radcliffe couldn't have cared less. Of course Hubert's friendship with me was only platonic.'

'So what were you getting out of it?' Mary said.

'Exactly. In the end, that's what I asked. But who would believe it if there was a scandal? And you know these houses at Nemi, it was Hubert's idea to invest this way; he found two houses for me, and of course he wanted one for himself on that piece of land. I don't regret the houses, they're all good properties and appreciating in value, only I want out, out, out, where Hubert is concerned. When I remarried I told Berto about Hubert still occupying one of my houses, and all the best furniture in it. Berto said, "You're crazy, Maggie, crazy. He's a hanger-on. Just get him out. Tell him to go." But it's difficult, you know.'

'Hubert has the nerve!' said Mary. 'The nerve of him! I heard that he had a house full of queers last summer.'

'Yes, but I stopped the money. When I married Berto he said, "Stop sending money. Stop the money order at the bank." I didn't really know what to do. It's really hypnotic when you get in someone's clutches. Berto said, "Why are you hesitating? What are you afraid of? Just write and tell him you're stopping the money." Berto said he would write himself, if I wanted. I said, "Well, Berto, he knows you don't need the money and neither do I, and I don't give him very much." So –'

'That's not the point,' Mary said.

'Right. That's precisely what Berto said. It isn't the point. But now Hubert's being so stubborn, I don't want a scandal, especially as you and Michael live here and like it so much. It's a problem.'

'It's a very, very big problem,' said Mary, eager to be entirely with Maggie. 'It's a tremendous problem.'

'And there's that lesbian secretary living with him,' Maggie said.

'Is she lesbian?'

'I guess so. What else would she be?'

'I guess that's right,' said Mary.

'She couldn't be normal, living there with him.'

'Well, it could be platonic like when you were friends with him,' Mary said, 'but I guess it isn't.'

'A lesbian,' Maggie said, adding, as if to make her real point, 'a penniless lesbian.' With that much off her chest, Maggie now started to praise Hubert by little bits, placing Mary, who also had a few pleasant memories of Hubert, in a state of assenting duplicity.

'He has been careful of the furniture,' Maggie said. 'He appreciates fine furniture and understands it. In fact he helped me choose it. And now I hear he still sends the Louis XIV chairs to an antique expert in Rome to be checked regularly and put right if there's any little thing loose or frayed, you know, and maybe the wood treated. I heard only the other day. In some ways, Hubert was very thoughtful for me.'

'It's expensive, the maintenance of antiques,' Mary said. 'My father's – '

'Oh, I know. He can't be all that short of money, can he?'

Mary said, 'I'll find out what I can.'

'Not that it matters to me,' Maggie said. 'Only, I mean, he can't be all that badly off if he's looking after my furniture, can he?'

'No, he can't.'

'He didn't open the door to the official whom my lawyer sent with a notice to quit. Pretended he was out.'

'But he'd have to let *you* in,' Mary said. 'Why don't you go yourself and have it out with him? A confrontation is always the best.'

'Do you think so?'

'Well, maybe. I don't know. I mean, most of the time a confrontation is healthy when a relationship goes wrong.'

'There's nothing wrong with the relationship,' Maggie said. 'On my side, everything's the same. I just don't want to go on keeping him, that's all. No explanation necessary. I just don't want to go on.'

'I hear he changed the locks on all the doors.'

'Who told you that?' Maggie said.

'Pietro, the Bernardini son. He told us their tutor learned it from Hubert's secretary. They changed all the locks so your keys won't fit.'

'I wouldn't dream,' Maggie said wildly, 'of breaking into the house without his permission. What's he think I am? He's not all that bad.'

'Sure, he's got very good points. Very, very good points.'

'It would be nice,' Maggie said speaking softly now, 'to think he wasn't in need of actual food. I hope he has enough to eat.'

'He couldn't afford a secretary if he hasn't enough to eat,' Mary said in an equally low voice.

'Well, I don't know,' Maggie said, 'and it makes me thoughtful. There are some young secretaries foolish enough to work free for a man if they believe in him. And Hubert's secretary, the little time I saw her passing in that station-wagon of his, it was only once, for a second, well, I don't know . . . She may have ideas for the future.'

'But she's a lesbian!' Mary said.

'Who knows? Lesbians like to hook a man too, you know. Sex isn't everything. She might want a cover. And so might he.'

'Well, if he hasn't enough to eat he'll be starved out,' Mary said.

'Then there's the electricity, the gas and the telephone. They'll be cut off if the bills aren't paid,' Maggie said, and her voice had taken completely to a whisper, as if an utterance of such things could be unlucky.

'That will solve your problem, then,' Mary said. 'He'll have to leave.'

'Do you believe in the evil eye?' said Maggie still speaking very low.

'Well, no,' said Mary whispering back in concert, 'I believe I don't.' She bent closer to Maggie.

'It's possible,' Maggie breathed, 'that if there is such a thing, Hubert has the evil eye. His name, Mallindaine, is supposed to be derived from an old French form, "malline" which means of course malign, and "Diane" with the "i" and the "a" reversed. He told me once, and as he explained it, the family reversed those syllables as a kind of code, because of course the Church would have liquidated the whole family if their descent from a pagan goddess was known. And they always worshipped Diana. It was a stubborn family tradition, apparently.'

'It sounds very superstitious,' Mary said in her hush.

'I wouldn't think Hubert was malign, would you?' Maggie whispered.

'No, I wouldn't think that. I think he's a bum, that's all,' Mary said, shifting in her garden chair, while the treetops on the slope below their house rustled in a sudden warm gust of air and the dark lake showed through the branches, calm, sheltered by the steep banks.

'It makes me uneasy,' Maggie said. 'Could you keep a secret?' She moved her chair a little nearer to the daughter-in-law.

'Sure.'

'Even from Michael?'

'Well, if it wouldn't make any difference to our marriage . . .' Mary said.

'I don't see how it could as it only concerns Hubert and me,' Maggie whispered.

'Oh, sure I can keep a secret,' the girl whispered back eagerly, as if the confidence might otherwise be withdrawn altogether.

'I want to send Hubert money from time to time. But he mustn't know it comes from me,' Maggie said. 'I also have to think of my marriage. Berto insists that I throw Hubert out. Well, I have to keep trying, and in a way I want to.'

'You don't have to tell Berto everything, do you?'

'He wants to know everything,' Maggie said. 'He's the old-fashioned Italian, it's part of the charm.'

'I can see that,' said the girl.

'How can I get this money to Hubert without him guessing?'

'Is it a lot of money?'

'Well, if I decide on a sum . . . enough for him to live on here at Nemi while I'm trying to get him out of the house.'

'I don't think I follow, really,' said Mary. 'But I see what you mean in a way.'

'It's a paradox,' Maggie said. 'But Hubert mustn't know how I feel.'

'He'd think you were frightened of him.'

They talked in hushes late into the afternoon.

'We're going a long way but we aren't getting anywhere,' Maggie said as the air grew cooler.

'I wish I could talk it over with Michael.'

'No! Michael would put a stop to it.'

'So he would, I guess. I'll try to think of a scheme.'

'You have to help me.'

'I'll help you, Maggie.'

They looked down on the incredible fertility beneath them. A head and small flash of face every now and again bobbed out of the trees as the country people came and went; one of these, approaching up a path through the dense woodland, presently emerged clearly as Lauro returning. He appeared and disappeared ever larger, seeming to spring from the trees a fuller person at every turn. A little to the north was a corner of Hubert's roof, and under the cliff below him at a point where the banks of the lake spread less steeply into a small plain lay the cultivated, furrowed and planted small fields of flowers and the dark green density of woodland that covered what Frazer in *The Golden Bough* described as 'the scene of the tragedy'.

The scene of the tragedy lay directly but far below Hubert's house, and meanwhile the stars contended with him. 'Hoping to inherit the earth as I do,' he said, 'I declare myself meek.'

This tragedy was only so in the classical and dramatic sense; its participants were in perfect collusion. In the historic sense it was a pathetic and greedy affair. The recurrent performance of the tragedy began before the dates of knowledge, in mythology, but repeating itself tenaciously well into known history.

The temple of the goddess Diana was, from remote antiquity, a famous pilgrim resort. To guard her sanctuary, Diana Nemorensis, Diana of the Wood, had a court of attendants ruled over by a powerful high priest. Legends and ancient chronicles have described this figure and it was upon him that J. G. Frazer's great curiosity was centred. Here is Frazer's celebrated account of the priesthood of Diana and its 'tragedy' :

In the sacred grove there grew a certain tree round which at any time of the day, and probably far into the night, a grim figure might be seen to prowl. In his hand he carried a drawn sword, and he kept peering warily about him as if at every instant he expected to be set upon by an enemy. He was a priest and a murderer; and the man for whom he looked was sooner or later to murder him and hold the priesthood in his stead. Such was the rule of the sanctuary. A candidate for the priesthood could only succeed to office by slaying the priest, and having slain him, he retained office till he was himself slain by a stronger or craftier.

The post which he held by this precarious tenure carried with it the title of king; but surely no crowned head ever lay uneasier, or was visited by more evil dreams, than his. For year in year out, in summer and winter, in fair weather and in foul, he had to keep his lonely watch, and whenever he snatched a troubled slumber it was at the peril of his life. The least relaxation of his vigilance, the smallest abatement of his strength of limb or skill of fence, put him in jeopardy; grey hairs might seal his death-warrant . . . According to one story the worship of Diana at Nemi was instituted by Orestes, who, after killing Thoas, king of the Tauric Chersonese (the Crimea), fled with his sister to Italy, bringing with him the image of the Tauric Diana hidden in a faggot of sticks. After his death his bones were transported from Aricia to Rome and buried in front of the temple of Saturn, on the Capitoline slope, beside the temple of Concord. The bloody ritual which legend ascribed to the Tauric Diana is familiar to classical readers; it is said that every stranger who landed on the shore was sacrificed on her altar. But transported to Italy, the rite assumed a milder form. Within the sanctuary at Nemi grew a certain tree of which no branch might be broken. Only a runaway slave was allowed to break off, if he could, one of its boughs. Success in the attempt entitled him to fight the priest in single combat, and if he slew him he reigned in his stead with the title of King of the Wood (*Rex Nemorensis*). According to the public opinion of the ancients the fateful branch was that Golden Bough which, at the Sibyl's bidding, Aeneas plucked before he essayed the perilous journey to the world of the dead. The flight of the slave represented, it was said, the flight of Orestes; his combat with the priest was a reminiscence of the human sacrifices once offered to the Tauric Diana. This rule of succession by the sword was observed down to imperial times; for amongst his other freaks Caligula, thinking that the priest of Nemi had held office too long, hired a more stalwart ruffian to slay him; and a Greek traveller, who visited Italy in the age of the Antonines, remarks that down to his time the priesthood was still the prize of victory in a single combat.

Rigid and frigid as was the statue of Diana the huntress, still, after all, it became personified as a goddess of fertility. But how, Hubert would demand of his listeners, did the mad Emperor Caligula have sex with a statue? It was an orgy on a lake-ship: there must have been something more than a statue. Caligula took Diana aboard his ship under her guise as the full moon, according to Suetonius. Diana the goddess, Hubert explained, was adept at adding years to the life of a man – she had done so with her lover Hippolytus. She bore a child to the madly enamoured Emperor, added years to the infant's life so that he became instantly adult, and it was this young man, and not a Roman hireling, whom Caligula sent to supplant the reigning King of the Wood, the priest of Diana.

Hubert descended, then, from the Emperor, the goddess, and from her woodland priest; in reality this was nothing more than his synthesis of a persistent, yet far more vague, little story fostered by a couple of dotty aunts enamoured of the author-image of Sir James Frazer and misled by one of those quack genealogists who flourished in late Victorian times and around the turn of the century, and who still, when they take up the trade, never fail to flourish.

Modern Nemi, at the end of the last century, as more recently when Hubert Mallindaine settled there, appeared to Frazer to be curiously an image of Italy in the olden times; 'when the land was still sparsely peopled with tribes of savage hunters or wandering herdsmen'. Diana's temple had been feared by the Church. The long wall of high arched niches, once part of the temple-life, have perfectly survived antiquity, and these, at a later time, had been named 'the Devil's Grottoes'. Hubert, beating his way through the undergrowth along the rows of remaining cliff-chapels, would come upon the relics of traditional disrespect and of outcast life. There was a rubbish dump, incredibly rubbishy with the backs of yellow plastic chairs, petrol tins, muddy boots and cast-off rags piled up in those enormous Roman votive alcoves which soared above their desecration with stony dignity. And from this view the plateau was beautiful; it contained the rectangular site of the sanctuary itself, now filled up with earth and cultivated with a chrysanthemum crop.

Very few people now visited this spot as a temple. Hubert had seen reported in a recent article that it was 'still lost as far as the ordinary tourist is concerned'. 'No local folk,' complained the author of the article, 'seem to know where it is.' Which, of course, was instinctively the way with local people. Chrysanthemums enjoyed a commercial popularity in Italy on one day of the year, the Day of the Dead; otherwise they were considered unlucky.

The site of the rectangular sanctuary was marked unobtrusively by a withered tree in one corner. A rim of the temple wall still protruded a few inches from the ground on three of its sides. The reason the peasants had cultivated the soil once more over the late dig was that 'the money for the excavations had stopped', as one of them explained to Hubert.

One spring, when he was supervising the building of the house then destined by Maggie to be his, Hubert had walked down the cliff-path and talked to a man who was pruning a pear tree on the site of Diana's temple. The man was about forty-two. He remembered the excavations, he said, when he was a boy. Very beautiful. Red brick paving. A fireplace. Yes, said Hubert, that was for the vestal virgins; it was an everlasting flame. The man went on with his pruning. My ancestress, Diana, was worshipped here, Hubert said. The man continued his work, no doubt thinking Hubert's Italian was at fault.

Again, standing one winter day alone among the bare soughing branches of those thick woodlands, looking down at the furrowed rectangle where the goddess was worshipped long ago, he shouted aloud with great enthusiasm, 'It's mine! I am the King of Nemi! It is my divine right! I am Hubert Mallindaine the descendant of the Emperor of Rome and the Benevolent-Malign Diana of the Woods . . . ' And whether he was sincere or not; or whether, indeed, he was or was not connected so far back as the divinity-crazed Caligula – and if he was descended from any gods of mythology, purely on statistical grounds who is not? – at any rate, these words were what Hubert cried.

Chapter Six

Mary had not yet got used to the Italian afternoon repose. Her hours were the Anglo-Saxon eight in the morning till midnight with a two-hour break for lunch. That Maggie went to bed between three and five in the afternoon she attributed to

Maggie's middle-age. That nearly all Italians rested during that period of the day she attributed to Latin laziness. What her husband did with himself in Rome during these hours she had not begun to wonder; if she had done so she would have assumed that he regularly returned to his office after lunch, keeping American hours in lonely righteousness. In fact, Michael had a mistress in Rome in whose flat he spent the customary hours of repose; it was not unusual for Italian businessmen to spend the long free hours of lunch and after-lunch with their mistresses, but if Mary had suspected that Michael had acquired the habit, especially so early in their married life, she would have considered her marriage a failure beyond redemption.

Maggie was sleeping successfully that afternoon. Mary had, with some scruple, for she was a girl of many scruples, plied her mother-in-law with white wine. They had lunched together on the terrace, talking of next week. Then Maggie had given Mary the smart jewel-case of black calf-skin, slightly wider than a shoe-box, which, when opened, was dramatically and really very beautifully packed with gold coins of various sizes, dates and nationalities. 'There are no absolute collectors' items,' Maggie explained. Their two heads – Maggie's shimmering silver and Mary's long and fair – bent over the glittering and chinking hoard. 'But,' said Maggie, 'the collection as a whole is of course worth more than its weight in gold. Coins always are. My real collection is worth a great deal.' Mary's long fingers shifted the coins about. She lifted one, examined it, put it down and took up another, then another. 'Queen Victoria half-sovereign, King Edward sovereign, South African sovereign – whose head is that?' 'Kruger,' said Maggie. 'Kruger. Are these worth a lot of money, then?' 'Well,' Maggie said, 'it depends who you are, whether they are.'

The coins tinkled through Mary's hands, then hearing the coffee-cups being brought she shut the box, put it on her lap and looked over her shoulder. Lauro appeared, his eyes intent on the tray although he must have seen the black box on Mary's lap.

When he had left, Maggie said, 'Hubert mustn't have a clue who sent them.'

Mary said, 'I really don't see why he should have all these.'

'I have my own important collection,' Maggie said, 'and I can get more. Any time I want.'

'I know. But it's crazy . . .'

'Yes, it's crazy. But it's a way of getting rid of him in my own mind.'

'Oh, I do see that.'

'A cheque would tie him to me even more. I could never get rid of him.'

'No, I see that. He'd think he was in with you again. But gold is appreciating in value, isn't it?'

'Such a damn cheek,' Maggie said. 'I hate him.'

Later, in Maggie's room, they counted the coins and made a list. It was Mary's idea to make a list. She made lists of everything. A good part of her mornings was spent on list-making. She had lists for entertaining and for shopping. She listed her clothes, her expenditure and her correspondence. She kept lists of her books and music and furniture. She wrote them by hand, then typed them later in alphabetical or chronological order according as might be called for. Sometimes she made a card index when the subject was complex, such as the winter season's dinner parties, whom she had dined with and whom she had asked, what she had worn and when. Now she was making a list of the coins while Maggie took off her clothes, and got right into bed for her afternoon rest. Mary took her unfinished list and the coin-box quietly out of the room when Maggie fell asleep, and now she was in her own room sorting and writing seriously. She felt useful. Even though it was to be a secret from Michael, this help she was giving to Maggie was almost like helping Michael. Maggie, asleep in the next room, was much the same as if Michael were lying down there, having an afternoon sleep.

'Q. Vict.,' she wrote, '½ sov. 1842.'

She grasped quickly that there were no numismatic rarities; the value of the coins was largely commercial. At that, they added up to a considerable amount. They were mostly English half-sovereigns, early and late Victorian, bearing the Queen's young head and her older head. Mary found a sovereign of the reign of George IV and, realizing its extra value, wondered if Maggie had put it in by mistake. She put the coin aside, then, on the thought that Maggie might think her critical or stingy, put it back in the box and marked it on her list. The main idea was to please Maggie and show she understood her position. Maggie, after all, was being very delicate in her treatment of Hubert. Mary began to consider various means of conveying this treasure to him without betraying its origin. When she realized how impossible it would be for her to simply drive or walk over to the house herself and hand it over to him, she felt a waif-like longing to do so; she saw herself for a brief moment as an outcast from what appeared to her as a world of humour and sophistication which Hubert had brought with him during those few months she had known him, when he was still in Maggie's good favour. At the same time she disapproved of him as a proposition in Maggie's life. He really had no right to this golden fortune. Her mood swivelled and she imagined with satisfaction a dramatic little scene of handsome Hubert being thrown out of Maggie's house by the police.

Her list was complete. She closed the box and stood up. From the window she caught sight of a shining black head in the greenery below. She recognized Lauro and at the same time the idea came to her that, obviously, Lauro would be the person to carry this box to Hubert. She was convinced of his discretion and, after all, he had worked for Hubert once.

Mary went immediately to Maggie's room clutching the box. Maggie was still asleep. Her mouth was open and she slept noisily. The girl felt guilty, watching this uncomely sleep. Maggie, if wakened, would know she had been watched. Mary retreated, deciding to act on her own and rightly perceiving how gratified Maggie would be to wake up and find her plan accomplished; she would feel free in her heart and mind to turn Hubert out and give him hell and know that at least he wasn't starving. Mary was already on her way to meet Lauro, leaving the house by the back door. His white coat was hanging on the back of a kitchen chair. Mary swung down the hot winding path with her long brown legs and sandals and, seeing Lauro's black head once more below her, called to him, 'Lauro!'

He stopped and waited. She found him sitting down in the shade of the woods just off the path. 'Lauro,' she said, 'I've got something important to ask you. I want you to do something.'

She expected him to stand up immediately she approached but

he let a moment pass before doing so. He was smiling as if he enjoyed the lonely scene, and as if the woods belonged to him. She felt strangely awkward as she had not been before when she had been alone with him in the house or in the car, or walking with him to the shops in the village street.

She spoke rapidly, as if giving some domestic instructions while her free mind, as it might be, was on something weightier. 'You have to keep a secret, Lauro,' she said. 'I have something here for Mr Mallindaine but he must not be told who sent it.'

'Okay,' said Lauro.

'I want you to take this box to Mr Mallindaine's house. He mustn't see you as he mustn't know where the box has come from. Find some way of leaving it where he's sure to find it. Do you know the lay-out of the house?'

'Sure, I know the house well. I lived there all last summer. What's in the box please, Mary?'

Mary opened it, trembling at what she was doing. 'They're old coins,' she was saying. 'I've made a list.' She displayed the rich tumble of gold with an expression which conveyed both her naïvety and the pleasure of showing off to the boy.

The sight of so much golden money in the rich, very rich, tall girl's hands inflamed him instantly with sexual desire. He grabbed the box and pulled her into the thick green glade. He pulled her down to the ground and with the box spilling beside them he would have raped her had she not quite yielded after the first gasp, and really, in the end, although she protested in fierce whispers, her eyes all over the green shrubbery lest someone should see, she put up no sort of struggle. 'That wasn't no good because you didn't relax,' Lauro said, his face, satyr-like, closing in on hers, his eyes gleaming with automatic hypnotism as he had seen it done on the films and television from his tiniest years, and acquired as a habit.

Mary, in a crisis of breath-shortage and an abundance of tears, pulled at her few clothes and managed to articulate, 'My husband will kill you.'

'He sooner screw me,' Lauro said.

'That, too, I'll tell him,' she said. 'I would hit you on the face if you were not a servant.'

He jumped up; flash and flutter went his eyes closing on her face, and tight went his hands on her bare arms, as if he were directing the film as well as playing the principal part. 'Next time, you relax,' Lauro said, smiling through his teeth. 'For the first time, no good.'

Mary closed her mouth tight and pushed back her hair with a gesture of every-day indifference. He turned and took up the jewel-box whose contents were half-spilled on the earth, and with her help scooped up the lurking gold. He laughed as if the coins were some sort of counters in a party-game, while Mary, still trembling and crying, stood up; she tugged at her clothes and smoothed her hair; she said, 'Give me that box.'

'I'll take it to Hubert,' he said, and started off in that direction.

Mary caught up with him. 'Are you sure you'll find the right place to leave it? It's not mine, it's Maggie's. Hubert mustn't know.'

He smiled, and turned to put his face close to hers again, smiling. 'Leave it to me, Mary,' he said. He clutched the box under his arms as if it were a man's business, and looked as if he had earned the takings within.

She turned and ran back to the house, not sure how far she was guilty, or what she must do next. She became uncertain whether Lauro could be trusted with those coins. She was perplexed about the relationship in which she stood with Lauro now, and above all she was anxious to take a shower.

Hubert was at that moment counting some coins which he had found in a curious way at six o'clock that afternoon.

Pauline had gone in to Rome in Hubert's station-wagon, taking with her, wrapped in lengths and strips of sackcloth, a second Louis XIV chair of Maggie's to be delivered to the address in Via di Santa Maria dell'Anima where the copies were made. Of these transactions Pauline knew nothing, thinking only that the chairs were being examined and repaired, and that the bill for this service would be sent to their mysterious all-pervasive owner, Maggie. Pauline had never seen Maggie; to Pauline she was a hovering name, an absent presence in Hubert's house and his life.

She delivered the chair, with its penitential sackcloth secured by a winding string round its beautiful legs and tied over its seat and back, ordering the man who carried it up the stairs to take care, great care. She left it with him while she went to find a legitimate parking place for the car. When she returned the man was with a younger man, tall, in blue jeans and a smart shirt; the chair had already been unshrouded and they were examining it with pride.

As Pauline approached the younger man disappeared into a back room from where he carried a chair identical in appearance to the one Pauline had brought. She had been instructed to fetch this back to the house; apparently it was the first of Maggie's best chairs to be sent for inspection and overhaul and, apparently, it was now in perfect order. In reality, it was a new and very clever fake; one of its legs was all that remained of Maggie's former chair. Most of these clever fakes contained at least one limb of the original, and in that way the dealer was entitled, or felt entitled, to proclaim it 'Louis XIV'. To Pauline, it did not matter very much what period the chair belonged to. She had her orders to collect it and she was anxious to get back to Hubert quickly. She asked the men to wrap the chair carefully, which they duly did, with new rags, and much wadding placed over the sparkling green silk of the seat. It was carried to the car.

'Tell Mr Mallindaine to pass by early next week,' said the smart young man in blue jeans.

'He isn't leaving Nemi much, at the moment,' Pauline said, thinking of Hubert, how he was afraid to leave the house in case Maggie should come and reclaim it in his absence.

But the man repeated his request.

Meantime Hubert, at Nemi, was counting the gold coins he had found at six o'clock. It was his usual tea time and he had gone into the kitchen to make it. As he had fetched down the teapot from the shelf he heard a strange rattling inside it. He took off the lid. He had found a quantity of gold money inside the pot.

He sat down at the kitchen table, looking inside the teapot. Then he looked round the kitchen to see what else, if anything, was amiss. Nothing seemed to be out of place. He wished for Pauline to return. He had emptied the gold coins on the table, and now was counting them.

4

There were, in fact, far fewer than the amount entrusted to Lauro who had kept the black box and more than half the gold. Indeed, his sense of prudence in carrying out Mary's orders was mixed with a feeling of decided benevolence that he had deposited any of these coins in Hubert's teapot. It had sunk into his mind that Mary had told him she had made a list of the coins. It had seemed to him both a fruitless thing to do and a suspicious thing, as touching on his honour.

By the time Hubert, at his customary hour for tea, was puzzling over and re-counting the coins, Lauro was back at the Radcliffes' house, and had changed into his smart houseman's coat. He filled the ice-buckets, arranged the drinks and the glasses, set the terrace furniture to rights, then, chatting with the cook in the pantry, he waited for the cocktail hour.

On her return to the house, after her careful shower and before going down to dinner, Mary had sat for a long while in her room, with her head in her hands, thinking God knows what. Then she skipped to her feet and changed into a long skirt and a blouse. She took up her list of coins, where it was lying on the writing table, and put it down again. She sat down at the table, and pulled out another piece of her list paper. At the top of the page she wrote 'Michael' and underneath it she wrote 'Lauro'. She settled for the thought that she could not have been faithful to Michael all her life, but she felt it was too soon because a year had not passed since her marriage. But then she considered how she had not herself planned the incident with Lauro. One way and another, she tidied up her mind, aligned the beauty preparations in their bottles on the dressing table, and put away the paper she had just written Lauro's name on with Michael's together with the coin-list, her guest-lists and her other lists, locking them up in her desk. Mary had then patted her face with a paper tissue, and had gone down, passing Michael, home from the office, on the stairs. Maggie was already sitting on the terrace waiting for her husband to arrive and her son to come down. Lauro came forward to hover till they were ready to say what they wanted to drink.

'Oh, Lauro,' Mary said very uppishly, 'did you remember that errand?'

'Yes, Mary,' he said in his usual friendly tone, 'how could I forget?'

Mary turned to Maggie and said in a decidedly natural voice, 'He's delivered the box. You see, Lauro knows the house so well, I sent it by him.'

'Oh!' said Maggie. 'But then Hubert will know where it came from and who sent it, and – '

'He didn't see me,' Lauro said. 'I got in through the bathroom window while he was sleeping upstairs. I put the box beside the teapot, so when he came to make his tea he'd be sure to find it.'

'That's brilliant. Lauro, you're brilliant,' Maggie said. 'Mary, darling, you're brilliant. I feel so much relieved now he's at least not likely to starve, because you know I have to get him out of the house. How I've been in the past to Hubert is no guide to how I shall be in the future.'

'Get the police and have him thrown out,' said Mary rather impatiently. 'Lauro, a Campari-soda, please.'

'Well, in our position we can't have a scandal. You know what the Italian papers are like, and all those Communists,' Maggie said.

'We do it discreet,' Lauro said.

'That's right, Lauro. A gin and tonic. Lauro's got the right ideas. Lauro, you're brilliant.'

Hubert, meanwhile, having counted the coins and made his tea, taking it outside on the handsome terrace, gazed out on the panoramic view and pondered. He then began an inspection of the house and decided that one of the ground-floor windows had been entered. There was a narrow pantry window and a narrow bathroom window. The bathroom window was open. It had not been forced. He decided to put bars on the ground-floor windows. He went on a tour of the whole house, opening drawers and cupboards. Nothing was disarranged, nothing missing; it seemed to Hubert that his burglar had been motivated by sheer benevolence towards him. It was a pity to have to bar the windows. Nothing could have been more clearly intended as a personal and rather touching present than those golden coins in his own teapot. For the first time for nearly a year, Hubert started to feel, singing within him, innocence and happiness.

He spread out the coins on the terrace table in the late bright sunlight: Queen Victoria still with a firm young profile and high curly bun, on the coin which was dated 1880 although she was born in 1819. St George and the Dragon, 1892, whose Queen Victoria on the reverse had now been minted with an incipient extra chin, a little coronet and a veil. Gulielmus IIII D: G: Britanniar: Rex F: D:, drooping jowls, a thick neck, a curly quiff on top of his head, 1837. Who, thought Hubert, adores me enough to send me all this glittering mint? And here's Nero wearing a laurel wreath tied with a pretty ribbon at the nape of his neck, or rather, it's Georgius IIII D: G: Britanniar: Rex F: D: 1833. And now, Sub . Hoc . Signo . Militamus – a Knights of Malta ten scudi, 1961. Another juicy young Victoria D: G: Britanniar: Reg: F: D: – darling Victoria, 1880, and that poor downtrodden dragon on the reverse. Render unto Caesar the things that are Caesar's and I wonder, thought Hubert, what utterly charming gentleman hath rendered these things unto me? It then occurred to Hubert that the actual bearer of the coins was hardly likely to be the sender. Hubert had instantly formed an image of largeness, if only of heart, for the sender; he was certainly rich, anyway, and would most likely have young men at his beck and call. Only a young man and slim could have got through the bathroom window so silently and softly. Then, it was someone who knew Hubert's habits and who knew the house. Someone rich. Who? He scooped up the many dozens of coins and took them into the kitchen, where he spread them out and looked at them again.

Pauline returned with the fake chair which they placed in the drawing-room and admired. 'He wants you to call in and see him. Better go soon,' Pauline said. 'I hope it isn't about the bill.'

'I hope not,' Hubert said. 'Maggie gets the bills for this servicing of her stuff. However, if you'll hold the fort I'll go and see him very soon. Always hold the fort. Let no one into the house. I'm thinking of getting bars put in these lower back windows as it seems to me someone might easily get in that way. Once they're in, they can take possession of the house and we're done for.

It was in any case his intention to call on the furniture restorers and collect payment for the genuine parts of Louis

XIV. It would be a considerable sum. Hubert looked at Pauline in a kind of dream, wondering how he could explain to her the good supply of drinks and food he intended to bring back from Rome with him. She had brought back a chicken and some meat and wine from Rome, the good girl; she had spent her own money and was about to prepare a special supper.

After a glass of wine he was moved to tell her about the gold coins.

'It's my opinion,' he said, 'that the spirit of my ancestors Caligula and Diana are responsible for this.' He gave Pauline two sovereigns.

She accepted them after a little hesitation. 'They could have been stolen,' she had said.

'Well, *we* didn't steal them. They were in my teapot, so they're plainly mine. My dear, they are our crock of gold and we have come to the end of the rainbow.'

'Someone must have got into the house.'

'Through the bathroom window,' Hubert said. 'So tomorrow we arrange to have the windows barred.'

'Then your ancestors won't be able to come again,' Pauline said, looking at her sovereigns.

'Those are not on account of wages,' said Hubert. 'Wages I'll pay later and in good measure. I don't like that touch of scepticism in your voice. Remember that my ancestor Diana is very much alive and she doesn't like being mocked. But of course if you're going to express doubts and behave like a French village atheist – '

'It could have been one of those boys who worked for you last summer,' Pauline said, looking at the pile of gold on the table and touching the coins tentatively from time to time.

'Not on your life,' said Hubert.

'It's someone who wants to help you,' Pauline said. 'A well-wisher. Why didn't they send you a cheque?'

Hubert found himself suddenly irritated by this speech. Her kindergarten teacher's tone, he thought. All this being penniless, he thought, has lowered my standards. I should have better company, witty, good minds around me. I find a pile of sovereigns in the teapot and all the silly bitch can say is, 'Someone wants to help you. Why didn't they send you a cheque?'

He took up the newspapers and weeklies she had brought in with her, and, leaving the gold coins littering the kitchen table, went off to his study to take a couple of tranquillizers and further hypnotize himself with the current American government scandals of which everyone's latent anarchism drank deep that summer.

Lauro left for Rome very early next morning with his list of shopping at the supermarket. His first stop, however, was at one of the little cave-like shops in the village, filled, as they were, with the richest of fruits, plants and cut flowers. It was perhaps unusual, but not noticeably so, that he locked the car when he left it outside the door on the village street. Lauro went in and waited his turn.

Figs, peaches, strawberries, all so local and proudly selected, there was not one inferior fruit to be seen. The flowers were mainly of the aster family, huge, medium-sized and smallish, in white, yellow, mauve and pink. Among them were some deeply-coloured small roses and a variety of ferns and leafy plants. The woman who was serving and she who had just been served looked at Lauro with the look of curiosity which comes over the faces of people to whom nothing much happens, and which, to people of more elaborate lives, looks likes hostility. The Radcliffes had their own orchards and rarely shopped here. However, the local people knew very well who Lauro was, and of his recent transference from Hubert's mysterious home to Mary Radcliffe's spectacularly rich one. Lauro, in his smart clothes, the transparent beige shirt and fine-striped pink trousers, was to be treated with a touch of deference. What would he desire? Grapes, peaches fresh this morning, fine tomatoes . . . ?

Lauro desired some plants, strong and lasting, with the roots, for transplanting.

What type of plants? What did the gardeners at the Radcliffes' advise?

'Oh, no,' Lauro said, rather impatiently, almost as if to suggest that not any roots, not any plants, would do, 'they're for my mother's grave. I'm going to visit her at the cemetery.'

The woman who had been served, although she had received her change, made no sign of leaving, but entered the discussion.

Surely the Radcliffes had plenty of plants and to spare . . . ?

'For Mama,' said Lauro with a haughty masculine bark that sent the women scurrying, 'I prefer to pay.' And he bought four chrysanthemum plants not yet in flower and rattled his money while they were being carefully wrapped in newspaper and placed in an orange-coloured plastic shopping bag. He left, and was watched to his car. It was only when he was seen to unlock the empty car, there on the harmless street, that he looked behind him and saw the two women exchanging glances. Carefully, he spat on the pavement. Then he got into his car and drove away too fast. Suspicious old fat cows, what did it matter if they knew what he might be up to, and he knew that they knew that he knew, since, if he put his mind to it he could easily make as many accurate guesses about their doings as they about his. It was for this reason that he had not even bothered to take the precaution of buying his plants in Rome: in Rome they were twice the price, whereas in Nemi they were cheap and he didn't need to care what the people thought. So ended one of those telepathic encounters that go on all the time among compatriots who have foreigners in their midst.

Arriving in Rome, Lauro made first for the cemetery. He found his mother's grave, well-tended and neat, with its hovering marble angel and the little inset photograph. There was room here for his father; their five children would later buy their own burial-plots in the new cemetery, since this one would then be fully occupied. 'Cara Mama,' said Lauro. He had brought his packages in the bright orange plastic shopping bag from the car. He had unpacked the healthy plant-roots, the little strong trowel and another newspaper-wrapped package containing the black leather box with most of the coins that Mary had given over to him the afternoon before.

Some people passed, old people on the way to visit their dead. They gave Lauro a muted 'Buon giorno', inclining their heads towards him with approving piety. Lauro, on his knees, dutifully digging and tending his mother's flower-bed, looked up and returned the greeting with wistful repetition, one quiet 'Buon giorno' for each of the three figures who passed. He was a nice boy in their eyes, which made him feel nice as he dug. The figures, a fat woman in black, a thin man and another, less fat woman with difficult-walking feet, passed from his life. When he had dug enough and laid on the grass verge some of the flowers and plants he had dislodged in the process, he opened up the sheets of newspaper which contained the black leather box. He had almost thrown away the box, keeping only the coins to bury, but it was such a well-made, a well-bred box, such as Lauro sometimes saw in the shops and boutiques of Rome, and it was so connected, now, with the desirable coins and the casual and exclusive quality of Mary and Maggie in their inherited wealthiness, that he had decided to bury the box along with the coins, despite the nuisance. He opened the box, lifted the paper-tissues which he had stuffed inside to keep the coins from rattling, sifted a few of the beautiful golden disks through his brown fingers, quickly replaced the lot, put the black box in the orange plastic bag for safe preservation and, seeing that it was well-covered, he buried it deep. On top of this he replaced some of the short shrubs he had dug up.

He began also to plant the new chrysanthemum roots he had brought, working his way around the grave and, tidying up the border, tastefully arranged the colours; there were already a few nasturtiums, some asters in pink and purple shades and some dark green shoots the nature of which would not be revealed till the autumn. While he was at it he dug up, examined, and replaced two well-wrapped little parcels, one containing a huge sapphire ring and the other a pair of mono-grammed cuff-links, these being objects he had picked up some-where along the line from two earlier periods and encounters of his young life.

When the grave was ready, Lauro stood up and looked at the picture of his mother whom he remembered as deserving and energetic. Her huge voice had commanded until she died. She looked out unsmiling with her bold eyes and her short hair shining and fresh from the hairdresser's. The costly angel who spread his wings above her little oval picture looked frightened by comparison, and the downcast eyes of that pale, church-going, feathered adherent of the New-fangled Testament seemed shiftily afraid to meet those of the living Lauro.

Nobody except the family was permitted to touch the grave. Lauro had taken on this work exclusively to himself; the rest of the family, from whom, in any case, he had nothing to fear, were all too busy elsewhere to tend it. His father had married again and lived in Milan; his two sisters were married with children and lived in Turin. One brother was married in America, and the other, who lived with his father in Milan, was a student. Once a year at the beginning of November, on the Day of the Dead, those of the family and their spouses who were not in America or, as it might happen, confined in labour wards, came to visit Lauro's mother at the cemetery, bearing with them large bunches of long-petalled white and yellow chrysanthemums. These would be piled on the grave. The family would hover and weep, some lustily, some merely wetly. They would say how nicely Lauro kept it, how good he was, sparing them the expense of the cemetery-attendant's services. They kissed Mama's picture but did not touch the grave and asked no questions, not even of themselves. They felt Lauro was getting on quite well and admired his clothes. After the visit to the cemetery on the Day of the Dead the family would troop out with the other thousands of ancestor-visitors, get into their cars and proceed to a trattoria where they had booked a long table for a five-course family meal. Once a year.

Lauro looked round the cemetery, now, in early August, nearly deserted. Only one or two heads moved behind one or two tombstones. Lauro wrapped the leafy rubbish in a piece of his newspaper and the trowel in another. An attendant passed and wished him good morning. Lauro looked around with pleasure. What secrets lay buried in these small oblong territorial properties of the family dead!

Chapter Seven

Dear Hubert,

We are leaving for Sardinia next week – out of this frightful heat! I expect you too will have plans to go to the sea. After Sardinia I plan to return with Mary to the U.S. to spend some time on our own beautiful Atlantic beaches. Berto (my husband – he looks forward to the pleasure of meeting you one day!) plans to join me on the Emerald Coast for a few weeks and then goes on to Le Touquet to join his brother. They plan to look over some horses he plans to buy. I plan to join him in Rome, then Nemi for a week on October first after which our plans take us back to the Veneto.

What I am writing about mainly is, if you can plan to vacate the house during the summer so that we can occupy it from October first, that would suit our plans. Will you let me know, please? Address your letter up till the end of August:

La Marchese Adalberto di Tullio-Friole,
Villa Stazzu,
Liscia di Vacca,
Costa Smeralda,
Sardegna.

After that my New York address (address me there Mrs Maggie Radcliffe as the apartment is still in my old name!) till the end of September. Please leave the key with Mary's maid Agata, if you vacate in the month of August. Agata is coming in every day to feed the cat and dust. September, Lauro will be back so please leave the key with him if you have to vacate as late as the month of September. August would be preferable as this would enable me to plan for the decorators to come in from Rome in September so the house would be in shape for us.

A little bird told me you have been looking after my precious chairs! It was thoughtful of you and very, very simpatico. Bill me with the cost, of course. Maintenance is so very, very important.

One day when all the trivialities of life are settled I hope you will come and visit with me and Adalberto and tell us about your big project that you plan as I am sure you do. I hope it's shaping up!

Happy summer!

As ever, love,
Maggie.

Hubert took a large whisky and two Mitigils. He re-read the letter, paying less attention to what she actually said than to the tone and implication. A mass of ideas moved like nebulae in his mind. It was not until later in the day, after lunch, that he was able to isolate the germ: it was Maggie who, two days ago, had caused the gold coins to be placed in the teapot. The reason: plain guilt. But why buy him off in such an exotic manner?

And why, if she really wanted to make it easy for him to leave the house, had she sent so comparatively little? For, after all, small fortune though they amounted to, they were hardly the value and dimension of what one would call a settlement.

A settlement. In any case, for no money at all would he leave the house.

Again he read the letter. Over lunch he had read it out to Pauline Thin. 'Does she always go on like that about her plans?' Pauline said.

'Not in conversation so much as in her letters. She has an epistolary style which denotes an hysterical need for stability and order. In conversation she counts on her remarkable appearance to hypnotize the immediate environment into a kind of harmony. She learned about planning at college, I should think. It's a useful word in American education. She never understands the rules of anything, however, and her emphatic use of the word 'plan' when she writes a letter is nothing but self-reassurance. Naturally, she will not stick to her plans. If she goes to Sardinia at all, she'll probably only stay one night. That's Maggie.'

Pauline said, 'If you look at things in her light, you wonder why she doesn't get her lawyer to press on with the eviction.'

'She doesn't want a scandal and it's difficult to evict.' Hubert, who was always impatient with others who failed to keep pace with his leaps of logic, conveyed impatience now.

Pauline found herself regretting the appearance of the gold coins; Hubert had been sweeter during their recent weeks of meagre living.

'Well, we should still go very carefully,' Pauline said. 'It may be a trick to lure us into carelessness. We mustn't leave the house unguarded in case they suddenly swoop and stage a take-over.'

Hubert considered this. 'You're a clever girl,' he said.

'And we should still be careful with the money. Are you going to sell the coins?'

'Tomorrow,' Hubert said, 'I shall go into Rome and sell a few. You'll have another present, too.'

'Oh, no,' Pauline said.

'Why not?' said Hubert. His mind was on the money he was going to collect for the chairs. He would have to leave early for Rome to give him time to collect the money comfortably and, in the event they didn't pay in cash, change the cheque before the banks closed. It was an exceptionally hot August. He didn't like Rome in the heat. 'I'll leave early in the morning,' Hubert said.

'Then I'll iron those shirts of yours,' she said, the wifely girl.

'Shirts? I've got plenty of shirts,' Hubert said absently, for his head had lifted to hear the sound of a car coming up the drive. A green Volkswagen that he did not recognize presently drew up at the door.

Pauline said, 'It's the Bernardini daughter.' She stood beside Hubert behind the locked glass doors of the terrace.

'Those people who live in one of Maggie's other houses?'

'Yes, she's the daughter, Letizia.'

Letizia had evidently brought a friend. She got out of the car in front of the house and went round to the other door. Presently, partly by persuasion and partly by force she brought out of the front seat before the eyes of Hubert and Pauline a tall lanky young man with a mop of reddish hair very like a giant chrysanthemum out of which peered a peaked and greyish face. He was trembling and wobbling, and obviously was in a bad way.

'That's Kurt Hakens,' Hubert said.

'Who?'

'One of my secretaries from last summer.' Hubert locked the terrace door. 'He looks drugged, and my laughter demon, which resides somewhere inside me, has ceased to laugh.' He stood back from the glass door of the terrace. 'Let them in,' he said. 'See what they want. Tell them I'm busy and can't be disturbed.'

The secretaries from last summer were not, in themselves, of any particular account to Hubert. There had been other secretaries and other summers in plenty. And other winters.

Once, at a New Year party, in those days when Maggie was discovering the wonders of Bohemian life through him, one of his secretaries deliberately burnt Maggie's hand, that right hand with which she had signed the cheques, and such grand and frequent cheques. 'Hold this,' had said the young man who, Hubert reflected as he recalled the scene, must now be thirty, maybe with a secretary of his own. 'Hold this,' he had said, out on the terrace of that other villa of those days. It was a firework.

He put it in Maggie's hand then lit it; it was the live end of the firecracker that she held in her hand. It flared in her palm before she dropped it. She looked at the young man's smiling face and fuming eyes. 'He burnt my hand!' she screamed out to Hubert across the dark terrace. 'He did it purposely. I'm in agony.' She bent with pain. Hubert was dancing to the distant bells. He seemed to have lost his head to the New Year, and it was another secretary who took Maggie away to treat her hand with some type of cream. Helplessly, Maggie asked for her chauffeur. Another young man joined them. Both secretaries said the chauffeur was asleep in the servants' quarters. They wouldn't call the chauffeur. It was recounted thus later to Hubert first by Maggie and then by the two young men who had helped dress her burns.

'Where were you, Hubert?' Maggie had said. 'Why didn't you help me?'

'I didn't realize what had happened. I thought you were throwing a temperament,' Hubert replied. And he asked her, 'Why didn't you go into the kitchen yourself and demand your chauffeur if you wanted to go home?'

'I couldn't. I felt paralysed. Something just prevented me.'

Maggie had slept in Hubert's bed. They had given her a strong pill. She slept till the party was over at five in the morning, then had got into the car with her bandaged hand, without having seen Hubert around anywhere. The rooms had been littered with used glasses and piled-up ash-trays. Hubert had gone to someone else's bed long before.

When he heard this story later, he saw it all swiftly from Maggie's point of view; he weighed up her nightmare-like experience of being unable to move of her own will to call her chauffeur, and her retiring to a deep sleep on his bed, and decided she was fairly hypnotized by him. For about five years after that, apparently indispensable to Maggie in practical affairs, he had been able to do what he liked with her until that time when gradually, at first unnoticed by him, she began to withdraw. In the meantime there had been secretaries, waves upon waves, season upon season of them. Last summer Kurt Hakens was a secretary, but that was when Maggie had already begun to retreat and was vaguely nowhere to be found. It was plain, now, that last summer she had actually been plotting. She was already getting rid of her ineffectual and purely nominal husband, preparing to marry the new one, and was emerging as a society woman, well-groomed, fully using her enormous wealth which had been lurking there in her favour all the time.

Pauline Thin was at the drawing-room door, apologetically. Hubert looked vexed but in reality he was relieved to see her, imprisoned as he had been, merely sitting it out on one of the still unfaked chairs, out of sight and earshot of his visitors. He had a paranoiac feeling that he was being discussed behind his back and, at the same time as he was very eager to know what was going on between the Bernardini girl, the very ill-looking Kurt Hakens and Pauline, he was afraid to know. Pauline came softly over to him, apologizing in low tones. She pointed to the floor and said, 'They're still down there. Letizia says couldn't you please come down a minute. It's very urgent.'

'What do they want?'

'She says Kurt used to be your secretary and he's an old friend of yours. He needs help.'

'I can't have him here,' Hubert said.

'I'm awfully sorry,' Pauline said.

'You mean you can't cope with them yourself?' Hubert said nastily, rising.

'Yes,' said Pauline humbly.

Hubert took his reading glasses from his pocket and followed her downstairs, looking very much as if he had been torn from his desk.

Letizia was on the terrace, drinking tea. Kurt was stretched out on the long canvas chair beside her, his eyes closed, his mouth quivering. 'How do you do?' Hubert said to the girl.

Letizia stood up, affably showing her teeth and fixing her clear eyes steadily on his face. 'I did not phone,' she said, 'because we haven't met. It was less complicated to come. My father is your neighbour, Emilio Bernardini. I am Letizia.'

Hubert said again, 'How do you do?'

They sat down, looking at the view which seemed always to ask to be looked at like a much-photographed actress. Kurt Hakens continued to lie with closed eyes and quivering lips.

In a while Hubert said, 'What's the matter with him?'

'He's taken an overdose of a drug. I occupy myself with these cases. Now I find me in a predicament because we leave to-morrow for our vacation. This man is a foreigner and he's a friend of yours – '

'Yes, in a way,' Hubert said. 'I gave him a job last summer. A few weeks, then he left. You shouldn't abandon your patients, you know.'

'Papa has made arrangements.'

'Is he getting treatment?'

'I don't know.'

'How does he live?'

'I don't know.'

'Then you want to leave him with me?'

'Yes.'

Pauline said, 'We'll have to call a doctor.'

'Do you know what would happen?' Letizia stood up, agitated. 'They would take him to the Neuro.' The 'Neuro' was the mental hospital in Rome where all cases of mental, nervous, psychopathic and psychotic sufferers who could not afford private clinics were indiscriminately housed in conditions, it was said, rather worse than the Rome prisons, which were reputedly infernal.

'What can I do with him? My dear girl, it's a year since I last saw him,' Hubert said, looking down at Kurt. 'He needs treatment and care. I have no money, my dear. Are the police looking for him? Nemi is in fact my ancestral home. It may be difficult for an Italian to realize, but it is so. My landlady is trying to put me out of the house. How can I take in this poor boy? – I can't do it.'

'Well, yes, as I say, we will do our best,' Hubert said.

Kurt had been helped, half-pushed, upstairs, crying, and without any resistance; he did not seem to know where he was but he knew his way instinctively to the bedroom he had occupied last summer. From time to time a small noise would come from his room to the three sitting downstairs on the terrace; he was faintly whining through his nose; he sounded like a young horse or a dog dreaming in its sleep. Hubert looked at the cheque Letizia had given him. He passed it to Pauline.

63

'I really don't like taking it,' he said.

'It's from our fund,' Letizia said. 'Papa gave me it for our funds, because I had Kurt on my hands and I didn't know what to do with him for the vacation. I would have had to send him to a clinic, then they would ask him questions and maybe he would be in trouble.'

'It will go straight from your fund into ours,' Hubert said. 'I assure you we have a fund, too, for our unfortunates. Pauline, please put it in the fund.'

'All right,' Pauline said. 'Do you want a receipt, Letizia?'

'Oh, no!' She made a gesture of pushing away the offer with her open palms as if alarmed lest the exchange of any document should continue to bind her to the bought-off Kurt. She said, 'Papa was only too happy to help. We leave tomorrow on the boat for Greece and Turkey. Then we go to Ischia. Papa wants you to visit us when we come back.'

'If I'm still here,' Hubert said. 'Our padrona is trying to put us out.'

Pauline was upstairs trying to converse softly with Kurt and at the same time to persuade him to stay in bed. She sat near the door in a soft armchair, in a casual attitude, but ready to flee because Kurt, from time to time, demanded his clothes. Pauline had agreed with Hubert in family-type whispers to keep watch over him while Hubert continued his conversation with Letizia downstairs. Letizia had begun to interest him on the subject of Maggie and this, together with the good big cheque she had handed over, made up for the actual infliction of Kurt upon him; the actual problem of Kurt could be solved later.

The intermittent sound of Kurt's argumentative demands and Pauline's soothing replies seeped down to them. Letizia had accepted a sherry. Her face was lightly tanned, her eyes clear blue.

She paused in her account of the night that Maggie dined at her house, and Hubert, thinking she was troubled about Kurt, said, 'Oh, don't worry. We'll calm him down. I know a couple of Jesuits who'll give me advice. American Jesuits. They'll know how to cope with him.'

But Letizia was not, apparently, at all troubled by Kurt; he had become yesterday's problem. She had paused to consider whether, after all, it was wise of her to repeat how Maggie had tried to get her father's help to put Hubert out of the house. 'Yes, Jesuits, that's good,' she said.

'I suppose she wants your father to gang up with her,' Hubert said, coaxingly. The phrase 'gang up' was beyond her, and after it was explained she rattled on obligingly. 'Of course,' she said, 'we've no intention of making the gang with her. I mean, I have no intention and Papa will listen to me. At Casa Bernardini we're on your side. Papa has to think this way : if she can get one tenant out then we'll be the next.'

'This has the best view of all three houses,' Hubert said, wishing to establish a banal, greedy reason why Maggie should want to be rid of him.

'Oh, is that why she wants it? Well, Papa has spent a fortune in reconstruction so our house is now more worth than it was when we rented it.'

'Maggie,' pressed Hubert, 'covets the view.'

'She says you must go because her husband insists.'

'I dare say. He, too, appreciates the situation of the house. But I shan't go. I have an ancestral claim, you know, my dear.'

'I know! I know!' The girl jumped up and sat down again. 'Tell me more, please, about yourself, how you belong to Nemi and your – '

'Nemi . . . ' said Hubert, leaning back in the chair with his legs stretched out wide in front of him. 'Nemi is mine. It belongs to me, as a matter of fact. The offspring of Diana and Caligula became the high priest of Diana's sanctuary and I am his descendant.'

Kurt's voice could be heard in some sharp protest from above, joined with Pauline's impatient tones. It appeared, now, that Pauline had left the bedroom and was turning the key in the lock. Her footsteps could be heard coming down.

'I'm interested, so interested, Mr Mallindaine. Our English tutor and your English secretary have talked of your family tradition. I love so much the traditions. You shouldn't be sent away from your house.' She made her hands into fists and thumped one on top of another in a way most alarming to see in a young girl. 'My friends and I,' she shouted coarsely, 'will

5

put the son of that American Marchesa out of his house. They will not send you away from your house. The farm-house of the son is Italian property. The Curia had no right to sell it to her. The land where she built this house for you is Italian property. We want things Italian kept in the hands of the Italian people, we must remember our origins!'

Her oration finished, she breathed heavily with an overflow of indignation. Pauline had entered in the course of this speech and looked rather impatient of the rhetoric, in her English way. But Hubert, whatever he felt, looked impressed. He said, 'More Italian in origin than me you could not be . . . a direct descendant of a union between the Roman Emperor Caligula and the goddess Diana, here at Nemi. She must, of course, have been more than an idea; she was flesh, miraculous flesh, be sure of that. – Pauline, my dear, refill our glasses and help yourself. Letizia looks so like the very Diana of the Woods, she looks a true goddess of ancient Latium.' He shoved his glass towards Pauline who had sulkily fetched the sherry bottle. 'Diana, huntress, chaste and fair . . . ' Hubert said. 'It's true. She remained chaste at heart even after she became the great goddess of fertility of all Italy.'

'Do you have documents,' said practical Letizia, 'relating to the family?' Pauline was holding out the refilled glass of sherry; her hand wobbled and a few drops fell on Letizia's pink cotton skirt.

'Documents!' Hubert said, over and above the exchange of Pauline's squeal of apologies, Letizia's reassurances, and the sound of Kurt upstairs banging on his bedroom door. 'Documents! I have an avalanche of family letters and documents. We are working on them now. We're working against time. What do you think Pauline's here for?'

Pauline looked downcast, and indeed she felt so. Letizia, so very young and full of opinion, so very rich and so planted on her home ground, simply by her presence put Pauline in the position of an inferior. Upstairs, minding Kurt like the employee she was, while Letizia relaxed with Hubert on the terrace, Pauline had felt aggrieved. Letizia did not know quite how much *au pair* Pauline was; Pauline had been lending Hubert money to live on. She had paid his electricity bill. She had filled up the station-wagon with petrol to go back and forwards to Rome with those chairs.

Pauline sat silent, not being at all helpful to Hubert on the subject of the documents, because in the first place the documents she was putting in order had so far failed to prove, really, Hubert's ancestral claim, and secondly she did not feel in the mood to support him by so much as a misleading grunt. Hubert thought her obtuse. 'Pauline's been working on the documents,' he said. 'And I have sent for the important ones, which have been kept in England and in Malta. The Mallindaines lived for a long time in Malta.'

'It sounds most interesting,' said Letizia.

'It is most interesting,' said Hubert Mallindaine, and the words brought once more to mind his two aunts having passed the window on Lady Day. 'It sounds most interesting,' said the vicar who stood looking straight out from the bow-window with his hands in the pockets of his summer-grey clergyman's suit, rocking to and fro from his heels to his toes, while his mother sat sewing in the window-seat. The aunts had passed, without hats, which was strange for ladies in Hubert's childhood; their hair, moreover, was cut short, straight, grey and untidy. They were walking hand in hand, and his mother had finished explaining to the vicar that her sisters-in-law were convinced 'Mallindaine' was a corruption of 'maligne Diane'. 'Which is Old French,' his mother said. The aunts had not cared to turn their heads towards them as they passed the window. ' . . . on their way to Hampstead Heath; they do it every Lady Day,' his mother said, still intent on her embroidery. 'They light a bonfire and offer up prayers to the goddess Diana, and I expect there are other rites. They could be had up. Very eccentric. My poor husband could do nothing with them.'

'It sounds most interesting,' said the vicar.

'I dare say it is most interesting,' said his mother, 'but it's embarrassing for me, because of the boy.'

'Have they means?' said the vicar, gazing out on the sunny Hampstead pavement.

Hubert had a few letters referring to these aunts and their

special eccentricity. He had come across the letters some years ago, in Paris, while sorting the first batch of his papers for his memoirs. From that moment he had cultivated the fact of these long-neglected aunts, one of whom had died in the meantime, allowing their fantasy to grow upon him. It may be that in those days he had felt a premonition, even before he had any outward sign, of Maggie's ultimate defection. Those were the years when he still had full control of Maggie's mind and it was he who convinced her to acquire the houses at Nemi 'where Diana, my ancestress, got laid by my ancestor the Roman Emperor'. It wasn't every woman whose escort and protector could make such claims. Submissively and carelessly Maggie had acquired two of the houses at Nemi and had the third built to Hubert's special stipulations; in the meantime she started an affair with a fine-looking young man who was a plain-clothes policeman and part-time actor, the very scourge of those other young men preferred by Hubert. She handed over the fretful details of the purchase of land and buildings at Nemi and had telephoned to Hubert from Rome in that special jargon used by people who at that time woke and took breakfast, as it might be, in Monte Carlo, flew to Venice for a special dinner, Milan next evening for the opera, Portugal for a game of golf and Gstaad for the week-end. 'J'ai compris – toute à Nemi – un avocat . . . called Dante de Lafoucauld, yes, really. – What do you mean, "my policeman lover", Hubert? – Il était gendarme, c'est vrai mais, mais . . . Well, darling, he's handsome. I have to sleep with someone, je dois – ma vie . . . Va bene, va bene, Hubert, ma cosa vuoi, tu? I tuoi ragazzi . . . I don't say a word about your boys, do I? Hubert, after all these years pensando che siamo sempre d'accordo . . . Look, I have to go . . . My maid has the luggage . . . ' Maggie always travelled with her maid and now, for a short while, until the affair of course ended, with her policeman.

Hubert's aunts, in the meantime, grew in the grace of his imagination. They sprouted ancestors before them, springing from nowhere into the ever more present past, until Hubert had a genealogy behind him. He started corresponding with the surviving aunt who in her poverty and dotage was greatly consoled by Hubert's complicity in her life-long belief. He had brought the aunt to meet Maggie in her flat in Paris. Maggie's son, Michael, was there, and Mary whom he was shortly to marry. 'Our forebear Diana,' said Hubert's aunt, 'sets us rather apart. That was why I never married, nor my sister. Hubert will always be a bachelor, too.'

He sat, now, on the terrace of the house at Nemi, secure in this lineage in which he could truly be said to have come to believe, seeing that his capacity for belief was in any case not much. He managed very well without sincerity and as little understood the lack of it as he missed his tonsils and his appendix which had been extracted long since.

He sat half-facing Letizia. 'Documents . . . Yes,' he said, 'the documents exist, of course. Pauline is sorting out the documents. I'm writing my memoirs, you know.'

Letizia turned her head to look uncomfortably inside the house where Kurt's noise was coming from.

'You know how to handle him?' she said.

'Of course. Don't worry,' said Hubert.

Pauline helped herself to sherry and sat down.

Hubert said, 'I was good to him before. He wasn't on drugs then.'

Kurt sounded as if he would break down his door. Pauline did not move. She was watching Letizia who was ready to leave, and was standing, now, a little way off, gazing up at Hubert with her young face. They walked off to the car, talking. The girl obviously was extremely relieved to get rid of Kurt, and was gratefully attributing to Hubert a kind of broad-shouldered glamour which Pauline just for that moment realized he did not possess. That Hubert, walking Letizia to her car, was assiduously playing up to this role made Pauline impotently furious. She could not hear what Hubert was saying as he smiled down at Letizia, held her hand, kissed her hand, laid his hand reassuringly on the girl's arm, and held open the door of her car for her. Letizia turned to wave to Pauline who, after a slight pause, waved back in the laziest way she could manage. Then Letizia was off, back to her sheltered privilege, her Papa and her holidays by the sea, while Hubert, really looking very handsome, strode back and up the steps to the verandah. Kurt was shouting and banging louder still. Hubert looked for help towards Pauline.

'What'll we do with him?' Hubert said.

'Get a doctor, I suppose,' Pauline said, not moving. 'It's your job. You've been paid to look after him.'

'Look, Pauline, we can't get a doctor. You know he'll be put straight into the loony-bin; my house will be searched; I'll be questioned by the police, you'll be questioned – '

'Oh, no I won't,' Pauline said. 'I'm leaving tonight. Going back to Rome tonight and tomorrow I'm going to the sea. If your bouncy admirer can get rid of her responsibilities and flip off to Greece tomorrow morning, why shouldn't I?'

'Pauline, it would be very dishonourable of you to let me down at this moment. Listen to him, up there!'

'How honest are you?' Pauline said, the words coming out in an unpremeditated access of insight. She had never questioned his honesty before.

Possibly suspecting that she already knew more about him than she actually did, he said, 'Dishonest I may be when pushed to it; it's a relative thing. But dishonourable, no.'

Pauline was by now very much upset, and this verbiage confused her. She said, 'We should go up and get him. Bring him down, and try to do something with him.'

'Come on, then,' said Hubert, loftily and pained. 'Let's see what we can do.'

The boy's panic subsided when they opened his door. He was laughing and crying as they brought him downstairs, Pauline holding him by the arm and Hubert following, exhorting him to keep calm, not to worry and to relax.

There was a canvas chair on the terrace that converted into a full-length couch. Hubert arranged this and they got Kurt stretched out on it crowing through his tears. His voice had the effect of ventriloquism, sounding sometimes from a point above and behind him, sometimes from the ground beside him. No words were distinguishable among these doom-like cries and sob-like spasms of laughter. He bayed like an animal. He fell back exhausted. Hubert fetched him a glass of mineral water and two of his Mitigil tranquillizers which the boy took with upturned mad eyes.

Pauline was trembling. 'Either you call a doctor or I do,' she said.

'He can't be seen by a doctor here in my house.'

In the end Hubert agreed to take him to Rome to see a doctor he knew who might even get Kurt into a private clinic. 'It will cost a fortune,' Hubert said roughly.

'Isn't Letizia's cheque enough for the clinic?' Pauline was eager to know how much.

'Barely,' Hubert said. 'We must hope for the best.'

It was nearly eleven that night when Hubert arrived in Rome with Kurt, who was somewhat stunned by a further dose of tranquillizers and trembling at the wrists and knees, in the front seat beside him. Hubert drew up at the foot of the Spanish Steps in the Piazza di Spagna, pressed a golden Victorian half-sovereign into Kurt's hand, told him it was exchangeable for a week's lodgings, and put the young man out on the pavement. Kurt made his way without looking back to a crowd of young vagrants and hippies who were sitting or reclining on the steps in the warm young night.

'That's that,' said Hubert when he returned. Pauline had waited up for him.

'A clinic?' she said.

'Yes, a clinic.'

'What clinic?'

'It's better you shouldn't know what clinic. If there are any questions, you know nothing. Just mind your own business, my dear.'

'It's Letizia Bernardini's problem. You should phone and let her know what's happened before she leaves for Greece.'

'Don't be disagreeable, Pauline. Let the girl go in peace.'

'She hates foreigners, actually. She's that type of Italian. She's only using you.'

'She appeared to be very charming. She's entitled to her bit of folk-schmaltz, it's fashionable among the young.'

'I don't need to be told by you what it feels like to be young.'

'But you can be taught by me, I see, what it feels like to be jealous.'

'How could I be jealous,' said Pauline, 'when you don't care for women, anyway? That's what you told me.'

'I do care for women. I don't have sex with them.'

Pauline started to cry. 'There was something passed between

you and Letizia. I could see it. All that tenderness. I don't know what to believe.'

Hubert put his arm patiently around her shoulders, meting out an almost equal balance of tenderness. 'You can't leave me,' he said, 'because we're friends, and I need you.'

Chapter Eight

'Now you priests,' Hubert said, 'give me my money's worth. Ours is a friendship based on mutual advantage and so I expect some intellectual recompense for this materially superb dinner that we are about to receive.'

Father Cuthbert Plaice said coyly, 'Oh, Hubert!' Father Gerard gave a jocular smile to Pauline and lifted his fork.

'Pass the wine,' said Hubert. Pauline was wearing a long lavender-blue dress of floating chiffon; Hubert wore a deep purple patterned shirt of transparent cotton with expensive-looking blue jeans; the smart dining-room had been opened and the silver and fine glasses brought out; a cold buffet of elegant rarities was laid on the sideboard.

Cuthbert, having tasted his chilled salmon mousse, looked at Pauline across the candlelit table and said, 'Everything looks very sumptuous this evening.'

'He means opulent,' Hubert said, for no other reason than to be difficult.

'It's only a semblance of opulence,' said Pauline, warily; she was evidently thinking that their golden windfall must inevitably reach a point of exhaustion.

'But what is opulence,' said Hubert, 'but a semblance of opulence?'

'Well,' said Gerard, 'I would say there is a very, very great difference.'

'How ingenuous you are!' said Hubert.

'I don't understand,' said the young priest. 'How? – "ingenuous" . . .'

'If you imagine,' Hubert said, 'that appearance may belie the reality, then you are wrong. Appearances *are* reality.'

'Oh, come, Hubert,' said Father Cuthbert. 'Pauline has just said that you have here a semblance of opulence. "Semblance" was her word – wasn't it, Pauline?'

'Yes, it was,' said Pauline, 'and Hubert knows what I mean.'

'A vulgar concept,' Hubert said. 'Tonight we have opulence.'

'But it might not be everybody's idea of opulence,' ventured Gerard. 'I mean of course you're making reality out to be something very subjective, aren't you? People differ in their perceptions.'

'Reality is subjective,' said Hubert. 'In spite of what your religion claims, I say that even your religion is based on the individual perception of appearances only. Apart from these, there is no reality.'

'Try having a scientist agree with you,' said Cuthbert, making little excited movements in his chair.

'The more advanced scientists do agree with me; in fact they're almost mystics,' Hubert said. 'As am I.'

'Can you come to the sideboard?' said Pauline. 'Take your own plates and help yourselves.'

'It looks delicious,' said Gerard, following her to the sideboard. 'And you look very nice in that gown, Pauline.'

'It's new,' she said.

'Is Maggie back from her holidays?' Cuthbert meanwhile inquired softly of Hubert, as if treading a mined field.

But Hubert ignored the question, standing back and beckoning the guests towards the spread of cooked meats and the choiceworthy range of salads. When they were seated Hubert produced a different wine, recommending it with a grand and far-away voice.

It was mid-September and still the heat of summer hovered far into the nights of Rome and its surroundings. Tonight at Nemi there was a faint hill breeze, hardly enough to flicker the candles through the open doors of the dining-room balcony.

'Delicious,' said Cuthbert. 'Delicious wine.'

'Delicious,' said Gerard.

'And Maggie,' Cuthbert plodded on, ' . . . have you heard from her?'

'Not a word,' Pauline said, warming up to communicability which, with a little more wine, would presently become volubility. 'We had a letter from her before she left Nemi. She told us all her movements up to the end of this month. She should have been in America at the moment but I believe she didn't go. She's still in Italy. She wants us to get out of this house by the end of September, but – '

'Pauline!' said Hubert. 'Don't you think you might be boring these learned Fathers with this trivial gossip?'

'No, it isn't boring at all,' Cuthbert said.

'Isn't your chair comfortable, Cuthbert?' Hubert said.

'My chair? – Oh, yes, thank you kindly, it's quite comfortable, Hubert.'

'Cuthbert very often motionizes,' Gerard explained with well-wined pleasantness, 'while verbalizing, depending upon the emotive force of the topic in its relation to the scope and limitations inherent in the process of verbalization.'

'I see,' said Hubert, inclining himself very slightly in aristocratic acknowledgement of this exposition and with the same movement lifting his glass of deep red wine. He sipped and looked at a point above Pauline's head, as one who savours.

'Well, I wasn't being boring,' Pauline said. 'I was only saying that Maggie – and I've never seen her, mind you, I haven't met her at all – is simply impossibly spoilt. Too much money. She had a gentleman's agreement with Hubert and – '

'Maggie is not a gentleman,' Hubert said, 'and I find personalities a boring subject of conversation, Pauline, if you please.'

'What else is there to talk about?' Pauline said. 'Everyone reads the papers and we hear the news; I think it's boring to discuss what everyone's heard already. The point about Maggie is that she's holding this threat over our heads while she's sunning herself on some beach. We only have two weeks to go, and – '

'Pauline, enough!' Hubert said, loudly.

'Maybe we could be of help?' Cuthbert said. 'We found Mary, her daughter-in-law, a very charming, human person. Could I have a word with her? Gerard was in Ischia with them the beginning of August, you know. He – '

'Ischia – I thought they were going to Sardinia,' Pauline said.

'Maggie changed her plans,' said Gerard. 'I had an invitation from Mary to go study the surviving ecological legends of Ischia,' Father Gerard said. 'I stayed with them, it was very comfortable. And I must say that area is rich in legends of nature worship. Mary listed for me many cases of surviving nature-practices and superstitions in that area. They're devout Catholics, of course. I'm not saying anything against their faith; those peasants are great Catholics.'

'But they worship the tree-spirits and the water-spirits,' said Hubert.

'No, no, I wouldn't say worship. You've got it wrong. The Church continues to absorb many pagan nature-rituals because the Church is ecology-conscious.'

Pauline, who had been engaged in conversation with Cuthbert while the other priest was expounding all this to Hubert, suddenly broke in and, hurling the words across the table, said, 'Hubert – listen to this! Lauro, that Italian boy who was your secretary and works for the Radcliffes – well, he went to join them in Ischia and he's sleeping with Mary *and* Maggie. What d'you think of that?'

'Well, perhaps,' said Cuthbert, bouncing in his chair, 'I shouldn't have mentioned it. But, well, maybe – don't you think, Gerard? – it's something that Hubert and Pauline ought to know.'

Gerard, somewhat shaken, said hastily, 'Why, yes, in confidence, of course. As I told Cuthbert on my return from Ischia, this state of affairs arises from an impression, as it was indicated to me by primary coadjunctive factors, that formed in that location with the Radcliffes. But still, as I said, I found Mary very intelligent to be with and very, very helpful. I think, in her case, it's only a passing phase and that young Lauro should never have been allowed the freedom that he has. Mary was very helpful with her documentational listings.' When he had finished this speech he looked at Pauline reproachfully, as if by her outburst she had been a confessor who had burst out of the confessional proclaiming the outrage of a penitent's sins.

Pauline was not apparently concerned with his feelings. She was looking intently at Hubert. He looked back in aloof silence.

'Gerard,' said Father Cuthbert, 'is really very perceptive; since he told me about it, I thought about it and I decided this is something that you ought to know, Hubert, because both Lauro and Maggie have been friends of yours.'

'Personalities bore me,' said Hubert. 'I've spent too much of my life on perishable gossip. Cuthbert, let me change chairs with you; I can see that there's really something wrong with yours.' He got up and started moving his chair. Cuthbert looked bewildered.

'It's only a reflex of Cuthbert's,' said Father Gerard.

Hubert replaced his chair and before he sat down refilled their glasses. He said, 'Gossip and temporal trivialities. Whereas the intellectual principle endures. Cuthbert, be intellectual, for God's sake.'

Pauline took up her plate, holding it at arm's length from her new dress, and moved to the sideboard for a second helping.

'I thought you'd be interested, Hubert,' said Cuthbert, getting up to follow Pauline.

Pauline said, 'We've been hard at work all day. It's nice to relax at night.'

'Do you find it relaxing to think of Lauro busying himself with Maggie and Mary by turns?' Hubert said.

The priests giggled coyly.

Pauline said, 'I do.'

'Then you have a sexual problem, my dear,' Hubert said.

'Whose fault is that?' said Pauline.

'Maybe we'd better keep off personalities, as Hubert suggests,' Gerard said. 'There was a lot of that going on in Ischia, I'm afraid.'

'There always has been,' Hubert said. 'That's where your studies in pagan ecology should begin. Copulation has always been part of the worship and propitiation of nature.'

'Well, Christianity has given all that a very, very, new meaning,' said Cuthbert.

'To us,' said Hubert, 'who are descended from the ancient gods, your Christianity is simply a passing phase. To us, even the God of the Old Testament is a complete upstart and his Son was merely a popular divergence. Diana the huntress, the goddess of nature, and ultimately of fertility, lives on. If you poison her rivers and her trees she takes her revenge in a perfectly logical way. The God of the Christians and the Jews – where's the logic in him?'

'Hubert,' said Pauline, 'you know I'm a Catholic. I don't mind helping you but I won't have my religion insulted.'

Father Cuthbert said, 'Good, Pauline!'

'My dear, I knew you would take it personally,' Hubert said, 'and you look adorable tonight in your new dress. Go and get the sherbet ice out of the refrigerator and mind your frock.'

When the visitors had left, greatly cheered by the wine and liqueurs, the pleasant food, the physical prettiness of the evening and Hubert's exciting insults, Pauline went to change out of her new dress into a cotton nightdress in which she descended to join Hubert at the kitchen sink where he was stacking the dishes into the dish-washer. They started the machine buzzing, then Hubert poured whisky for both, and they sat at the kitchen table, sipping and sizing each other up for a silent while. Eventually Hubert said, 'Lauro and Maggie. Lauro and Mary. When will it be Lauro and Michael?'

'Just what I was wondering myself,' Pauline said. 'Only a few months ago I wouldn't have thought of it. But now since being here alone with you, Hubert, and sharing the trouble, we seem to think the same thoughts. I feel there's a real bond between us. An everlasting bond.'

'Everlasting!' said Hubert. 'A bond, my dear Miss Thin, is not very far from bondage. Don't frighten me, please.'

'Well, Hubert, you don't have to go back to calling me Miss Thin, suddenly, just at this moment. It's not very nice of you after all we've been through.'

'When I feel the bonds tightening, Miss Thin,' said Hubert, 'I break loose from them.'

'All right, I'll go away,' said Pauline.

'What have I done?' said Hubert. 'What have I done to deserve this?'

'Nothing,' said Pauline. 'That's the trouble. You've done nothing at all because you're a confirmed queer. Proximity to a man who does nothing gets on one's nerves after a time. I'm at the end of my tether and I'm leaving.'

'Before one speaks of sex I should have thought one considered the aspect of love,' Hubert said.

77

'I've got a boy-friend in Brussels working for the Common Market,' Pauline said. 'I can go to Brussels and consider the aspect of love with him.'

'Pauline, Pauline, how heartless you are! Love takes time,' Hubert said. 'And if you think you have a right to describe me as a queer when you don't know the first thing about my physical inclinations, then you've got a stupid and a common mind. If I were to impart to you the erotic details of what goes on in my mind they would excite you but *per se* would consequently cease to excite me.'

Pauline, successfully perplexed by this collage of clues, replied sulkily. 'Well, you once told me that you'd never slept with a woman; you said so yourself – '

'Which is not to say I can't.'

'Well, if you haven't, how do you know if you can?'

'Have you ever eaten blubber?'

'No,' said Pauline, ready to be very annoyed.

'Whale-blubber. I ate some once in a little fisherman's café in Normandy. It was on the menu so I thought I'd try it,' Hubert said. 'It tasted all right – fat and fishy – but I suppose there might be ways in which one could prepare it to make an absolutely delicious dish. However, you say you can't eat it – '

'I said I'd never eaten it. What's whale-blubber got to do with sex?'

'Practically everything, if you're an Eskimo. Survival first, sex second.' As he spoke Hubert, noticing a two-inch quantity of champagne at the bottom of the bottle, poured it into his own glass. He now drank it and waited for Pauline to snap back some reply to him, which she failed to do.

Hubert repeated dreamily, 'Blubber!'

'Do you mean to insult women by saying they're like blubber to sleep with?' Pauline said.

'I don't know what they're like to sleep with. But just because you haven't done a thing doesn't imply you can't.'

'Well, I've never eaten blubber and I'm damn sure I couldn't,' Pauline said. 'What has all this got to do with sex?'

'I thought we were talking about love,' Hubert said, persuasively. He considered it was time to go to bed but on the whole he decided another bottle of champagne between them would be a good investment and a good idea. It was appalling, he thought as he undid the cork, how much she wanted a lover and how much he needed a secretary-accomplice.

'What are you doing?' said Pauline, sitting winefully and sulkily in the corner of the big sofa.

'Opening another bottle of expensive champagne. With you in this mood, Miss Thin, I can't afford not to.'

'May I bring my lover in Brussels to stay with us for a while? He gets leave soon,' Pauline said.

'No,' he said, crossly. If she can try to be clever, he thought, I can be really clever. He filled their glasses, sank into his chair and raised his glass slightly to her before he sipped.

'You're using me,' she said.

'Of course. You'll be paid as soon as I have the money, Pauline.'

'I don't want to be paid.'

'You want to use me?' he said.

'No, I want to leave. Your behaviour . . .'

'You want,' said Hubert, 'to use me to satisfy your dreams. Which is wicked. I only want to use you as a secretary, which is perfectly reasonable behaviour. Are you in love with your lover in Brussels?'

'That's my business. Why do you keep talking about love?'

'My dear, it was you who started –'

'No, it was you.'

'Look,' said Hubert, 'one can't have sex with one's secretary. It doesn't work.'

'Now you're talking about sex,' she said.

'Well, it was you who started talking about sex, Miss Thin,' Hubert said, and refilled their glasses.

'We have to get new locks put on the doors tomorrow. The man's coming,' Pauline said, sleepily.

'Why are we getting new locks?'

'You told me to have them changed every month in case Maggie got hold of a key or something. Tomorrow's the six-teenth. I told the man to come tomorrow. Shall I put him off?'

'It's expensive, everything's expensive,' Hubert said, 'but no, my dear, don't put him off. You're very efficient.'

'Thank you,' she said. She put down her glass and started to walk carefully to the door, weaving only a little from her surplus intake of wine.

'Aren't you going to kiss me good night?' Hubert said when she reached the door. He made no motion to get up.

She looked back and felt the start of a drunken haze. She decided to use what lucidity remained to her to climb the stairs, clutching the banisters. 'No, of course not,' she said. 'What do you think I am? A piece of blubber?' She achieved an exit, leaving him to think over what she had said.

What he thought was that the worst was over for the time being. She had got out what was in her mind and might even regret having done so. However, the air was a little cleared and he could count on the *status quo* continuing until it was possible for him to develop a better and more stable *status quo*. Hubert finished the champagne, so musing, and enjoying the solitude of the night. He thought of Maggie in İschia. She had not told him of her change of plans. He didn't know her house in Ischia. 'Maggie . . . ' mused Hubert, 'Maggie . . . ' At about three in the morning he had a sudden desire to telephone Maggie and wake her up, hear her voice. The Marchese would probably be snoring by her side in one of those huge matrimonial beds so prized by Italian families. Hubert felt he didn't care. He half rose from his chair to go into the study, get her number from the exchange and ring her up. Then he recalled with great sadness that the telephone of his house had long since been cut off.

Chapter Nine

'No reply from Hubert,' Maggie said. 'I should have had the phone bill paid if only to keep in touch with him. But I didn't see why he should have the use of it free, calling San Francisco, Hong Kong, Cape Town, you name it. And that lesbian. I had the phone cut off. Anyway I sent him a telegram two days ago to ask if he's ready to vacate the house, and he hasn't replied.'

Her husband, Berto di Tullio-Friole, was intent on listening to a Beethoven symphony on the gramophone and frowned across the room at Maggie to keep her voice down; he made an irritable gesture with his hand to accompany the frown; he was not in the least disenthralled with Maggie; he only wanted very much to savour the mighty bang-crash and terror of sound which would soon be followed by the sweet 'never mind', so adorable to his ears, of the finale. He was a sentimental man. Maggie and Mary lowered their voices.

Berto closed his eyes till the record came to an end. Then he went to join the women at the other part of the long paved room with its windows opened to the sunlight of October and the sea beyond. Lauro appeared from nowhere and was ordered to fetch a whisky and soda for Berto. 'Si, Signor Marchese,' said Lauro. No first names with Berto, nor would Berto have tolerated his wife, her son and her daughter-in-law to be addressed by their first names by any servant in his presence. Lauro, understanding this perfectly, had not even tried. They were nearly ready for lunch, already missing the past summer's days with their morning rhythm of laze and swim, laze and swim, on and off their private rocky beach. This beach, a small promontory, was not entirely private by law, only the elevated rock was private. The pebbly shore where the waves lapped was like all other beaches in Italy, public property, a fact well-known to the blithe visitors who ostentatiously intruded whenever the whim seized them to bring their little boats ashore. It had happened that, one day during the summer, Maggie's swim had been disturbed by a girl in a rowing boat; she was washing her long hair over the side with a shampoo which bubbled Maggie's way. Maggie, aware of her impotence in territorial rights, shouted at the girl, 'You can't wash your hair in sea-water.' Whereupon the girl shouted back, 'It's a special sea-water shampoo.'

Maggie had been very upset and after a hard day's work on the telephone to the mainland had procured five private coast-guards who still lounged along the rim of the shore below and on the rock and in front of Maggie's house, dressed up as 'intruders', thus to keep at a distance the real ones. 'The time is coming,' Maggie said severely, 'when we'll have to employ our own egg-throwers to throw eggs at us, and, my God, of course, miss their aim, when we go to the opera on a gala night.' She had sighed; a deep sigh, from the heart.

Meanwhile they sat in the room with the blinds lowered against both the fairly bright sunshine and those hired intruders, who Maggie thought were making a noise beyond the call of realism, while Berto waited for his drink and the two women continued their discussion of Hubert.

Berto, who was less rich than Maggie, but rich enough to understand the excessive and rather mysterious concerns of rich women of Maggie's generation, and did not object to them, listened with a touch of tolerance and another touch of jealousy. The war of 1973 in the Middle East was just coming to an end. Things would never be the same again, as Berto had been told by the owner of the only newspaper he read. Once when he had entertained at a shooting-party a journalist of considerable fame, descendant of a noble family from Verona, who had ordered the delivery of three newspapers of conflicting politics, Berto had been highly indignant; his roof had been insulated and his hearth befouled; how could anyone read a Communist or a slightly left-wing newspaper, how could any friend of his read anything but the established paper of the right wing with its news reported fairly and its list of important deaths? The mild and middle-aged gentleman of Verona had tried very hard to point out that his profession required him to read all slants of opinion, but had not succeeded in conveying this to Berto who was convinced that all the needs of objectivity were supplied by the one and only newspaper permitted within his walls and whose owner he had known all his life. The journalist gave in and cancelled his wild order, being a man of agreeable temperament, and a desire to shoot some animals being one of the purposes of his visit.

'By law,' Maggie was saying to Mary, 'when you turn someone out of a furnished house in Italy, you send a certain number of warnings, then the authorities send a van for the stuff. By law they have to leave behind the bed, the washing machine and the contents of the files. I would love to take everything away and leave him with the bed, the washing machine and his ridiculous papers and let him share them with Miss Thin.'

'What about the man himself?' Mary said. 'How do you get rid of the person?'

'It's a different process and it's difficult because first of all the neighbours gang up to protect the guy, and then you have the Press and the photographers and the police. But before it comes to all that you have to – '

'Maggie dear!' Berto said. 'Maggie, my love, you'll just have to forget it, you know. Leave him alone; starve him out. He'll leave of his own accord one day, you'll see.'

'Now, Berto, you know you advised me to turn him out!' Maggie said.

'Yes,' said Mary. 'Berto – you did say to turn him out.'

'But,' said Berto slowly, exasperated by their lack of his local logic which he fully thought to be the universal logic, 'if the lawyer has told you the law, and it's going to make a scandal, then you can't succeed. You have to face the fact that the man has tricked you and has stolen your property. And you have to put that man right out of your mind because you can't put him out of your house and make a scandal for the Communists to make capital of in the papers.'

'Italy is a strange place,' Maggie said.

'It's the same everywhere,' Berto said. 'Times are changing rapidly and things will never be the same again.'

'I hate Hubert Mallindaine!' Maggie cried out. 'I loathe Hubert Mallindaine!' And as she exploded further about her feelings against Hubert, her husband was overcome by a tremendous jealousy; Maggie's emotions against Hubert were stronger by far than any she displayed towards himself; and Berto, suspecting in his jealous anxiety that she did not love him with the intensity that she hated Hubert, was too agitated to care whether she expressed love or hate; he cared only lest Maggie felt something for Hubert and nothing for him.

'Hubert,' Maggie said, 'is a man that I despise, loathe and hate, and absolutely detest.'

'He is very contemptible,' Mary said.

'The servants will hear you, Maggie,' Berto said aimlessly, while staring at her as one appalled at his own fate. Lauro, representing the servants, appeared to inquire if he should serve more drinks. Berto had cancelled his trip to Le Touquet to buy horses. He had thought well before doing so; he had thought well, all the time knowing that he would decide to cancel the trip. Maggie had watched this process of decision with the eye

of one watching a horse race, knowing full well which ho se
ought to win, and seeing it win.

'I'm thinking of getting married,' Lauro said.

'Really? To anyone in particular?' said Maggie.

Lauro looked put out. 'She's a fine girl from a very fine family.
She did a year at the University of Pisa studying sociology, and
she's only twenty.'

'And what does she do now, then?'

'She works in a boutique in Rome. Her mother also works in a
boutique. Her father is dead; I don't know where he is.'

'What do you mean ... ?'

'I don't know anything of the father. Maybe there isn't a
father. The mother's family has land at Nemi, two fields.'

'Well, Lauro,' said Maggie, 'you're a lucky man. Is she
beautiful?'

'Oh, yes,' said Lauro as if it went without saying.

'Well, why don't you bring her here to see us?' Maggie said.

'The Marchese wouldn't mix,' Lauro said with a laugh.

The Marchese had gone out and Lauro was sitting on the arm
of one of the blue cotton-covered armchairs in the long paved
room. He had opened the blinds to let in the mild sunlight of the
late October afternoon. Berto was upstairs asleep. Mary and
Michael had also disappeared upstairs where their voices
sounded faintly in a continuous everyday tone. The rest of the
staff had dispersed, some to the cottages behind the villa where
their quarters were, others to hang around with their local
friends at the bars which stretched along the quayside and
where the incoming ferries brought ever-new talkative life from
Naples, and the outgoing ferries carried away those multilingual
visitors who had done their day, or stayed their weeks, on the
islands of Ischia. Lauro perched at his ease, in a fresh shirt and
blue jeans, sipping from a glass of cloudy grapefruit juice and
talking to Maggie. She sat back in her immaculate bright-
coloured house-pyjamas, against the blue cotton covers of her
chair, and smiled through her bright eyes and even as it seemed
through the deep bronze of her skin.

Maggie was wondering whether Lauro had decided to talk of
the girl he wanted to marry from the sheer naturalness of his

kind, or whether he wanted to assert his male pride and put her in her place in some way, since he made love to her often in Berto's absence and when Berto returned was so very much the old-fashioned servant; or did he, thought Maggie, smiling still, want a sum of money on the excuse that he needed it for his wedding and in the knowledge that, so far, she had always been generous to him with money? Maggie pondered on these alternatives as Lauro spoke in his casual manner about his girl and the boutique where she worked, and how she was unaware that he was employed as a domestic. 'I am Mary's secretary,' Lauro advised Maggie, who murmured gaily, 'Quite right, Lauro.' Meantime Maggie's mind ran on the alternatives of Lauro's motives, mistakenly assuming that they were in fact alternatives and that Lauro was capable of analysing his own motives, or bothered to do so, since it had never been in the least necessary for him to find one reason only for doing any one thing.

Then Lauro said, 'I hope that Mary will not take it to heart.'

'Oh,' said Maggie, 'she won't object to calling you her secretary. She'll play along. What's the difference?'

'I mean that I hope my marriage will not upset Mary.'

Maggie was about to ask, 'Why should it?' But, thinking quickly, she refrained. She gave a little laugh instead and said, 'There's no question of upsetting Mary.' And she was gratified to see that Lauro was put out. He's trying to upset me, she thought.

'You know about Mary and me?' Lauro said.

'I know you're a very active boy,' said Maggie, laughing softly again and gazing openly in his face.

'Well, you Americans . . .' Lauro said, gazing back.

'What about us?'

'Strange women,' he said, and in Italian repeated, 'donne strane.'

'Look, Lauro, I'll give you a wedding present, a handsome one. Mary, too, will give you a present; from her and Michael. Isn't that what you're talking about?'

'No, it isn't what I'm talking about,' said Lauro. He was furious and began to shout, 'You think you can buy everything, don't you? I was a secretary to Hubert Mallindaine and now I'm only the butler.'

'Well, I wouldn't say "butler",' Maggie said. 'A butler is a very special type of professional with a very special training. You wouldn't fit in as a butler, really. I always thought of you as our friend who looked after us, as – '

'As a servant,' Lauro shouted. 'I have to wear that white coat, those black pants.'

'Well, Lauro, that's the custom and we pay you well. You do better with us than you ever did with Hubert, and besides you were only his houseman, really, among other things. The word "secretary" – ' She stopped and motioned towards the staircase where footsteps descended.

Lauro stood up and Berto appeared in the bend of the staircase. 'What's going on?' he said to Maggie. 'Who's shouting?'

'Lauro wants to be known as our secretary from now on,' Maggie said. 'I don't see why he shouldn't be a secretary. He's going to get married.'

'Secretary? What do you mean? I don't understand,' Berto said.

Lauro stood in a state of confusion. He was exasperated by Maggie's coolness and quickness of mind and by the fact that he had put himself in the wrong by raising his voice. Maggie, smiling in her chair, was fully conscious that even if the younger man burst out at this moment with the wildest truths about his relations with Maggie and, possibly, Mary, he would be disbelieved on principle; and in fact he would be in deep trouble.

Lauro stood looking at Berto's angry face. 'I finish being a servant,' is what he said.

'All right, all right,' said Berto. 'You can go. Take your things and go. Come back tomorrow morning and I'll give you your wages and your severance pay and your holiday pay and all your other damned communistic rights for domestics, but don't stand there abusing the Marchesa. You don't raise your voice in my house, understand.'

The thought flitted into Maggie's mind that Berto was behaving out of character, but then the thought flitted away in the heat of things.

'Now, you listen a minute,' screamed Lauro, ready for a long hysteria-match such as he had been involved in several times before in his life, not only with Hubert but with the owner of a nightclub, with another Marchese, with a policeman known familiarly as Contessa, with his late mother and very many others. In torrential Italian he listed the indignities he had been subjected to in the service of the Radcliffes and threatened to denounce to the Ministry of Inland Revenue the family's faulty tax returns, this being a safe guess; he said he would sue for being overworked and having to keep late hours with the result that he now suffered a nervous crisis. Tears came to his eyes as he bawled his accusations, convincing himself by his own voice, more and more, how humiliated he had been and how Berto had even done the unspeakable by addressing him with the familiar 'tu' instead of the third person 'lei' required by the law.

'Go!' screamed Berto and gave him the 'tu' again: 'Vai!'

Maggie now stood up majestically, spreading her golden arms in a peace-appeal. From upstairs Mary called down, 'Maggie!'

Maggie went to the foot of the staircase, leaving the two men glaring at each other, and called up, 'It's all right, Mary.'

Michael looked over the banisters. 'What's wrong?'

'Stay there, both of you,' Maggie said. 'Nothing's wrong.' Then she returned to the combatants. 'I haven't understood a word of all this Italian,' she said, 'but it sounds awful. Berto, I have to speak with you privately. Lauro's only a young man and they're all like that these days.'

Lauro spat on the floor between them and left the scene, mounting the main staircase to his room where he banged the door hard. Against the further banging of Lauro's cupboard door and his suitcases, Maggie settled once again in her chair with her hand to her head.

'I'm sorry, Maggie,' said Berto gently and quite surprisingly.

'Oh, these things happen.'

'Can I get you a drink?'

'Yes. Anything.'

He brought her a whisky and soda and she could hear the clink of ice in the glass as he brought it over. His hand was trembling.

Upstairs, Michael could now be heard in urgent conversation with Lauro, possibly trying to calm him down.

Berto brought over his own drink and perched where Lauro

had lately perched. The ice in his glass pelted against the sides. He was agitated. 'I'm sorry,' he said.

'Well, Berto, it's sweet of you to feel sorry for me, but really he wasn't so bad before you appeared.'

'I'm sorry.'

'I don't want him to leave,' Maggie said. 'At least not yet. He might start saying things and cause a scandal.'

'Did he say anything about me? What did he say about me?'

'Nothing,' Maggie said, smiling again, 'except what he said to your face, and that was enough.'

'Oh, I just wondered if the little swine had said anything about me, as you say he might go around talking –'

'I mean Mary. He might talk about Mary.'

'What can he say about Mary?'

'I don't know. Between ourselves, Berto, I don't know if Mary hasn't been foolish with Lauro. He seemed to hint something like that.'

'Mary!' he said.

'Yes, Mary.'

'I can't believe that. These boys are capable of saying anything. They're dangerous. What did he want? Money?'

'I guess so. But you know he's proud and he went a long way round to ask for it.'

'He went the wrong way round.'

'I guess so.'

'He has to leave this house,' Berto said, rather factually and with a melancholy tone which invited contradiction.

'Maybe it will blow over,' Maggie said. 'I don't mind calling him our secretary. I don't see that it makes any difference what he's called. He says he's going to get married and the girl thinks he's a secretary.'

'I don't believe there's a girl.'

'No? Why not?'

'There are things you don't understand, Maggie. You know, at least, that he was Mallindaine's boy.'

'I dare say he goes with boys and girls regardless.'

'Amazing,' said Berto, obviously not much amazed.

'You should talk to him like a father, Berto.'

'Me?' he said. 'Look, I don't want any more to do with him.

He's a whore. Coming into my house and raising his voice to my wife . . . Are you sure of what he said about Mary?'

'Well, he hinted. I don't remember the actual words.'

'He's a liar. I'm sorry.'

Maggie, suddenly unable to resist the impression that Berto had said 'I'm sorry' rather often, threw out a small bait. 'If we let him go, what could he say against *you*, Berto?'

'Anything,' he said. 'Anything. But it wouldn't be true, naturally.'

'Then we'll throw him out,' she said. 'Servants are a boring subject. So that's settled. Michael can drive him to the ferry.'

'He'll make a scandal of it,' Berto said. 'I think, in fact, he'll calm down.' He looked up to the ceiling. 'Michael seems to be dealing with him.' Berto was agitated, speaking softly and loudly by turns. Loudly now, he said, 'And he'd better apologize.'

Maggie said, 'I'm going to have a shower.' She put down her glass and got up, looking back at her empty chair. Berto stood up politely beside her, hovering and anxious to please. What a lot one can learn, she thought, just by sitting still for one hour in a chair. She recalled the long gaze of anger that had passed between Lauro and her husband a short while ago. It had been a knowing anger. She said to herself that she had not seen Berto lose his temper with the other servants or with any of his business employees whatever their stupidity, or however much they lost theirs; Berto habitually subdued them by placing a thousand miles of ice between himself and them. On the other hand, she had seen him involved in brief shouting and glaring exchanges, like that with Lauro, when discussing a horse with his brother or politics with an acquaintance.

'Michael seems to have done the trick,' Maggie said, smiling as she went to the stairs. There was silence above. 'I'm sorry, Maggie,' said Berto as she left him.

Lauro came along the passage from the farther end, where his room was, and confronted her before she could reach her room. She put a finger to her lips. Michael threw open the door of his room, meanwhile. 'Mother,' he said, 'you upset Lauro.'

Mary appeared behind him. 'We have to call Lauro our secretary, Maggie,' she said. 'It's only fair.'

'I quite agree,' Maggie said. 'After all, Lauro is our secretary in a very real sense. A secretary is one who keeps secrets. What is the Italian for "secretary" anyway?'

Nobody answered her. She went into her room, glancing swiftly at Michael. God knows, she thought, what next to expect; anything might have been going on under my nose, anything. She took off her clothes and went to turn on her shower. But of course, she thought, it hasn't been under my nose. It's been somewhere I wasn't. Lauro with Mary. Lauro with Berto, of all people; Berto. Michael . . . God knows.

Berto, she mused to herself as she took her shower, is in love with me all the same. Mary and Michael I suppose love each other. Who loves Lauro? Who cares? And he knows he isn't loved in this little family; that's what the row was really about, I guess. She soaped her breasts and pummelled them between her fingers luxuriously. Lauro, she thought, knows a lot, and a man like that is useful to know.

By the evening their holiday guests, the Bernardinis, had returned with their English tutor from a three-day progress to various friends along the Amalfi coast. By the time Berto returned from the chemist's with medicine for Lauro's migraine, the visitors were sitting out on the terrace overlooking the sea. Berto handed the bottle of tablets to one of the maids and told her to take it to Lauro in his room: two with a glass of water; then he rubbed his hands, cheered up and kissed Letizia Bernardini and Nancy Cowan, once on each cheek, both girls. Then he went and fetched a shawl for Maggie.

At dinner they spoke of Hubert, and of Nemi to where they were all planning shortly to return. It was not in their minds at the time that this last quarter of the year they had entered, that of 1973, was in fact the beginning of something new in their world; a change in the meaning of property and money. They all understood these were changing in value, and they talked from time to time of recession and inflation, of losses on the stock-market, failures in business, bargains in real-estate; they habitually bandied the phrases of the newspaper economists and unquestioningly used the newspaper writers' figures of speech. They talked of hedges against inflation, as if mathematics could contain actual air and some row of hawthorn could stop an army of numbers from marching over it. They spoke of the mood of the stock-market, the health of the economy as if these were living creatures with moods and blood. And thus they personalized and demonologized the abstractions of their lives, believing them to be fundamentally real, indeed changeless. But it did not occur to one of those spirited and in various ways intelligent people round Berto's table that a complete mutation of our means of nourishment had already come into being where the concept of money and property were concerned, a complete mutation not merely to be defined as a collapse of the capitalist system, or a global recession, but such a sea-change in the nature of reality as could not have been envisaged by Karl Marx or Sigmund Freud. Such a mutation that what were assets were to be liabilities and no armed guards could be found and fed sufficient to guard those armed guards who failed to protect the properties they guarded, whether hoarded in banks or built on confined territories, whether they were priceless works of art, or merely hieroglyphics registered in the computers. Innocent of all this future they sat round the table and, since all were attached to Nemi, talked of Hubert. Maggie had him very much on her mind and the wormwood of her attention focused on him as the battle in the Middle East hiccuped to a pause in the warm late October of 1973.

Letizia Bernardini, with her youth dedicated to an ideal plan of territorial nationalism, had she been able to envisage at that moment the reality to come would have considered it, wrongly, to be a life not worth living. At any rate, at Berto's table in Ischia that evening, Letizia conversationally embarked once more on the leaky ship of Hubert.

'There's a certain magic about him,' Letizia said, causing Maggie to glare at her and her father to smile. 'There's something of the high priest about him,' Letizia went on. 'I want to see more of him when we return to Nemi.'

Nancy Cowan said, 'I think he's pure fake.'

'What!' said Letizia.

'Why?' said Maggie at the same time as her husband said 'Fake what?'

One way and another, Nancy's quiet little words produced an uproar of argument, all about Hubert, so that they hardly noticed the good food they were eating or heard the very professional robbery of Maggie's summer jewels going on upstairs in the meantime. Here are the details of the burglary :

Maggie's summer collection of jewellery was worth a vast fortune, even although it was far less valuable than her winter jewels, and considerably less again than the jewellery she kept in the bank summer and winter, except for the rarest and most important occasions. Her jewellery was difficult to insure against theft in any way that meant business; the insurance companies' requirements for so large a risk were not only so expensive as to defeat the purpose of insurance, but inconvenient as well. The companies insisted on the jewellery being housed in all types of safes and secured by innumerable safeguards, and even then were becoming more and more unwilling to insure jewellery of Maggie's sort. Generally, she avoided hotels and when she did stay in one she took very little jewellery, which she lodged in the hotel safe when she was not wearing it. Maggie's main problem was to prevent jewel-robberies at home. Burglar-alarms had become less and less effective as the burglars themselves became more and more adept at inventing, patenting, selling and subsequently exploiting them.

Two summers ago, Maggie had thought up a scheme to outwit the burglars, provoked as she had been at that time by a passing thief's discovery that she kept some of her jewels in a hot-water bottle. Her new scheme was to have a tiny kitchen built on an upper landing of every house she owned and frequented. This kitchen, complete with stove, refrigerator and sink, was ostensibly for the use of house-guests who wanted to be independent and who might take it into their heads to cook bacon and eggs in the middle of the night, or mix a drink. These upper kitchens were never used but were always elaborately stocked with food and drinks. They were always approached by a little step about four inches in height. This step was in reality a drawer, and in this drawer went Maggie's jewellery, unlocked and unnoticed.

Maggie had not been robbed for two years until this evening at Ischia during dinner. Lauro was sleeping off his migraine, heavily dosed with the pain-relieving drugs that Berto had brought from the chemist. The other servants were occupied downstairs with the serving. A boat drew up quietly and unremarked on the rocks below Maggie's villa from where a lift ascended to the top of the house. One man was left in the boat on the look-out. Two others, young in their T-shirts and blue jeans, went up in the lift with fixed and sad expressions on their faces. They got out precisely at the landing where the little upper kitchen stood. The dinner proceeded downstairs and Lauro slept heavily in his room.

They left the lift door open, went straight to the kitchen door and within a few seconds had opened the drawer in the step. They emptied it and stuffed most of it bulgily under their shirts. All the rest, enclosed in their leather cases, they held in their hands and tucked under their arms as they sadly and expertly descended to the waiting boat. This operation was the fruit of six weeks' research into Maggie's habits, casual questioning at local bars of builders connected with the latest construction of Maggie's upper kitchens, of boatmen connected with the villa, of unwitting servants who chattered about how ridiculous it was that the Marchesa had kitchens built at the top of her houses, always unused, and of simple deduction from a builder's boy's remark that she had quite unnecessarily called in a different builder from Milan to construct the step up to the kitchen. Summer jewellery though it was, the haul was high in the chronicles of summer robberies that year.

It was just towards the end of the dinner, with feelings and exchanges still vibrating across the table on the subject of Hubert, and Nancy Cowan quietly insisting that he was a fake, and Letizia rowdily defending him, with a murmur of scorn and an exclamation of despair here and there from Maggie, that the sound of an outboard-motor rapidly leaving the site of their landing-stage caused one of the servants to run out on the terrace and look over the cliff at the departing boat below. Suspicious of what he had seen he called out to one of the maids and ran to the lift. He pressed the button. Nothing happened. It was stuck down at sea-rock level, with the doors open.

It was when the maid returned to the terrace outside the dining-room window and started calling down vainly to Maggie's house-guards that the diners at the table were aware that something had happened.

'What's going on?' said Maggie, waving her arm towards the beautiful night outside the open french windows.

The maid and the manservant both appeared together in the dining-room, worried. 'There's a boat seems to have just left here, Marchesa. It left with great speed and we can't find the house-guards. Those boys are terrible. I always say they're negligent. They must have gone to a bar, Signora Marchesa.'

'Go down and find them,' said Maggie.

'And the lift doors have been left open,' said the girl. 'The lift's stuck downstairs.'

'Then go down the steps,' said Berto, rising, bothered by the fuss. The man and the girl made off across the terrace to the winding steps that led down the cliff to Maggie's rock-beach. Berto stood looking after them.

The boat had already disappeared across the bay, heading probably for another island or some remote inlet of the Neapolitan shore. Maggie said to the others at the table, 'Don't get up. Letizia, Nancy, go and get the fruit, please, will you? These servants are hysterical.' The cook had joined Berto on the terrace and was shouting inquiries to the maid and the manservant who had now reached the rock-beach. They were presently joined by those two of the five house-guards who were supposed to be on duty; they were amazed that their absence should have caused such a stir. Berto called roughly down to them to ask where they had been while the cook sent down vilifications of a rich and strange Italian variety.

Nancy and Letizia brought fruit and cheese to the table, but Maggie was standing now, and Emilio Bernardini with her, his pale smooth oval face gleaming beside her brown and splendid one. She looked from the terrace to him, then to the terrace again, and then back to Emilio, into his brown eyes behind his judicious spectacles. 'Do you know,' she said, 'I'm going upstairs to check my jewellery.' Emilio looked anxious but he smiled and said, 'Oh, I hardly think . . . '

Maggie was still upstairs when another visitor arrived, by car at the front door. He rang several times before Emilio let him in. A short man with very black dyed-looking hair and a taut, very cosmetically-surgeoned face. He seemed understandably surprised that no servants had appeared at the door to take his luggage and he greeted Emilio, who was obviously an old friend, with an absent-eyed geniality.

'Maggie's upstairs; she'll be down soon. The servants have made some mystery about an unknown boat that took off from the landing-stage in a hurry. Berto's down at the shore, investigating. Leave everything in the hall. Come in. Have you had dinner?'

The man said he had already eaten in Naples. Nancy and Letizia had left the table and were on their way down the sea-steps to join Berto and the servants. Emilio took his friend into the drawing-room where his son Pietro sat, sulkily uninterested in the fuss and ostentatiously unmoving. Emilio helplessly pressed a bell. As if in answer to it, Maggie appeared with her arms waving and her lips moving silently up and down in an effort of dumbstruck wild speech. Her arms waved and her dress glittered. On her arms and round her neck she wore the jewellery she had put on for dinner: bracelets and long necklaces of sea-shells which she had taken the whim to have set by a jeweller in conjunction with rubies and diamonds. These jewels. which were now all the summer jewellery she had left, made a sound like little dolls' teacups being washed up in some toy kitchen as her arms waved and her mouth gasped. She sat down on a sofa as Emilio came to help her. His friend had also stood up, quite bewildered by the whole business. Pietro sat still with a supercilious air.

'What happened, Maggie?' said Emilio, sitting down beside her.

Maggie pointed at the stranger, and this time her voice came through. 'Who is that?' she said, her pointing arm outstretched with its expensive shells.

'Maggie, what's happened? You've had a shock.'

'Who is he?' Maggie said. 'Call the police. Arrest him.'

'Maggie, don't you remember, you asked him to stay. He was expected, Maggie. What's wrong with you, my dear? This is my friend Coco de Renault.'

Berto returned followed by Letizia and Nancy. 'Nothing down there,' he reported. 'Someone took the lift down to the water and left the doors open. Must have been one of the servants, though of course they deny it.'

'Arrest him!' Maggie said, still pointing to Coco de Renault, who said, 'What the –'

'He's stolen my jewellery!' Maggie said.

At this moment Coco de Renault took charge. 'This lady,' he said gently, 'has had a shock.'

'I think so,' said Berto, while Emilio said, 'What's happened, Maggie?'

'My jewellery has gone,' Maggie said. 'It was upstairs in the kitchen step and it's gone. Call the police and arrest this man.'

But Coco de Renault was already pouring out a brandy and soda for Maggie. He came and stood over her like a doctor and said in a firm, almost harsh, voice, 'Drink this.' Maggie took the glass and drank. Monsieur de Renault then ordered the two girls to help Maggie stretch out on the sofa; on the strength of Maggie's words, 'My jewellery . . . the upstairs kitchen . . . ' and assuming his hostess was unbalanced by nature and in a mixed-up mood, he ordered Berto to go up to Maggie's room and investigate, and he ordered Emilio into the kitchen to investigate. He then ordered Pietro to have his luggage taken to his room and unpacked. Maggie lay on the sofa, moaning. Looking cross, Berto none the less went upstairs and Emilio with alacrity went into the kitchen where the servants were complaining and arguing loudly amongst themselves. Pietro did not move from his chair but stretched out his hand and tinkled a little china bell which was to hand. 'The servants are spoilt in this house,' Pietro remarked.

Monsieur de Renault stood in the middle of the room watching his orders being executed. His head was poised like the conductor of an orchestra. Lauro then appeared in the doorway, bare-chested and bare-foot, wearing only his day-time jeans. 'Who are you?' said Coco de Renault.

'I'm the Marchesa's personal secretary,' said Lauro.

'Then go and put on some respectable clothes,' barked the stranger-in-charge. Lauro fled.

At this moment, Berto's voice preceded his footsteps down the staircase. 'There's been a robbery! Maggie's jewels have been taken from their hiding-place. Call the police, call the – '

'Call the police,' Coco de Renault said to Pietro. 'Quickly, your mother's jewellery – '

'She isn't my mother,' Pietro said.

'Then who are you?' said de Renault as if he owned the place, and his question was so imperative that it seemed to include Berto himself who had now appeared in a state of agitation. Pietro said, 'I'm Bernardini's son,' and Berto said, 'I'm Tullio-Friole, the Marchesa's husband.' Pietro dialled the emergency number.

'How do you do,' said Coco de Renault to Berto. 'I'm Emilio's friend – '

'Oh, yes, Maggie was expecting you. I'm sorry about all this . . .'

Emilio returned from the kitchen and said, 'There's nothing missing from there. The servants are – '

'Please come immediately,' Pietro said into the telephone. 'Casa Tullio-Friole, the Marchese. There's been a robbery.'

Lauro appeared again, still half-dressed, and this time ready to express his summoned-up indignation. Maggie feebly pointed at Coco de Renault. 'He stole my jewellery . . . ' she murmured.

'Maggie,' said Emilio patiently, 'this is Monsieur Coco de Renault, my friend from the Argentine whom you invited here. Your jewellery has been stolen by someone, probably common thieves who have got away by boat. Monsieur de Renault has just arrived in this distressing situation, but I'm naturally very embarrassed – '

'Maggie, Monsieur de Renault is our guest,' Berto said, while Nancy pressed a table napkin folded round ice from the drinks-trolley on to Maggie's forehead, and Letizia held her hand.

'I really am not embarrassed,' said de Renault. 'I understand shock. It's hardly conceivable that anyone would seriously take me for a jewel thief.'

The servants were questioned by the two policemen who presently arrived. Coco de Renault's documents were looked over as were Nancy Cowan's. The police took the numbers of the passports. They looked with a certain scorn at the drawer in the upstairs kitchen step. They expressed their doubts that the thieves would ever be found: 'The jewels will likely be broken up by now somewhere in the *quartieri* of Naples.' They inquired if the jewellery had been insured. Then they inquired why not. And on learning that its value was beyond the range of the insurance companies, exchanged glances. They assured Berto they would do their best, and Berto assured them, quietly, that

7

there would of course be a reward if the jewellery should be found. The elder of the policemen exchanged some wry Italian colloquialisms with Berto: the stuff would never be found, and they knew it. Lauro, however, was taken away to the police station, in a fuming rage, to be questioned, much against Maggie's protestations but very much with Coco de Renault's approval.

'You can't trust *anybody*,' said de Renault when the police car had gone. And there was in fact this much in what he said, that he himself, within the next year, was to trick Maggie into handing over to him the bulk of her fortune, such a bulk as to make the more entirely absurd her concern about Hubert's occupancy of the house, or the little earnings of Lauro, or the theft, that evening, of her summer jewellery.

None the less, later that evening Maggie had so far recovered as to sit clanking her remaining bracelets on her arm as she reached for her drink, and asked Coco de Renault's advice as to how Hubert should be removed from the house at Nemi. Lauro returned from the police station by this time, soothed by the fact that Berto had followed the police car and had gone right into the office of the Commissioner himself to vouch for him, and had telephoned to the Prefect at Naples, and had altogether given Lauro such a good name as to be almost equal to promotion from private to general in the army. Lauro sat, now, in his jeans and the light cotton sweater he had put on to go to the police. He sat arrogantly, as arrogant as young Pietro.

Chapter Ten

'Truth,' said Hubert, 'is not literally true. The literal truth is a common little concept, born of the materialistic mind.' He raised his right arm gracefully from the lectern before him, and with it the sleeve of his green and silver liturgical vestment. The raised arm seemed to signal an expectancy; the congregation obediently drew its breath; Hubert's eye rested on Pauline Thin in the third row, and he proceeded as if uttering a prophecy directed to all the world, but aimed especially at her.

'Brothers and sisters of Apollo and Diana,' Hubert went on, with his eyes focused defiantly on Pauline, 'we hear on all sides about the evil effects of inflation and the disastrous state of the economy. Gross materialism, I say. The concepts of property and material possession are the direct causes of such concepts as perjury, lying, deception and fraud. In the world of symbol and the worlds of magic, of allegory and mysticism, deceit has no meaning, lies do not exist, fraud is impossible. These concepts are impossible because the materialist standards of conduct from which they arise are non-existent. Ponder well on these words. Hail to the sacred Diana! Hail to Apollo!'

'Hail!' responded the assembly. 'All hail to Diana and Apollo!'

In the second row, the Jesuit Fathers Cuthbert and Gerard whispered together excitedly.

A little over a year had passed since the Middle East war of 1973, and Hubert was fairly flourishing on the ensuing crisis. He had founded a church. It cultivated the worship of Diana according to its final phases when Christianity began to overcast her image with Mary the Mother of God. It was the late Diana and the early Mary that Hubert now preached, and since the oil trauma had inaugurated the Dark Ages II he had acquired a following of a rich variety and ever more full of numbers.

It was the autumn of 1974 and Maggie had not succeeded in turning Hubert out of her villa, partly because she had been distracted throughout that year by little thumps of suspicion within her mind at roughly six-week intervals concerning the manipulation of her fortune, with all its ramifications from Switzerland to the Dutch Antilles and the Bahamas, from the distilleries of Canada through New York to the chain-storedom of California, and from the military bases of Greenland's icy mountains to the hotel business of India's coral strand. Brilliant Monsieur de Renault was now the overlord of Maggie's network. Mysterious and intangible, money of Maggie's sort was able to take lightning trips round the world without ever packing its bags or booking its seat on a plane. Indeed, money of any sort is, in reality, unspendable and unwasteable; it can only pass hands wisely or unwisely, or else by means of violence, and, colourless, odourless and tasteless, it is a token for the exchange of colours, smells and savours, for food and shelter and clothing and for representations of beauty, however beauty may be defined by the person who buys it. Only in appearances does money multiply itself; in reality it multiplies the human race, so that even money lavished on funerals is not wasted, neither directly nor indirectly, since it nourishes the undertaker's children's children as the body fertilizes the earth.

Anyway, back to Maggie's fortune: Coco de Renault had reorganized her financial network throughout the past year; he had made something of a masterpiece of it. Like so many others in that year he began using the new crisis-terminology introduced by the current famous American Secretary of State; Coco de Renault's favourite word was 'global'. He produced an appealing global plan for Maggie's fortune, so intricate that it might have been devised primordially by the angels as a mathematical blueprint to guide God in the creation of the world. It was quite unfathomable, but Maggie, whose rich contemporaries were beginning to look at each other with wild alarm, at first felt a great satisfaction at having acted in time. She felt that brilliant Monsieur de Renault from the Argentine was a sort of perfected bomb-shelter. But as the months of 1974 passed from those of spring and summer into the autumn, she had experienced these intervals of anxiety, sudden little shocks. On one occasion she realized that her administration headquarters, which previously occupied an entire floor of offices in a New York block, with three full-time lawyers, twelve accountants and a noisy number of filing clerks and secretaries who fell silent on the few occasions that Maggie made a visitation thereupon, was now all disbanded. Pensions and parting gifts had been bestowed on the staff. The lately administering lawyers had lawsuits pending against Maggie for breach of contract, but Coco de Renault was dealing with such trivial nuisances out of court. Coco explained to Maggie, the first time she had one of her little shocks on realizing her estate had no business headquarters any more, that a headquarters was the very thing she had to avoid. He was her headquarters and she must realize he was dealing with her affairs globally. Maggie calmed down. Another time, she failed to find him on any of his telephone numbers on the globe. She went frantic, rattling the receiver for long hours over a period of three days and a half, in the course of which a strike of the international telephone service took place in the Veneto, from where she was calling. Vainly dialling the Minister of Posts and Telegraphs in Rome, Maggie looked out of the window of Berto's Palladian villa and saw her husband talking to the groom as if the world were not coming to an end. It came to her that if she were to die there would be an enormous lachrymose funeral with the Italian nobility speeding up to the Veneto to attend it and lay her in Berto's family tomb; then two days later Berto would be out in the garden as usual talking to the groom, while her son Michael would be busy on the question of her fortune. Maggie drove off to Venice and booked into an hotel from where she tried to telephone to Coco. The strike on the international exchange still prevailed. She looked out of the window and saw a placard which said 'The Postal Strike of the Veneto Must Be Confronted Globally'. She remained frantic after the strike was over, and still in the hotel room tried one number after another in search of Coco and her power of attorney. She tried San Diego, California, Port au Prince, Hong Kong, London, Zürich, Geneva and St Thomas in the Virgin Islands. Then she tried Madras. She had been in Venice two days when Berto called her to ask what she was doing. Had she been to the del Macchis' masked ball? How was Peggy? She said she was trying to find Coco de Renault. He replied that he thought there had been a call from de Renault if he wasn't mistaken. Maggie returned to the villa and located Coco within a few more agonizing days. The fear passed once more. 'I've been at Nemi, at Emilio Bernardini's,' he said, and laughed at the news that she had looked for him everywhere.

These distractions took her mind off Hubert but every now and again she was brought back to her frustration over his stubborn occupancy of the house. At the beginning of the summer of 1974 unknown to Berto she had handed the whole story of Hubert, in her own revised version, to an obscure lawyer in Rome, with instructions to get Hubert out of the house and to do it without a scandal. The lawyer promptly agreed to do it, and not only did he point out that the new Italian laws made it difficult to turn anyone out of any habitation whatsoever, but he exaggerated the difficulties. Maggie duly paid the man the large deposit he demanded to match the exceptional difficulties of the job he had undertaken. As it happened, this lawyer, having sentimental sympathies towards the political left wing, although no longer the extreme leftist he had been in his poor student days, loathed what he conceived Maggie to stand for at the same time as he was put into an ambivalent state of excitement by her glowing and wealthy presence. The one time she presented herself with her case in his absolutely ordinary office became an obsessive memory; as the months passed and the unseen presence of Maggie lingered here and there, with her voice on the phone to remind him on the one hand of his undertaking and, on the other, of her vital self and her money, his office and his life seemed in his eyes to be even more sad and ordinary. So that he was more short-tempered now, with his wife and with his secretary, than before. The secretary, indeed, left and he had to make do with another, inferior one; meantime Maggie was living her life all unaware of the effect she had produced on the lawyer. As to getting Hubert out of the house, the lawyer had written him a letter in a somewhat vague manner. Hubert had sent it back scrawled at the bottom with the message, 'Mr Hubert Mallindaine is at a loss to understand this missive and, assuming that it is misdirected, returns it to the sender.'

'You see,' explained the lawyer on the telephone to Maggie, 'he knows well the Italian laws. If you take out a court order even, this makes two years before you can disencumber him. He will make the newspaper scandal that your husband fears and he might win the case if he proves that the house was built by his instructions for his own use. The laws are now on the side of the tenant, always. And if he loses the case everyone will assume he has been your *amante* and you are tired of him.'

'Don't you know,' Maggie said, 'there's a big recession on? We can't afford to give away houses and there is valuable furniture inside. My Louis XIV furniture . . . '

'You have said he had them restored?'

'I believe he's looking after my things. Yes. There's a Gauguin painting, too. I want it.'

'If he is spending money to care for the property he could argue that the property was his, else why should he spend the money?'

'Are you my lawyer or his?' Maggie said.

'Marchesa, I see the case objectively and I will try. I have my heart's sympathy with your side. Everyone knows what our laws are like in the world of today. I have landlords and proprietors at my office lamenting every day that they cannot remove their tenants and they cannot raise the rents – '

'But he's paying no rent, and it's fully furnished, my house.'

'That is all the more argument for him. Marchesa, you permitted him to stay too long. Now is probably too late, in effect. In effect, I will try and I can only promise to continue to try. If you are not satisfied with my efforts, Marchesa – '

'Oh, please carry on. Please do. I quite understand the difficulties,' Maggie said. 'But I have many problems just at this terrible moment in the economical situation of the world and I do wish to have the house to be near my son.'

'The law says that if you already have a habitation, Marchesa, you cannot evict a tenant on the grounds that you need the house. Only if you are homeless – '

'I know. I know. Go ahead, please; I have complete faith in you – '

'If you would care to lunch with me on your visit to Rome, I could better explain my plan of next procedure, or you could call in again at my office – '

'No, it won't be necessary – '

'It would be a pleasure. Or could I come to visit you at the Veneto? It is a country I well know – '

'What do you mean, "country"? It's still in Italy.'

'That is our manner of speaking. In Italy are many countries. I would be happy to visit – '

'Just at the moment I can't make plans,' Maggie said. 'Please go on trying and keep in touch with me.'

The lawyer wrote again to Hubert, a strong firm letter, cunningly phrased with many citations of law, number this and section that, including the commas. It was the sort of letter that would send the civil courts of Italy into a frenzy of sympathy for the tenant, at the same time as it left the lawyer professionally irreproachable. To this bureaucratic communication Hubert replied from the local bar at Nemi, by telephone.

'Look,' he said to the lawyer, 'this house is mine. The lady gave it to me. I've nowhere else to go. Why don't you just take me to court?'

'What number are you calling from?' said the wary lawyer, anxious about a possible telephone tap.

'The bar,' said Hubert, 'here at Nemi. Can't you hear the noise? I can't afford a telephone at my house. The Marchesa had it cut off.'

'Tell me the number and I'll call you back,' said the lawyer. He checked the number that Hubert gave him, and rang back to the bar.

'Now,' said the lawyer, 'it's like this. I have to do my duty, and I have sent you a letter. You have nothing to worry about.'

'I have plenty of things to worry about,' Hubert said, 'but the house isn't one of them. Why do you send me these absurd letters?'

'I am at the Marchesa's command,' the lawyer said. 'You want my advice? You write me a reply that you are not well and enclose a medical certificate. When you are recovered you will see your lawyer.'

'I'm in the best of health,' Hubert said. 'No doctor would give me a certificate, and anyway, I don't know any doctor in Italy.'

'Write me the letter,' said the lawyer, 'and I will arrange for the certificate.'

'This is unusually kind of you,' Hubert said. 'Why don't you come here and have a chat? I should be delighted to show you my house and my wooded grounds. And then, after all, I don't know how far involved you are with Maggie. I'd like to be reassured.'

The lawyer, who was fat, laughed with the full fruition of the fat. 'Sunday,' he said, 'I could make a little escape and getaway. After lunch, Sunday. Good?'

'Good,' said Hubert.

By the autumn, all the Louis XIV chairs had been replaced by very beautiful fakes, the Gauguin had been replaced by a copy for which Hubert had paid a very high price, but not, of course, a price of such an altitude as that fetched by the Gauguin, now safely smuggled into Switzerland. He had also replaced a Constable with a fair enough copy, the original of which, in any case, had been kept in a dark corner so that the many fine points of difference between this and the fake were obscured by the gloom. A Sickert painting still awaited treatment because the price of a good copy was by now reaching excessively blackmail proportions and Hubert was investigating another organization which provided a discreet art-copyist and export service. He had similar plans for an inoffensive Corot in the lavatory, with its little red blot in the right foreground, and also an umbrageous Turner which, although it was small, overpowered the wall of the upstairs landing, but this, one of the experts in clandestinity had informed Hubert, was already a fake; an expensive fake, but not marketable enough to have copied.

In this way, Hubert was very comfortably off by the time the collapse of money as a concept occurred. 'I refuse,' he said, 'to eke out my existence or change my philosophy of life according to the cost of oil per barrel – '

All the same, he took care to continue changing the locks on the doors of the house frequently. He did not flaunt his newly-acquired money. The telephone remained cut off, the garden was weeded to the minimum and the paint on the outside doors and windows was left to peel and flake with poverty.

The expert self-faker usually succeeds by means of a manifest self-confidence which is itself by no means a faked confidence. On the contrary, it is one of the few authentic elements in a character which is successfully fraudulent. To such an extent is this confidence exercised that it frequently over-rides with an orgulous scorn any small blatant contradictory facts which might lead a simple mind to feel a reasonable perplexity and a sharp mind to feel definite suspicion.

Pauline Thin's mind was not particularly sharp. But in her second year as Hubert's companion and secretary she had acquired enough experience of him, of his documents and his daily sayings, that she couldn't fail to realize that something was amiss between Hubert's claims and the facts. It was just when, with the aid of his new ally, Maggie's plump lawyer, Hubert had founded his religious organization that Pauline had discovered among Hubert's papers clear evidence that his aunts, infatuated by Sir James Frazer and his *Golden Bough*, had been in correspondence with the quack genealogist; they had instructed him in the plainest terms to establish their descent from the goddess Diana.

Hubert had looked Pauline straight in the eyes and with some arrogance informed her that she was misreading his aunts' intention, that she was terribly ignorant on some matters, but that he entertained many fond feelings for her, none the less.

Impressed by his cool confidence Pauline read the letters again, and was again dumbfounded. And once more, Hubert, actually looking over the batch of letters that Pauline had placed in his very hands, said only that she was a nice little fool, threw them aside, and went off about some other business.

It was the next day, at the meeting of the Brothers and Sisters of Diana and Apollo, that Hubert was preaching his sermon on the nature of truth. He had turned the dining-room, which led off the entrance hall beyond the terrace, into a chapel. The new world which was arising out of the ashes of the old, avid for immaterialism, had begun to sprout forth its responsive worshippers.

'Truth,' Hubert repeated as he wound up his sermon, his eyes bending severely on Pauline, 'is not literally true. Truth is never the whole truth. Nothing but the truth is always a lie. The world is ours; it is in metaphorical terms our capital. I remember how my aunts, devotees as they were of Diana and Apollo, used always to say, "Never, never, touch the capital. Live on the interest, not on the capital." The world is ours to conserve, and ours are the fruits thereof to consume. We should never consume the capital, ever. If we do, we are left with the barren and literal truth. Let us give praise to Diana, goddess of the moon, goddess of the tides, the Earth-mother of fertility, and to Apollo, the sun and the ripener, her brother. Hail to Diana! Hail to Apollo!'

'Hail!' said the majority of his congregation, while Father Cuthbert Plaice whispered to his fellow-Jesuit Gerard, 'There's a lot of truth in what he says.'

'I like the bit about the earth being our capital,' replied Gerard, ever ecologically minded, 'but he mixes it up with a lot of shit, doesn't he?'

'Oh, well,' said Cuthbert, 'it's like manure and even if it's shit it gets people thinking about religion, doesn't it?'

'Yes, I suppose it's an experience, isn't it?'

Hubert, splendid as a bishop *in pontificalibus*, folded in his vestments of green and silver, proceeded up the aisle giving his benediction to right and left before disappearing into the downstairs bathroom which had now been transformed into a vestry.

'Miss Thin,' said Hubert as Pauline came in behind him, 'remind me to apply for an unlisted, repeat unlisted, telephone number.'

Chapter Eleven

'The trouble with Berto,' Maggie said quietly to Mary, 'is that his *tempo* is all wrong. He starts off *adagio, adagio*. Second phase, well, you might call it *allegro ma non troppo* and pretty nervy. Third movement, a little passage *con brio*. Then comes a kind of righteous and dutiful *larghetto*, sometimes accompanied by a bit of high-pitched *recitativo*, and he goes on, *lento*, you know, *andante, andante* until suddenly without warning three grunts and it's all over. What kind of an art of love is that?'

'Rhythm is very, very important,' said Mary reflectively, 'in every field of endeavour. What is the *recitativo* bit?'

'I don't understand dialect Italian,' Maggie said. 'Ordinary Italian is difficult enough, but this is some sort of dialect that Berto uses on these particular occasions. Afterwards he talks about horses, how a horse may go off his feed from too much exercise or too little or how sometimes horses get lumps on their skin from over-exercise or under-exercise, I forget which. Anyway, he frequently talks about horses afterwards. What kind of an art of love is that?'

'I could tell you a lot about Michael,' Mary said, 'but as he's your son it makes an obstacle.'

'I hardly think of him as my son any more,' Maggie said. 'Michael can be very inconsiderate. I think of him more as his father's son and if he's anything like Ralph Radcliffe then you have a problem there. Ralph was a problem but very, very attractive. Berto is no problem at all, but it's boring to go to bed with him, especially when you're my age. In your case you have your whole lifetime in front of you.'

'Not all of it,' Mary said. 'I feel I'm wasting my best years sometimes, and I know Michael's got a girl in Rome, too. But I want to make a success of my marriage, I really do.'

'You can always take time off,' said Maggie, 'while Michael's in Rome with the girl.'

'Well, I wouldn't like to.'

'You must think I'm pretty dumb,' said Maggie, 'if you think I don't know that you take time off with Lauro.'

Mary said, 'Oh, no! This is terrible. You mustn't say such a thing.'

'Keep calm,' said Maggie. 'Nobody else knows anything about you and Lauro.'

The girl started to cry. 'I wanted my marriage to be a success.'

'Go on wanting it, is my advice,' said Maggie, while Mary dried her tears on a paper tissue from the box beside her and drank a large gulp of her vodka and soda, spilling some of it on her body.

They were in bathing suits on the concealed sun-terrace of Berto's Palladian villa in the Veneto in the spring sunshine of 1975. They lay side by side on the dark blue mattresses soaking up the sunny vitamins of May in the hours between noon and lunch at two. Maggie reached out for her body lotion and smeared it over her legs, her breasts and shoulders, then, playfully, she smeared the remainder on her hands over Mary's belly, so that the girl became less nervy; she lay back somewhat becalmed and murmured solemnly, 'Lauro doesn't mean anything to me.'

'He satisfies the appetite,' said Maggie, 'but not the passions, I agree.'

A bright smile came suddenly to her face as Lauro himself appeared on the terrace, carrying a mute transistor radio and a bottle of Vermouth. 'Why, Lauro!' she said, 'I thought you were taking the morning off.'

'I shouldn't have come to this house at all. I repent it. The staff is terrible. They are vulgar domestics. They hate me. I came to help you out. I should have stayed at Nemi where

I work for Mary and Michael. I am not obliged to follow the family.'

'Oh, Lauro, you can go back to Nemi any time you like,' Mary said.

He removed his white coat, put the bottle on the drinks trolley and stretched on a mattress beside them, and then got some pop music on his radio.

'God, Berto will see you, Lauro!' said Maggie. 'And I'll get the blame for fraternizing.'

Lauro threw the radio to the other end of the terrace where it stopped playing; he jumped up in a neurotic fit, spitting Italian obscenities, put on his white coat, and left.

'Well, I've finished with him as a person,' Mary said. 'He really means to get married to that girl in Nemi.'

'You'd better keep him on as a houseman,' Maggie said. 'Trained servants are hard to get. And he is well trained, you know.'

So much could be recounted about the winter past, so many sudden alarms as to the whereabouts of Coco de Renault and so many frantic messages sent by telex to non-existent offices far away; always, Coco turned up with an explanation and enough ready money to put Maggie back in a stable frame of mind.

He had on one occasion gently and consolingly hinted that she was the victim of the menopause, and this act of stupidity on his part nearly finished his relationship with Maggie, so violently did she react. Berto had to intervene and explain away Coco's mistake. He told Maggie that Coco was probably in love with her. 'This is a way in which a man in love tries to provoke a woman,' he told Maggie. 'When there is no hope for him, he provokes.' And to Coco, privately, he said, 'If what you think is true, as it probably is, then the last thing you should suggest is the truth, since the truth is the original irritant.' Coco meekly humoured Maggie and presently told her that her financial affairs were blooming only a little less than her lovely self.

There had been so many bad scenes that past winter with Lauro, and a cruise with Mary and Michael for Christmas in the Caribbean, followed by a week together in New York where Berto joined them. Berto now expressed strong doubts about

Coco's integrity and escorted them home. Maggie defended Coco expansively; Coco was nagging her to have her portrait painted by a young artist friend of his.

And all along, Maggie had reverted to her passion for evicting Hubert from the house at Nemi. So much could be recounted. 'Eras pass,' said Hubert, in the new comfort of his life, 'they pass.' He had just read in the newspaper of 15 February that year that Julian Huxley and P. G. Wodehouse were dead: 'The passing of an era . . .' the newspapers had commented.

But this day in May 1975, in the sun of the north Italian spring, chose itself from among those others to be that sort of day when complications ripen, since inevitably there is always one particular day when discoveries come to being, when incidents put out shoots and start to bring into force from the winter's potentialities the first green blades of a crisis. Maggie and Mary stretched out on the sun-terrace before lunch while downstairs the probabilities foregathered to form what are the most probable events of all, which is to say, the improbable ones.

Meantime, Maggie said to Mary, 'We should go off to Nemi soon. I have to get Hubert out of the house. The Church authorities should be on my side. He's committing a great sacrilege in my house with that cult of his. He's got to be exposed, because of course he's sheer fake.'

'I'd like to go to one of the meetings,' Mary said. 'If only I could do so in disguise. You know, Letizia Bernardini says the services are terribly elating, really like magic.'

'Could we both go in disguise?' Maggie said.

'He'd be sure to find out. He's very, very discerning,' Mary said.

'I could kill that man, I really could,' said Maggie. 'It isn't so much the property, it's the idea of being done down that makes me furious with him.'

'Yes, and he wasn't even your lover,' said Mary, egging her on as usual, since the theme of Hubert had become one of Mary's favourite serialized entertainments.

'He wouldn't know what to do with a woman,' Maggie said. Twelve guests for dinner tonight; with Michael, Mary, herself and Berto that made sixteen. There were dinner parties practically every night. New friends, old friends visiting Italy from America, old and new friends of Berto's. Maggie sat for Coco's young artist; then it was Mary's turn. 'He's got you both out of focus,' Berto had said. In a world of jumping sequences, the problem of Hubert was a point of continuity, although Maggie herself had no idea how gratefully she clung to it.

Berto's Palladian villa was a famous one. It had been photographed from the beginning of photography and, before that, etched, sketched, painted, minutely described inside and out, poetically laboured upon, visited by scholars and drooled over by the world's architects. The Villa Tullio was indeed a beauty; the Villas Foscari, Emo, Sarego, D'Este, Barbaro, Capra, with their elegant and economical delights still in comparison with the smaller Villa Tullio, seemed to some tastes to be more in the nature of architectural projects and propositions. The Villa Tullio was somehow magically complete and at rest. It was a farm-house built for the agricultural industry of the original Tullios, for the charm of its position beside a reclaimed waterway and the civilized comfort of Berto's prosperous ancestors. Now, the plans of this house, every angle, every detail of its structure, being known throughout the world, photographs of the interior and exterior, and the original plan of the lay-out from every side having been published for centuries in studious manuals and picture books, it was hardly worth the while or the price for a gang of expert thieves to send their men to case the lay-out. However, they did.

It was ten minutes past twelve when two smart-looking men drove up to the marvellous front door in a white touring car. On to the upper balcony came Berto from the library where he had been glooming behind the french windows. Out he came into the shadows cast by the sweetness and light of that harmonious pediment. He did not recognize the people. They were too early for lunch, and therefore probably were not friends of Maggie's. Most likely, then, they were visitors come to inquire if they could see the house. Berto's arrangements for sightseers were very haphazard. He kept no porter at the lodge. While he was away his old butler was accustomed to use his sixth sense as to whom he admitted into the house and whom he sent away. There were no regular visiting days as had been established in the grand and more famous buildings of Palladio. Mostly, the visitors who wanted to see over the villa wrote in advance, or were written for by their universities or, as it might be, some friend of Berto's family. It was well known that Berto had changed nothing of the structure; only, over the years, in the interior, had new drainage systems been installed and bathrooms fitted in.

Berto was proud of his Palladian jewel, and his heart bent towards the two arrivals with such a desire that they should be educated tourists wanting to see the house that he invested them at first sight with various nice qualities. They mounted the fine steps, a tall, white-haired man and an equally tall youth, presentably dressed in fresh shirts and pale trousers; they approached the house with the right visitors' modesty and lost themselves under the balcony where Berto hovered and awaited their ring of the door-bell.

After a few seconds, during which Berto imagined them to be admiring the portico, that harmonious little temple, and the well-calculated panorama therefrom, the bell rang. Berto withdrew from the porch into the library and heard below the shuffle of Guillaume going to open the door. Guillaume was the old butler, who had been brought as a small boy from Marseilles sixty-two years ago by Berto's father and who, having had no surname that he knew of, was long since equipped with one: Marsigliese; he fairly ran the villa, and Berto who had grown up under his eye rarely questioned his judgement. Berto enjoyed with Guillaume a kind of reciprocal telepathy by which Berto understood precisely which of his friends Guillaume meant when he said that the French had telephoned, or the Germans had called, or that the Romans might be arriving, although, in fact, Berto had a good number of friends who might fit each definition. Guillaume Marsigliese likewise knew exactly which Americans were expected to dinner when Berto said he had invited 'the Americans'; no doubt there was a slightly different inflection of their voices for each designation, but no friend discussed between them in that way was ever confused with another. 'The Americans' also covered Mary and Michael, and, before her marriage to Berto, Maggie.

Now Guillaume had started to climb the beautiful sweeping staircase and Berto, to save him the fatigue, came out of the library door to meet him, leaning over the well of the circling banister.

Guillaume looked up. 'People,' he announced, without further elaboration – '*Gente*', by which he conveyed that the visitors were, as Berto plainly expected, people who wanted to see over the house. And the fact that he had invited them to wait inside and given them some hope that Berto would receive them demonstrated that he considered the newcomers not, so far, unworthy, without committing himself further to the road of positive approval.

'A few moments,' Berto said, giving himself time to put away the papers he had been studying and the visitors time, no doubt, to admire the care that had gone into the maintenance of the villa inside and out, starting with the hall and its superb outlook.

'Go down and tell them to wait.' His commands to the servants always struck Maggie and Mary as being on the abrupt and haughty side: they felt embarrassed and guilty when Berto gave orders to his old butler especially. But to Guillaume's ears Berto's tone was perfectly normal; the old man judged only what his master said, whether it was sensible or not sensible. Guillaume's life had been considerably upset by the fraternization that went on between Lauro and the Americans. Now, he turned and shuffled to the hallway, deeming Berto's orders to be sensible.

Berto descended in his own time and, courteously shaking hands with each of the men, inquired their names. At the same time he took in the well-silvered hair and the interesting light blue and white fine stripes of his trousers, the jacket of which he held over his arm. The younger man, who wore well-tailored fawn trousers of some uncrushable and impeccable material, was holding a shiny slim catalogue of an artistic nature. They gave their names, apologized for the intrusion, and asked if they might see over the exquisite villa. They bore no resemblance whatsoever to Caliban the beast, with intent to rape and destroy Prospero's daughter who, some have it, represents the precious Muse of Shakespeare. 'Come along,' said Berto. 'With pleasure, come along.' The younger man left his catalogue on the hall table, while Guillaume came forward to take the older man's jacket from his arm.

Meanwhile Maggie, on the sun-terrace, turned over her splendid body, winter-tanned from the Caribbean, and lay on her belly; she continued smoothing her arms with suntan oil. 'I want my house at Nemi and my furniture and my pictures,' she said. 'It's a simple thing to ask. That man makes me have bloody thoughts; they drip with blood.'

'Do you think he's practising some kind of magic?' Mary said.

'We ought to go to the police. But Berto's so conservative,' Maggie said. 'Berto would prefer magic to a scandal.'

Lauro appeared once more, and sulkily ambled over to where he had thrown the transistor radio. He picked up the battered object, tried it, shook it, opened it and readjusted the batteries, but apparently it was dead from violence. He threw it back on the terrace floor and went to pour himself a drink.

'Where is my husband?' Maggie said, nervously.

'Showing visitors over the house.'

'What visitors?'

'I don't know. They just came and asked to see the house. Guillaume let them in. Two men, well-dressed.'

'Berto will get us all killed one day,' Maggie said. 'They are all well-dressed. They could be armed. We could all be tied up and shot through the head while they loot the place.'

Mary dipped into her bag for her powder-compact and lipstick. She combed her long hair.

'Your husband is too much a gentleman,' Lauro told Maggie, 'and old Guillaume is too much an old bastard in all the senses of the word. He never knew his parents. He was off the streets. No family.'

'What recommendations do they have?' Maggie said. 'Who sent them?'

'I don't know. Perhaps nobody. They are art historians.'

'They are all art historians,' Maggie said. 'You read about them every day in the papers. And look what happened to me the summer before last at Ischia.'

'Those were boys from Naples,' Lauro said. 'These men here are Americans.'

'I wouldn't be surprised if Berto doesn't ask them to stay to lunch,' said Maggie.

Mary closed her powder-compact. 'There are only six of us for lunch today. Two more won't make any difference.'

'They could tie us all up, shoot us, take everything,' Maggie said.

'I got a gun,' Lauro said. 'Don't worry. I go now and get my gun.'

'Oh, we don't want any shooting!' said Mary. 'Please don't start carrying revolvers in the house. It makes me jumpy.'

'Lauro's wonderful,' said Maggie, standing up like a brown statue in her gleaming white two-piece bathing suit. She swung her orange striped towel wrap from the back of a chair and put it on, haughtily. Mary got up too, lean and long. 'I'm going down to the pool for a swim,' she said as she too wrapped herself up neatly in a bathrobe.

'I'm going to my room,' Maggie said. 'One thing they can't do is see over my bedroom. I just won't have it, even if it is one of the most interesting sections of the upper floor.'

'I bring you a drink at the pool, Mary,' Lauro said.

'Lauro, you're sweet.'

They descended from the sun-terrace together, listening for voices but hearing none.

'In fact,' Mary said, 'I think I heard them outside. Berto must be showing them the grounds.'

'Well, if you're keen to see them try to get rid of them before lunch,' said Maggie. 'I don't want them to stay.' She swung into the little lift that descended to her room.

'Maggie,' said Berto, 'these gentlemen are staying to lunch.'

Two middle-aged women, Berto's cousins who were expected to lunch, had already arrived and Maggie saw the two un-familiar men chatting easily with them in the hall. The younger man was saying 'Byzantium was a state of mind . . .'

Maggie came over regally to be introduced, on her way passing the console table where the young man had left his catalogue. Mary stood with her back to it and when she saw Maggie she murmured, 'The damn pool water wasn't heated – the gardener forgot – '

'How are you? Come on in,' said Maggie to her husband's cousins, and then she held out her hand to welcome the new visitors who stood with Berto. The little group at the console table parted and Maggie's eye caught the picture on the cover of the catalogue just as she had her hand in the elder art historian's. She let her hand drop and her smiling mouth formed a gasp. 'What's this?' she said, grabbing the catalogue.

It bore on its lovely cover, in tasteful print, the name Neuilles-Pfortzheimer, a Swiss auction house famous among collectors of paintings and fine arts. Under this was a reproduction of an Impressionist painting. 'What's this?' Maggie shrieked, and the circle of friends around her stood back a little as if in holy dread. 'What's *what?*' said Berto looking over her shoulder.

'My Gauguin!' Maggie said. 'It was in my house at Nemi. What is it doing in this catalogue? Is it up for sale?'

The younger of the visiting art historians said, 'Why, that was sold last week. We were there. You must be mistaken, ma'am.'

'How can I be mistaken?' Maggie screamed. 'Don't I know my own Gauguin? There's the garden seat and the shed.'

Everyone spoke at once with ideas pouring forth: ring the police; no, never the police, you don't want *them* to know what you've got; get your lawyer; ring the gallery, yes, call Neuilles-Pfhortzheimer, I know the director well; I know Alex Pfortzheimer; call your home at Nemi, who is the caretaker? . . . 'Art-thieves!' Maggie screamed, pointing at the two visitors who looked decidedly uncomfortable, having come predominantly to find the best means of entry to the little Chinese sitting-room with its rare collection of jade, to plan a future jewel-robbery at least, and certainly they were alert also to where Maggie's room, with its wall-safe, was situated, since it was known she had taken her large ruby pendant, part of the diaspora of the Hungarian crown jewels, out of the bank to wear to one or two of the season's balls, even though she ostentatiously insisted, as was the fashion, that it was a fake. The visitors had also noted, with an eye to its whereabouts, Berto's sublime Veronese about which they had already heard, at the top of the staircase. They were innocent, however, of Maggie's Gauguin and the more she cried out against them, there in the graceful hall among the astonished friends, the more it seemed how demonstrably wronged the strangers were; the only discomfort in the affair, for them, was the risk involved should the police be called in, for they were already in some embarrassment in France.

Berto looked at them and said, quietly. 'I *am* sorry. I do apologize. My wife is distraught,' at the same time as he put his arm round Maggie as if to protect her from the menaces of a malignant spirit.

Mary joined the group and, shortly, Michael too, seeming, as he more and more frequently did, that he had too much on his mind to take notice of a domestic emergency. He eyed his watch. Mary was looking rather enviously at Berto's gesture of concern for Maggie, for in fact he looked very handsome at those moments of spontaneous charm belonging as it did to his own type and generation; it did not occur to Mary how silly Michael would have looked, how affected, bending his eyes upon herself as Berto bent his, so frankly with love, over Maggie. She only admired handsome Berto and envied Maggie who, pouring out her accusations, did not, in Mary's view, really deserve so fine a solicitude. If Mary had suspected the theft of any of her property she would have gone about it silently and with a well-justifiable slyness. Maggie, in the mean-time, shrieked on, and Berto murmured over her as if she greatly mattered in the first place, the guests in his house next, and the Gauguin not at all.

Lunch was delayed forty minutes, but the hubbub had been whisked away little by little by Berto's tactics, and the guests had been waved into the green sitting-room, had been served drinks and their several troubled souls variously feather-dusted, while Maggie, refusing her room, lay on a sofa and allowed herself also to be somewhat becalmed. Berto was considerably aided in his efforts by the two cousins, women of authority and many wiles, who had pulled themselves together quickly for the purpose of family solidarity and the pressing need to avoid the threat of a lawsuit against themselves for defamation of charac-ter. Quite soon the embarrassed art historians were given new courage, full explanations, and were begged to stay; the elder remained slightly nervous, but both magnanimously overlooked Maggie's accusations which, from her sofa, she blurted out from time to time, ever more feebly, for thirty-odd minutes. A short space, and they went into lunch.

Berto had refused to do anything whatsoever about the Gauguin mystery before lunch. 'Later, later, it must wait,' he said. 'If the picture is stolen . . . well, first we have to make a plan of inquiry, and first we sit down and have a drink before lunch. Maggie, my dear . . . Love, be tranquil. We have a drink, all. Only the worst can happen. Only the worst . . . It is not so very terrible . . . The worst is always happening to many people everywhere. And only the worst can happen, Maggie, my dear.'

Now they sat in the perfect dining-room overlooking the artificial lake. Berto looked attentively towards his cousin Marisa; she was the newsbearer, grand as a Roman statue and anxious to get these pettifogging hysterics of Maggie's over and done with so that she could impart news of the world that mattered to the assembled company, whether they understood what she was talking about or not; for Marisa's world concerned the heavily populated cousinship of their family, and only she could know which of their Colonna cousins was in love with which Lancelotti, and how much the dowry would be; only Marisa could know who was expected to inherit when the ancient Torlonia should die, probably within the next few days; she alone knew that the Baring nephews had been staying in Paris with the Milanese Pignatellis in an endeavour to find a settlement about the companies in Switzerland; all this Marisa only was able to know since only she had the mornings on the telephone with a family information service from all parts. Very often, when the family themselves failed to telephone or were not to be found at home, she would get the required information from an old housekeeper. All these facts she was waiting to impart to Berto and her other cousin, the thin religious widow Viola, at lunch, for she had a strong sense of what was right for lunch, what to eat, what to wear, what to say; she expected fully that these family concerns would enthral every listener; if not, what were the strangers doing at Berto's table? She was as confident of the fascination of her subject to everyone as were the ancient dramatists who held their audiences with incessant variations on the activities of the gods and heroes of legend. And indeed, such was her confidence that she did manage to hold the attention of the outsider, for however unintelligible the substance of her talk she brought a sense of glamorous realism to the Italian mythology of the old families.

Maggie had brought her glass of strong rye whisky to the table, trembling still, but settling somewhat under the influence of Berto's solicitude and induced into an effort of self-control by a determination not to be overborne by the tourist-attraction, Marisa. Maggie now sat gleaming in her shaken beauty at the top of the oval table. On her right was the elder of the intruders who had been pressed to stay for lunch, and who went by the name of Malcolm Stuyvesant. Next to him, Mary, with Berto on her other hand, and next to Berto at the other end of the table his other cousin, the black-dressed pale little Princess Viola Borgognona, very thin of neck among her strings of seed-pearls; Viola was agog to hear Marisa's new serial in the family saga, for it always gave her an excuse to be morally scandalized and to recall the family scandals, misalliances and intrigues of the past. She, like Berto, was aware that this inter-family talk had little relevance to the world of foreign visitors or of newcomers to the family, but she felt that it should be common knowledge even if it wasn't and, anyway, it was plain that people were not bored by it. Marisa had already started talking. 'Dino is sure to get married again when the year is up. He goes every morning to the cemetery, and then rides with Clementine, but of course the parents think he's too old. What can one say?' She turned appealingly to her neighbours, Michael on her left and then, on her right, to the younger of the two intruders, George Falk by name. 'What can one say?' she asked first one and then the other.

Berto, however, was still concerned for Maggie, and now started on a course that was distinctively his own and which he reserved for occasions when the atmosphere required to be soothed. It consisted of the introduction of certain words into the conversation which formed a magic circle of sweet suggestiveness, and, such was his instinct and skill, that he managed to do this without definitely changing the subject. 'When I was young,' Berto now said, 'I was very much in love with a Spanish girl who had been married to a man much older than herself; he was killed in the war. But although I was very much in love I didn't marry her because I felt that she would always desire an older man, and I, of course, was not much older.'

'Well, in the case of Dino,' Marisa went on, 'let me tell you that he does ride with her every morning after visiting poor Lidia's tomb.'

'It is so fragrant and cool in that cemetery,' Berto said. 'You know, it's quite romantic. I went once to visit our German aunts who are buried in that little cemetery, tucked away in the Vatican, and I heard the nightingale, suddenly, as if paradise were there among the treetops. I also would have liked, afterwards, to have gone riding with a beautiful lady and kiss her.'

So he went on with his groupings of 'I was in love' and his 'fragrants', his 'heaven' and his 'beautiful lady' and all the pleasant numbers of romantic poetry – trite in themselves but accumulatively evocative of a better life than the actual and present one; so he went on, and presently he could see Maggie's wrists relaxing on the table and her shoulders responding as a cat which has been upset responds to the soft stroking hand.

He could see that the danger was past that she should again open her mouth and let forth accusations like the dead pouring out of their tombs, crazed, on All Souls' Night. If she had been a cat she would by now have started, against her better judgement to purr, and if an analytical critic had been taking a careful note of all that was said, Berto's magic technique would have been a feast more special than the very good lunch they were eating. Mary looked at Michael who alone among the company was brooding over whatever it was he had on his mind, and then she looked at Berto and once more thought how attractive he was in spite of his age; she hadn't noticed before how good-looking was Berto, what marvellous eyes he had.

'And before they went to Baden they were getting that new pool in the garden,' Marisa was saying. 'They had to dig much deeper, and do you know they found a marble head of the first century? Dino says they are now digging deeper to find the rest of it.'

'The Belle Arti will stop everything,' said Cousin Viola.

'They'll take it for the nation and someone will steal it and smuggle it abroad.'

'Well, they had to leave for Baden,' said Marisa. 'But I'm sure, I'm sure, that they haven't breathed a word to the Belle Arti.' Again she appealed to her neighbours. 'The Belle Arti,' she said to Michael on her left and to the young criminal who went by the name of George Falk on her right, 'is our cultural protection agency, but they stop work on anything the moment you report a find. In Italy you only have to dig a few metres and you have a find. If one reported every find to the Belle Arti nobody would get a house built or a swimming pool.'

'Can they trust the servants?' said Cousin Viola.

'It happened once to me,' Berto said, 'that I was helping Guillaume to put up a rabbit hutch as he was sure the rabbits we bought to eat were poisonous and he wanted to breed our own rabbits. We were digging a trench out there behind the orchard and I felt my spade touch on a stone, but not a stone. It felt not like the stones of the garden. So I put aside the spade and went down on my knees. Guillaume was amazed and he said, 'But what are you doing, Marchese!' I scratched at the earth with my hands and I saw a colour, blue, then another, red. It was a moment I could never forget, such a moment of all my dreams – you remember, Viola, the Byzantine vase. It was in fragments, of course.'

'It's in the museum in Verona,' said Viola, calmly eating.

'Oh, yes, it went to the museum.'

'You could have kept it,' Marisa said.

'How could I have kept it? But the moment of discovery, it's a moment that no one can take away from me, not even the Communists. I went back that night to look at the pieces in the moonlight. We left them where we found them, afraid to break them, and Guillaume constructed a little wire fence around them. I looked up at the clouds passing over the moon thinking of Guillaume's tenderness as he made the fence. It was *una cosa molto bella, molto bella* –'

'You have many fine things in this house,' said the younger criminal.

'Exquisite,' said Mr Stuyvesant, the older one, for whom under another name Interpol were looking to help them with their inquiries. 'It must have been wonderful to grow up with them.'

'I was not here very much as a child,' Berto said. 'I was a great deal in Switzerland, and then at school. But when I was a very young man just before the outbreak of the war I remember we had a masked ball here. It was considered a small house for a masked ball, but it was a summer night, you can imagine for young people in those days how exciting . . .'

The troubadour host turned inquiringly to Lauro who stood quietly by his chair waiting for him to finish speaking. Lauro had appeared unexpectedly, for he did not serve at table here in Berto's villa, clashing so much as he did with Guillaume and the cook. Berto looked up at the brown face with a little questioning smile. Lauro spoke in rapid Italian, very excited and happy and Berto listened with his eyes on Maggie till Lauro had finished, and had turned and left the dining-room.

'The masked ball,' said Marisa across the table to her cousin Viola, 'was where Mimi de Bourbon met Aunt Clothilde. She had just broken off from the Thurn and Taxis –'

'Maggie!' said Berto, 'do you know what Lauro has just told me? Your Gauguin is perfectly safe at Nemi; it's there in your house and hasn't been moved.'

'Oh, darling!' said Maggie, who was by now sweetly mellowed by the fragrant distillations of Berto's talk.

Viola, more mesmerized by her cousin Marisa than by her cousin Berto, set her pale head at a saintly angle, and said, 'Aunt Clothilde is still President of the Orphans of St Joachim. She does good work. She has not changed since the old days.'

'Well, she should have,' said Marisa, 'but that's a different topic. I remember – ' Meanwhile, Berto recounted how Lauro had telephoned to his girl-friend at Nemi, and she had gone on a pretext to Hubert's house, and there had seen the leafy Gauguin in its usual place.

'How did she know,' said Mary, 'where to look for that picture?'

'Apparently Lauro's fiancée goes to Mallindaine's dreadful meetings regularly. Moon-worshippers. You can imagine – '

Maggie turned to Mr Stuyvesant, 'Your Gauguin must be a fake,' she said, happily.

'It isn't my Gauguin,' said the art-thief. 'It belonged to

Neuilles-Pfortzheimers' client, and it has been sold as an authentic. One should inform them.'

'Could it possibly be,' said George Falk, the younger crook, 'that the Gauguin at your home is a fake?'

'It is authentic,' said Maggie, and rose to lead her guests into the garden-room for coffee.

Michael woke from his self-absorbed dream and said, 'Mallindaine could have had a copy made. He could have sold the original.'

'Oh, come,' said Berto, as he stood aside to let his guests move out of the dining-room.

'We should get the experts,' Michael said, 'and, anyway, get the picture out of Hubert Mallindaine's hands.'

'That I do agree,' said Maggie.

Berto was about to catch Maggie's arm, to waylay her before she left, and whisper in her ear that she really might, now that she knew her picture was safe, and her initial shock had blown over, apologize to Mr Stuyvesant and Mr Falk. He was about to say she really should, when he was himself waylaid by Guillaume, Maggie in the meantime sailing ahead. Guillaume, alone with Berto in the dining-room, now confided his change of mind about the two visitors of whom he had earlier approved. 'I think they're up to no good,' said Guillaume.

'But why, Guillaume? What makes you say so?'

Guillaume seemed uncertain what precisely to reply. 'The senior visitor spilled *ragoût* on his trousers,' he ventured somewhat wildly. 'It's embarrassing him – a great red stain, and he's trying to cover it up. Right in the front.'

Berto, stifling all reasonable thoughts, and only recalling that it is the easiest thing in the world to splash on one's clothes some of that tomato sauce swimming in which Italian cooks love to present their pasta, was immediately troubled. Plainly, Guillaume had merely only offered an outward symbol for an inward insight, and it was the insight that Berto trusted.

'See if you can do anything for his trousers,' Berto said. 'Offer him some talcum powder. *Ragoût* is always a messy dish. I don't see what it has remotely to do with trusting the unfortunate man, anyway. An accident can happen to the best of us. No reflection whatsoever on his character.'

In the garden-room Berto found Mr Stuyvesant sitting in a crouched position, leaning well forward, with his legs crossed, holding his coffee. But one could still see, on the pale thin-striped trousers that Berto had so much admired, numerous red blotches and smears. He was glad he had not asked Maggie to apologize to these men. It struck him, now, that it was strange how neither of them had seemed to expect an apology, even after news had arrived that Maggie's picture was still in her house. They had not been offended, only embarrassed, by Maggie's outburst. That could be a sign of guilt. One had to be careful who one let into one's house. He looked out of the french windows to where the young Mr Falk was walking on the lawn between Maggie and Cousin Viola, and he looked again at Mr Stuyvesant crouched over his coffee. Guillaume had come in to hover. 'Why don't you go with Guillaume to the pantry,' said Berto, 'and let him do something to your trousers?'

Mr Stuyvesant looked helplessly at his splashed suit and gave a short laugh. 'Not the pantry,' Guillaume said. 'If the gentleman will go to the guest cloakroom I will bring some materials to clean.'

Ah, yes, yes, thought Berto. Guillaume is thinking of the silver depository. Not the pantry, not the pantry. Stuyvesant rose to follow Guillaume while Berto, Knight of the Round Table, courteously remarked, 'Beastly stuff, *ragoût*.'

He hung around the window watching his guests and his wife wandering around the garden in the May sunlight. Lauro and Michael stood under the lovely portico which gave off to the back of the house. Lauro was talking quietly but urgently, Michael listening sullenly. Lauro glanced towards the french window, caught Berto's eye where he stood watching, grinned, and resumed his talk. Berto watched Lauro with tolerant resignation; he had little doubt that Lauro was raising a moderate sum of money every so often from Michael; not much, but a moderate amount, just to keep quiet about the mistress in Rome. Berto looked at Lauro's shining head with its expensive hair-cut. It was difficult to think of him keeping a secret or doing anything free of charge. 'Once a whore,' Berto mused to himself, 'always a whore. That's my philosophy.'

Guillaume's efforts to clean the trousers were not a great

success. Mr Stuyvesant asked for his coat, saying he would hold it over the stain to hide it. So his coat was brought, and holding it draped over his arm he collected his friend and said good-bye to the party very quickly. Berto, with Guillaume hovering behind, watched them leave from the front door. They revved up and left with unusual speed. 'Guillaume,' said Berto, 'I think you're right about those people. They drove off as if it was a getaway from a bank robbery.'

Guillaume muttered to himself in his French-Italian. Berto went to telephone to Alex Pfortzheimer.

Chapter Twelve

Dear Marchesa Tullio-Friole,

Having written in capacity your legal advocate to Mr Hubert Mallindaine at Nemi with regarding the opera of art painted by Paul Gauguin in view of your righteous inquiry in light of the sale of said painting in Switzerland, and having myself accompanied our expert to examine said painting at Nemi by Mr Hubert Mallindaine's request I have to report as it is suspected by the distinguished House Neuilles-Pfortzheimer that this picture at Nemi is a copy of original.

From which arises the complication which I myself have foreseen but not wishing to disturb without necessity have not mentioned to you since this moment. That is, the above-written Mr Mallindaine is hoping to claim of you the cost of original which he is declaring to be part of agreement settled upon him at your handing over to him in the year of 1968 the land and promise of house which he undertook for three years plus housebuilding to his requirements personally in accordance his needs; and the above-written Mallindaine was given contents in the year 1972, July 1, which makes, combined, the remuneration to his services of ten years adviser in your affairs. Always according to Mr Mallindaine's advice, the opera of Paul Gauguin was said at your moment of gift to be original which he has been accepting as such. This is the situation which naturally I hold off with every means from making a confrontation at the present time, as Mr Mallindaine has not yet employed legal offices in the case.

It is my hope you will approve my actions which I should explain you if you should be disposed to be my guest for lunch at the good restaurant that I most admire where we can discuss in tranquillity on the day of your choice.

Very soon hoping to have your telephonic communication my dear Marchesa,

Yours cordially,
Massimo de Vita.

Massimo de Vita, the obscure lawyer whom Maggie had engaged to evict Hubert from his house, sat in one of the copies of Maggie's Louis XIV chairs and looked out at the lake below, while Hubert read through this letter which the lawyer proposed to post from Rome next morning. As he gazed at the still green lake he thought of Maggie, and pictured her, perhaps bursting into his office, Queen of Sheba, making the secretary even more indignant than she constitutionally was, and demanding, with the rings flashing on her fingers, that Hubert be denounced to the police; whereupon, so the lawyer day-dreamed while Hubert studied the letter, one could have a beautiful time calming her down.

'Excellent,' said Hubert. 'The sentiments are accurate and the English is wrong just right. You must understand that with a woman like the Marchesa everything must be done in style. If your style wavers she takes immediate advantage of it and walks all over you. No doubt she believes the Gauguin is genuine. Certainly, she had it smuggled into the country along with many others, in the first place, so she can hardly make a public fuss. I myself have never doubted its authenticity or naturally I would never have accepted it in part settlement.'

'Style, style,' said Massimo de Vita grasping at the idea as if it were a crust, and he starving for it, as indeed he was. He was a brutally ugly man, which in itself could not be counted a disadvantage if he had not made it so by a continual unconscious betrayal of his thoughts which were low-pitched all the time and really quite base. He thought, in fact, that he exercised a quality which he called style, but was in reality an aggressive cynicism. Style, in the sense that he believed himself to possess it, needs a certain basic humility; and without it there can never be any distinction of manner or of anything whatsoever. 'Style,' he repeated, smiling at Hubert who, on occasion, did have a certain style.

'Send her this letter,' Hubert said, handing it back.

Some people could be heard coming up the stairs and presently Pauline entered the drawing-room with a lanky young man. Massimo de Vita got up and greeted her warmly while Hubert sat on in an expressionless way.

Pauline introduced the young man to the lawyer as Walter. He was her boy-friend from the Common Market Headquarters at Brussels, taking his vacation in Italy now that May was passing into June, and was staying in the house as Hubert's guest. He had yellow hair and a moustache of a darker yellow. Hubert tolerated him even though, as he said to Pauline, 'Walter is too occidental for my taste.' At first she thought he had said 'accidental', and was puzzled. He had repeated 'occidental', whereupon she was still puzzled but rather less so.

Walter now plonked himself, tired from his walk, on the sofa, while Pauline busied herself with the letter which the lawyer offered her for a second opinion.

'The English is all wrong. I'll put it right,' she said when she had read it through.

'You will leave the English alone,' Hubert said. 'It expresses Massimo's personality, and besides, if there's any real unpleasantness one can always fall back on the plea that there was some linguistic misunderstanding.'

'What misunderstanding could there be?' Pauline said. 'We thought all along the Gauguin was genuine. We could have counted on it for our bread and butter. Now it turns out to be a fake. I think that woman knew all along it was a fake.'

'I wouldn't be surprised,' Hubert said.

'And we spent all that money on getting it cleaned,' Pauline said.

'You had it cleaned?' the lawyer said.

'Yes, I took it into Rome myself. I was terrified of a hold-up and being robbed or kidnapped on the way. I needn't have been,' Pauline said.

'You needn't say anything to anyone about the cleaning,' Hubert said. 'It would make people laugh. Spending good money on cleaning a fake. It could damage the work of the Brothers and Sisters of Diana and Apollo. The Movement comes first.'

'If the picture went to be cleaned,' said the lawyer, 'this

should not be mentioned. The Marchesa must not believe you have money to burn.'

'It's a really lovely picture,' Pauline said. 'It's real to me, anyway.'

Walter said, 'That's all that matters,' and he looked at Hubert with an expression a little more sour than befits a guest.

Bulging Clara, the Bernardinis' chronically victimized maid, stopped in the main street of Nemi, and put down her plastic shopping bags, bulging like herself they were. Agata, the pretty housemaid from the Radcliffes' house, stopped too. She had approached from the end of the narrow street where the grey castle stood bulkily with its tall and ancient tower, looking like a crazed and bulging woman wearing an absurd top hat, ready to dive off over the cliff into the lake far away below her. Agata was decidedly swollen round the hips and belly, pregnant as a well-founded good hope.

'Well,' said Clara, 'Well, Agata, any news?'

Agata stood into the wall to let the men who were unloading fruit cases from a truck go about their business. She looked back up the haphazard street of fertile Nemi which, by some long-ago access of euphoria or wishful thinking, when Italy was still a kingdom, had been named, doubtless to the peal of bells and the high notes of trumpets, the Corso Vittorio Emmanuele. She already had her paper-tissue handkerchief to her eyes. Agata then named the private parts of numerous animals, including humans, and ended the litany by declaring that, to sum it up, the man was a ne'er-do-well.

'And all his dead!' responded Clara, meaning precisely that all the dead relations of the man in question should by rights endure damnation alike with him.

They stood talking in the sunny main street of Nemi while life bustled by them, the machines in the smithy went on grinding, the electrician skimmed by in his bright Opel, the fruit van backed up and then manoeuvred forward, backed up again and then was off while the fruit shop assistants noisily discussed where the fruit should go in the banked-up crates outside the tiny shop. Clara, with her sly eyes moving occasionally towards the fruit shop, to see how the prices were set on the newly-graded qualities, listened to the young wronged Agata; she listened with her sly ears and puffed out her breath with sympathetic paranoia. Across the street outside the recreation centre stood a carabiniere in his brown uniform, the town clerk in his pressed suit and clean collar and tie, looking on at an exchange of banter between a schoolboy and a white-frocked friar. The two women were greeted occasionally by busy shoppers who passed and swept a glance, along with their smiles, at Agata's hard-done-by belly of shame, while the whole of eternal life carried on regardless, invisible and implacable, this being what no skinny craving cat with its gleaming eyes by night had ever pounced upon, no tender mole of the earth in the hills above had ever discovered down there under the damp soil, no lucky spider had caught, nor the white flocks of little clouds could reveal when they separated continually, eternal life untraceable and persistent, that not even the excavators, long-dead, who had dug up the fields of Diana's sanctuary had found; they had taken away the statues and the effigies, the votive offerings to the goddess of fertility, terracotta replicas of private parts and public parts, but eternal life had never been shipped off with the loot; and even the lizard on the cliff-rocks in its jerky fits had never been startled by the shadow or motion of that eternal life which remained, past all accounting, while Clara and Agata chattered on, tremendously blocking everyone's path although no one cared in the slightest that they did so.

'Could it be anyone else's?' Clara said.

'No, it could only be Lauro's,' said Agata. 'He wants me to put it on Mr Michael but Mr Michael wasn't there at the time. It couldn't have been Mr Michael, but Mr Michael offered to pay for an abortion and Lauro says the offer is a proof of responsibility, and he's getting married to his fiancée right soon; anything to save himself the responsibility. I said, "Lauro, there will be a blood test and I can prove the paternity," but Lauro said, "Well, Michael's group O and I'm group O, so you can just go to *that country* and prove paternity." It was terrible to hear him swearing at me like that after all those times I was good to him when he needed it.'

Clara looked judicious about this. 'You shouldn't have been

good to him.' And she added, 'I'm never good to them,' as if she had plenty of opportunities. Then she observed the obvious: 'If Mr Michael wants to pay for an abortion he must have a reason.'

'I never went with him,' said Agata. 'But I know about his woman in Rome. I know all about that. He even brought her to the house once.'

'What did the Signora Mary say?'

'She was away. Anyway, he wants to help me, and maybe he wants me to keep quiet, too. Maybe he just wanted to help me, to be kind; I don't know. Anyway, I wouldn't have had an abortion, not even –'

'They never do anything just to be kind. Imagine it, just figure to yourself!' Clara said.

'Well, maybe Michael will give me something to help.'

'He'll have to. He'll have to,' Clara said. 'He has no option. The master of the house . . . Work it out for yourself and take my advice. Be advised by me.'

Lauro sat in the sitting-room of the new bungalow high on the terraced cliffs among the woods and caves of Nemi, one of a new group of small houses that looked as if they belonged to tidy Snow White. His relations-to-be sat around him, a good-looking, long-legged set, modern and, with the exception of his fiancée, slender. His future mother-in-law had a fine tanned face and streaked short hair, a woman who could pass, at sight, for any of the Radcliffes' friends. The same was not quite true of his fiancée with her long dark hair and slightly over-ripe figure dressed in a shirt and blue jeans; Lauro considered that he could slim her down after they were married. The two uncles, however, brothers on the mother's side, were also good-looking; one, in his late thirties, with lightish hair, well-tinted and cared for and of a length to cover his ears; and the other, about fifty years old, grey-haired, bespectacled and professorial of appearance. The latter's wife was a fashionably skinny woman with a close-cropped silvered hair-style. They all looked as if they worked in the fashion business or the film industry or else ran a night club, and went to the hairdresser a great deal for tints and cuts and for manicures. Lauro, gloomily perceptive, was proud enough of his new family's appearance, now that it had come to the point where he was goaded into actual marriage by the demands of the wretched servant-girl, Agata. It would have been unthinkable for him to marry Agata, a man of considerable pride like Lauro who had been accepted into the familiar confidences and the beds of the Radcliffes and the Tullio-Frioles, not to mention the distinguished and equally care-free company of the past. It was the lack of that very heart-easy quality in his new family, fine-looking as they were, that depressed Lauro. He flicked ash from his cigarette into a clean ceramic ash-tray, and as he did so his impending mother-in-law, good woman that she was, rose and took the ash-tray and shook the frail ash out of the window, so that Lauro was left with a clean ash-tray again to finish his cigarette with. It was like eating from a plate where they gave you a clean one half-way through the dish. To the tips of her red varnished finger-nails, the mother-in-law was spick-and-span. It made Lauro unhappy although he could not precisely say why, since Maggie, too, and Mary and all the others were always neat and well-groomed enough. It bothered him too that his fiancée, Elisabetta by name, called herself Betty. It troubled him deeply that these people were talking about the wedding-feast in the best trattoria in Nemi with grade one French champagne, seven courses, and at least two hundred people, counting all cousins and friends on both sides, at the expense of the bride's family, no matter how much per head, money no object on such an occasion and seven courses; seven, eight courses, light courses, Betty's sleek, smart aunt was saying, just as if she was a fat country woman, seven courses so that you start with the antipasto, maybe ham and melon; then the soup, a cold consommé very chic for summer; and for pasta you want two, three kinds, say a fine cannelloni of game or spinach and cream cheese inside and a lovely ravioli with tomato sauce and a good fettucine al burro with parmigiano over it, a choice; then you have to have the fish, scampi dipped in a batter; and then a salad, tomatoes and endives with condiments; you have to have the cold meat next, like for instance veal sliced thin and chicken breasts, or pheasant and for the next course something original, maybe a shish kebab which is to say beef on skewers surrounded by small carrots, green beans and rice; and then a green salad of lettuce and basil, very fresh, and so to a cream cake, for example St Honoré, and then the fruit, fresh fruit or macedonia, you could give them a choice, which could be served with petits-fours and some nuts on the table, too; then of course the cheese and coffee; the chocolates you pass round with the liqueur, sambuca, cointreau, cognac, and the bride cuts the cake which goes round; Betty's eldest relation should toast the *sposi* in champagne as the champagne glasses are always kept full throughout the meal, and the *sposo* replies to toast the relatives of the bride and Betty's eldest uncle toasts the relatives of the groom; and you give cigars; the waiters should come from Rome so they would know what to do and serve with white gloves. The bride should give away flowers from her bouquet, then you must remember . . .

Lauro looked at his young bride-to-be with panic on his face but she failed to notice. He panicked all the more that she was listening, enthralled, to her aunt, after all the two years' association with Lauro, and then becoming engaged to him and all the times he had described the sort of life he led, with Michael and Mary, with Maggie and Berto, and their friends in Sardinia, at Ischia, in the Veneto, at Mary's house at Nemi, with its well-served meals of which nobody ate very much so that it was all sent back to the kitchen for the servants to guzzle and drink, and the funny, quite outrageous, chatter and gossip with always little bits of laughter but never a real rowdy laugh. In the world Lauro knew, there was silence in between the talk, and afterwards music and space, and nobody talked of the food at all; they took the good food for granted and if the men discussed wines or the women certain dishes, it was all like a subject that you study in a university like art history or wildlife. For two years Lauro had distilled all this into Betty's ear, but now, it seemed, to no avail, for she was chattering away about the wedding-feast, as loudly and eagerly and rapidly as everyone else, breaking into the half-finished sentences of the others as indeed they were all doing. It was a big food-babble, rising louder and louder and dinning around Lauro's ears, he being only half able to isolate the source of his unhappiness since certainly the family looked very good and up-to-date and prosperous and distinguished. Lauro wanted to run, but he thought of Agata in the Radcliffes' kitchen with one hand on her hip and the other pointing at him, and her screaming accusations and all those tears threatening the vengeance of her father and her brothers. He had nowhere to run to; once he was married to Betty it would be too late and Agata would become a muttering bundle of impotent umbrage, violated for life.

The food affair died down and now they were discussing the money and the marriage portion and the financial arrangements for the couple and their house. Betty should keep her job in the boutique in Rome and she had her car. Betty's mother was about to open a new boutique in Rome, at which point Lauro could give up his job as secretary to the Radcliffes and get the money due to him for liquidation of the contract with a good bit besides; those people had plenty of money.

There came a moment when they let Betty's eldest uncle speak. It was a moment of gravity. Betty's mother filled the liqueur glasses with a sweet syrupy drink and handed them round accompanied each by a lace-edged napkin with a little lacey circlet to rest the glass on. The uncle spoke.

'Betty,' he said, 'is entitled to her share of the land. We have a bit of land.' And he pulled the black, smart brief-case that rested on the arm of the sofa beside him on to his knee, opened it, and extracted a folder. From this he brought a much-folded large document and a map which he spread out on the marble-topped dining-table.

Lauro began to take some notice, and the thought of Agata and his fury against her subsided, together with the memory of her accusations and the slightly older memory of the occasion when, just at the magic moment he had wanted to withdraw, the calculating bitch had told him she was on the pill, it was all right. These rankling images, as at the cinema, changed into that of the actual scene before him, Betty's uncle and her land.

Betty's family comprised her mother's side; the father was unknown and said to be dead. The grandparents, too, were dead and there remained only the uncles, co-proprietors of the fields represented in the big map open on the table.

Lauro bent over it with his arm affectionately round plump

Betty's shoulder. He played with her hair and touched her neck as he looked, for he was excited by the surprising idea that she had so much land of her own. They traced a line. Betty's portion was about ten acres, on a plateau among the cliffs of Nemi. 'But it can't be there,' Lauro said.

The uncle's finger traced the boundaries. 'Of course it's there,' he said, and patiently he took out of his brief-case the title deeds, tracing their history for five generations right into young Betty's hands.

'This is good land,' said the younger uncle. 'Better a few *ettari* of good land than a hundred kilometres of waste.'

'But some of that land has been sold. There's a house there. The Marchesa bought it and a Mr Mallindaine, an eccentric Englishman, lives there. I used to work for him.'

Betty's mother started to laugh and so did the uncle. 'She bought it, yes, but not from us,' said Betty's well-groomed mother. 'Some lawyer came along and sold it to her. He said he represented the Church and it was Church property. She got false deeds. We didn't protest, naturally, when she put up the house. It's just as well to bide one's time.'

'It isn't hers,' Betty said, 'and the house is illegal. It's *abusivo.* We can make them take it down.'

'Any time we like. If we like. We can denounce them.'

'Send the police along to that house,' said Betty's skinny aunt.

'Why should we? Better let them pay us than pay a fine to the State,' the elder uncle said. 'We can sue. But she won't take it to court; she'll pay.'

'Once you leave the job, Lauro,' Betty's mother said, 'you can give the Marchesa a piece of news: she's got an illegal house and is trespassing on your land.'

Betty's mother took Lauro's ash-tray, almost empty as it was, into the kitchen and brought it back clean.

'The title deeds of the land,' said Hubert, 'were transferred to Maggie on 8 February 1968, a date I can never forget; and at the end of April this house was started on cleared land where no house previously had stood. The house took three years and two months to construct.'

'The building permit?' said Massimo de Vita. 'Was that a fake, too, or didn't you have one?'

'Maggie had a building permit, of course,' Hubert said. 'I don't know what she's done with it. She probably has it in her company offices for safe keeping.'

'A pity she didn't come to me sooner,' said Massimo. He was growing a beard, as yet not long enough to cover the extra chins which would not go away. He looked excited and hastily dressed, as one who had been, as in fact he had, working long hours for several days. In that time he had established beyond doubt that the lawyer who had arranged for Maggie to buy the property at Nemi was not to be found and his name nowhere on the legal records of Italy. He had further discovered that Lauro's impudent claim that the land on which Hubert's house was built belonged to his fiancée was not impudent at all, it was true. The whole of the transaction had been a fake, including the documents, and the land presumed to have been Church property belonged to Lauro's prospective bride at this moment.

'She should have had me for her lawyer in those days,' said Massimo. 'Now I have to write her a letter and see how I can get her out of this mess.'

'She gave me this house,' Hubert said sulkily. 'It is mine. I supervised the building of it for three years and two months; it was agony; getting things done in Italy is agony; then I moved in and a few months later Maggie cut off the funds she had promised in order to maintain it. I can sue.'

'It's up to me,' said the lawyer, 'to say whether you can sue or not. Meantime, let us look at the facts. You occupy this house – no?'

'Yes,' said Hubert, meekly.

The library door opened and Pauline Thin put her head round it. 'Coffee?' she said chirpily.

'Get out!' barked Hubert. Pauline withdrew.

'But you had no building permit.'

'There was indeed a building permit,' Hubert said. 'I remember obtaining photo-copies from the lawyer to satisfy the building contractors. Everything was regular.'

'Well, it wasn't regular,' said Massimo, 'and the lawyer least of all. Dante de Lafoucauld, what a name for an Italian lawyer . . . You should have known . . . You should have – '

'What's the matter?' said an aggressive male voice from the door. It belonged to a skinny sun-bronzed chest, shoulders and pair of arms topped by a yellow-haired head: Walter, with his deep yellow moustache, having been called in from his sun-bath and, bored by Nemi and resentful of Hubert, being now only too keen to take up a quarrel on Pauline's behalf. Some other voices, male and female, questioned and commented behind him; Pauline had brought some of the local young people to the house for the day. She did this many, many days now, gradually building up something like a commune under the protective wings of the Brotherhood of Diana and Apollo; so far, Hubert had felt it wise to refrain from expressing all the alarm that he felt, even although these young people had seemed to take over the house, left a mess behind them all over the place and never did any work.

Hubert shouted at Walter, 'Get out! I'm discussing serious business with my lawyer.' He rose and lumbered over to the door, gave the young man a hefty push, slammed the door shut and locked it. A clamour of protest arose from the other side of the door, subsiding after a few minutes as the footsteps of the lithe and sandalled young set flip-flopped down the staircase into the overgrown garden where these people were wont to lie and watch the intertwining of the weeds and get their bodies ever browner by the good offices of Apollo.

'Now,' said Hubert when he had simmered down a bit, 'one problem at a time, if you please. *Una cosa alla volta*.'

'Precisely,' said the lawyer, on the defensive. 'It's hardly my fault that –'

'Down to business,' said Hubert. 'Presumably, when Lauro gets married, he will start putting me out of the house.'

'I don't know about that,' said Massimo.

'Or they will want some money. A lot of money,' Hubert said, 'to keep their mouths shut.'

'There could be several legal opinions,' said Massimo. 'The law is very contradictory. Certainly they will want some money. Certainly. But can they claim it? The house does not exist.'

'I mean this house,' Hubert said.

'It does not exist. How can it exist? It is not on the records. In

Italy if a house is not on the records, it has been constructed illegally and we call it *abusivo*. An *abusivo* construction does not exist in legal terms. The family who own the land can make the Marchesa pull it down.'

'But will they?'

'It depends on their frame of mind and if they can come to terms. It depends also on whether the land they own is only the top soil. In Italy, sometimes the sub-soil belongs to somebody else; it could belong to the Church or the State. At any rate the family can make trouble for the Marchesa.'

'She will have to pay,' Hubert said. 'Maggie will have to pay them off.'

'Even then,' said the lawyer, 'the police or the town council might discover that it is *abusivo* and cause the house to be destroyed, but it is unlikely they will know that the house is *abusivo* unless the family reports it.'

'Well, it's my house. Maggie gave it to me.'

'She had no right to do so. It doesn't exist.'

'She will have to make reparation if the house is pulled down,' Hubert said.

'Oh, certainly she would have to do that if she gave it to you. The legal transfer of the house to your name fortunately did not take place. Technically the house is still hers. Although of course I believe you, it is obvious that verbally she gave you the house. But now it is certain, anyway, that she can't put you out. There are many tenants in *abusivo* houses who cannot be put out and who need not pay rent, either. Because the house does not exist.'

'And the contents of the house?' Hubert said.

'It would be difficult,' said Massimo, moving his plump hands in the air as he spoke, 'to say anything about the contents of a house that does not exist. How can a non-existent house contain contents? How can it have a tenant? You don't exist when you inhabit a house that is *abusivo*.'

'Under Italian law?' said Hubert.

'It could be argued,' the lawyer said. 'It could be argued for a very long time and the longer you stay in a house the more difficult it is to get you out.'

'Italian law,' said Hubert, 'is very exciting. Positively mystical. I approve strongly of Italian law.'

Massimo laughed merrily and looked at his watch, very flat, very gold with its golden band encircling his plump wrist. He said something about lunch-time, but Hubert was musing on a private dream of his own from which he presently emerged to say, 'This house seems to me to be perfectly safe as the head-quarters of the Brother-Sisterhood of Diana and Apollo. We can ignore Maggie's protests about the use the house is being put to; that's my opinion.'

'And mine,' said Maggie's lawyer. 'I tear up the letter now which the Marchesa sent me to that effect. I never received it.'

He took a letter from his brief-case and tore it in small pieces.

'It doesn't exist,' Hubert observed.

'I never received it,' said Massimo. 'She did not register it and so it is easy never to receive a letter with the postal situation in our country being what it is.'

The door opened and Pauline stood on the threshold of the library. 'Why have you unplugged the telephone?' she said. 'Someone is wanting to use it.'

'I don't want to be disturbed,' Hubert said. 'Miss Thin, are you my secretary or are you not?'

'I'm hungry. We're all hungry,' she said, 'and the lunch is ready and the cook is getting angry.'

'How much pleasanter it was,' said Hubert to the lawyer, 'before we had our good fortune.' He rose with the lawyer and swept past Pauline, declaring that the blessings deriving from his ancestor the goddess Diana were mixed ones indeed.

As he descended the stairs Massimo loitered to grasp Pauline and press her against the wall of the landing; then he kissed her heavily whether she liked it or not.

Chapter Thirteen

'Have you read the papers?' Berto said, his eyes reposing on an abyss of horror.

Maggie was in Switzerland intently but vainly hunting Coco de Renault through the woods and thickets of the Zürich banks, of the Genevan financial advisory companies, the investment counselling services of Berne, and through the wildwoods of Zug where the computers whirred and winked unsleepingly in their walls, where the office furniture was cream leather in the tall buildings, and the dummy directors of elaborately-titled corporations entered the glass front-doors set into the marbled façades, walked up the staircases lined with the cedars of Lebanon, to take their places at their large desks at ten in the morning, after a massage and a swim in the pool.

Mary and Michael had gone to the Greek islands on a yacht, to get away from it all, to get to know each other again and for a number of other purposes described in similar phrases which Mary had written down on a list. They were gone and the house at Nemi was closed up, the pretty maid having left their service with her aunt who, in view of the girl's condition, had carried the suitcases, refusing all help from Michael and Mary, but serving them with polite but pregnant assurances that justice would be done on the girl's behalf and Michael would be hearing from their lawyer. Mary had stood beside Michael in a very positive way, cool and blonde, rich and loyal. She had said the right thing: 'My husband is innocent.' Then she had said the wrong thing: 'We're not afraid of your Communist lawyer.' This had brought a duet of retorts from the niece and aunt, to the effect that Mary would pay for those words, the politics of their lawyer were not her business; she had committed an outrage against the Republic of Italy by speaking disrespectfully of their lawyer and his politics; she was a whore who slept with everybody including Lauro and she had also been seen in bed with her mother-in-law. Mary had stood on, her arm in Michael's, cold-lipped, till the women got into the car and drove off.

Lauro, too, was away. He was on his honeymoon, having first spent a morning with Maggie, at Michael's house, breaking gently to her the news that none of her three houses at Nemi was really hers and that Hubert's in particular was built on the dowry of Lauro's bride. Maggie had assumed at first that Lauro was weaving a fantasy in some obscure desire to rouse her passions and end up with a love-making scene. She had been indulgent about his stories, assuring him sweetly that she held the title-deeds of all her properties everywhere, or at least Coco de Renault did; Maggie took her cheque book out of its charming little drawer and wrote out a very large cheque to Lauro for a wedding present, which he received graciously and lovingly. When they got up from the sofa, pulling their clothes straight, however, Lauro again came round to his incredible story. 'Really, Maggie, that lawyer was a crook. He can't be found in Italy. He's sold you land and houses that didn't belong to him. He chose a couple of abandoned houses and a piece of vacant land and falsified the papers, that's all.'

'The real owners would have come forward by now,' Maggie said.

'In the case of this house of Michael's,' Lauro said, 'it belongs to a large family, twelve, fourteen, cousins, all of them in America. That crook was clever. But when one of those cousins comes home for a visit you'll have trouble. In the case of the Bernardini house, it once belonged to a cousin of my fiancée who died, but his son is the heir; he has a job in England, a very important job in a chemical factory. He won't like to see someone occupying his house if he returns to look for it in Italy.'

'The Bernardini house was a total ruin,' Maggie said, 'a complete wreck, and I spent a fortune on the reconstruction; I put in the tennis court and the pool; I put in the lily-pond and I laid the lawns; then the Bernardinis started all over again making big changes. The same with this house here; Michael had it before he was married; we flew one of the best architects in Los Angeles over here to restore this house; it was a wreck when I bought it.'

'You didn't buy it, Maggie,' said Lauro, quietly. 'You only thought you did. Take Hubert's house which you put on Betty's land, for instance, well, it just doesn't exist officially.'

He comforted Maggie greatly that morning as she telephoned one after the other office in Rome to try and trace that lawyer Dante de Lafoucauld whom it now appeared nobody had ever heard of, and whom Maggie herself had met only twice, in Rome, in the Grand Hotel in the winter of 1968. Nobody had heard of him at all. Maggie rang the office of Massimo de Vita, who was out. She left her name with an answering service, and then went into hysterics, blaming Massimo for everything and saying how awfully suspicious it was that he didn't have a secretary any more, only an answering service attached to his phone. 'Only crook lawyers have answering services,' Maggie moaned, while Lauro poured her out a brandy and said, 'Maggie, Maggie, drink this, Maggie dear. I love you, Maggie. You didn't have Massimo de Vita for a lawyer in 1968, did you? You only went to de Vita for the first time a year ago, didn't you? How can he be to blame?'

'They're all in it together,' Maggie screamed. 'Why hasn't he got a proper office with a secretary? It was the seediest office I ever saw. Now he hasn't even got a secretary. I hate to deal with answering services.' The telephone rang just then, from Massimo de Vita in response to her message on the answering service. He was just about to write to her, he said.

'I have to talk to you,' said Maggie. 'Have you ever heard of an Italian lawyer called Dante de Lafoucauld?'

'Yes,' he said. 'I heard that name last week. He isn't any sort of Italian lawyer. I don't know who he is. He's a crook. Apparently, you see, Marchesa, you were badly advised, and this man, whoever he is, forged some documents for some houses which don't belong to you –'

'You know him?' Maggie said. 'Then you know the man?'

'I never heard of him till a week ago, when I was looking into the matter of the eviction of Mr Mallindaine. Then it all –'

'He had a beard,' wailed Maggie. 'He had a dark beard.'

'So have I,' said Massimo. 'Marchesa, since last we met, I have grown a beard. I will do what I can for you in this affair, although you realize, Marchesa, that when the houses are not yours –'

'Crooks, all of you!' Maggie yelled, whereupon her voice was immediately overlaid by that of Lauro who had taken the telephone from her hand. 'Doctor de Vita,' said Lauro, 'you must excuse the Marchesa. She's very upset. I will be in touch with you and arrange a meeting.'

The lawyer said a few words in Italian for Lauro's ears only, partly legal in substance, partly sexual.

'Si, si, Dottore,' said Lauro, and hanging up the receiver continued his work of calming Maggie down. He was somewhat successful until she got it into her head to ring Coco de Renault. The lines were engaged for every number she tried where Coco might be: Nemi–Paris, Nemi–Geneva, Nemi–Zürich. 'It's lunch time; it's one o'clock,' said Lauro. 'Everyone will be out. I'll fix you some lunch, Maggie. Leave the telephone and I'll tell you all you need to do in the case of Betty's land. It's simple and, after all, you can afford it.'

Maggie rang Berto and gave him the story, which he didn't believe. He replied quietly, thinking her to be temporarily deranged, and said he would join her shortly at Nemi. He sounded reluctant to do so; he said he was occupied with problems to do with the safety from robbers of his house in the Veneto.

'We can't stay here. There are no servants,' Maggie said. 'Lauro's getting married on Saturday and Agata's left. I have all these houses and nowhere to stay.'

'We can stay in Rome. Or we could stay with the Bernardinis,' said Berto. Maggie hung up and rang the Bernardinis. Emilio would not be home till six. The young people were out. Maggie collapsed into tears and presently let Lauro bring her a delicate lunch-tray.

That stormy morning over, Maggie set off the next day with Berto's car and driver for Rome where she had a full-scale massage treatment, then onwards, glowing and resolute, for Switzerland in pursuit of Coco de Renault. She was anxious to see him in any case about the lack of funds. Something was happening to her monthly cheques which were not arriving at the Rome bank as usual, so that she had been unable to pay her bodyguard. She said nothing to Berto. The bodyguard had left. That was embarrassing enough. And now it was imperative to get from Coco the title-deeds of her houses and so prove them hers.

Berto was staying with the Bernardinis meanwhile and had wearily realized the truth about the houses at Nemi. 'If I had met Maggie earlier,' Berto told Emilio, 'she would never have done anything so foolish. There's nothing for it but for Maggie to pay reparations or else surrender the properties; she can manage that all right. I wish she would try to see things in proportion.'

'It would be hard on us,' said Emilio Bernardini, 'to have to leave here after all the work we've put into the house.'

'I dare say something can be arranged,' Berto said.

'I dare say,' said Emilio, smiling to reassure his friend.

'Do you trust Coco de Renault?' said Berto, gazing across the trees towards the tower of the castle and the rows of little houses built into the cliff below it, huddled in half-circular terraces round the castle like the keys of an antiquated type-writer. He looked away from the view and into Emilio's face, suddenly realizing that the man was not quite his usual cool self.

'I did trust him, of course,' said Emilio. 'When I introduced him to Maggie of course I trusted him. He handled some affairs of mine, very badly as it has turned out. I can't say, honestly, that I trust de Renault now. It's very embarrassing, and I wish I'd never brought him together with you and Maggie. But I had no idea she would hand over so vast a part of her fortune to him to manage. In fact, I think she put everything in his hands, which was a foolish, an unheard of, thing to do. I would never have expected her to hand over *everything*.'

'Has she done that?' said Berto.

'I think so, yes.'

'And you have doubts about de Renault?'

'I do, yes. I have had quite a shock in my own case. There is something shady about him, and I'm very sorry, very embar-rassed.'

'Poor Maggie,' Berto said mildly, 'I hope she won't get any more shocks. I think only of Maggie herself, you know. A won-derful woman, a wonderful woman. She doesn't need money to make her a wonderful woman. It's only that she's used to it.' Berto added after a while, 'It's hardly your fault, Emilio. I should myself have taken more interest in Maggie's affairs. Perhaps I could have persuaded her not to put her trust in de Renault. For my part, how could I hold you responsible? After all, I've known you since you were a schoolboy.'

Emilio said, 'Thank you, but, you know very well, you can't trust every man who was at school with your son. These days, whom can you trust?'

'One's friends,' said Berto. 'You know, Emilio, you're too sad by nature. Why are you so sad?' And this question, the asking of which would have seemed quite absurd in another society, was really quite normal at Nemi, on the outskirts of Rome in the middle of June 1975, for Berto and Emilio.

'Why are you so sad by nature?'

'Life is sad.'

It was the next morning, reading the newspaper, that Berto said to Emilio, 'Have you read the papers?' This was an unnecessary question since the news, on that morning and the next, was a national event: the regional elections throughout Italy had confirmed a popular swerve to the political Left. It could fairly be said that Italy had turned half-Communist overnight. Both halves were fairly stunned by the results.

Berto, keening at the wake in those days, detained Emilio from going about his morning's business, with prophecies and lamentations. The Communists became 'They', the Italian 'Loro'. Berto said, 'Loro, loro, loro . . . They, they . . .'

'It's the will of the people,' Emilio said, but he spoke into heedless morning air, and Berto continued, 'Look how they write in the newspaper; they say one has the sensation that something is finished for always. And whatever they mean by that, it's the truth. Something is finished. Loro, loro . . . They, they . . . They will come and take away everything from you. They took away everything from us in Dalmatia. They will take, will carry away . . . Loro . . . ti prenderanno, ti porteranno via tutto . . . They will come and take . . . Everything you possess . . . ' The gardener's son, passing by and catching these words, wondered how that could be, his possession being a motor-scooter. 'They will kill . . . ti liquideranno . . . ' said Berto. 'They will take over, and they will – '

Emilio, who, although not himself a Communist adherent, had none the less voted Communist in these elections to express his exasperation with Italy's government-in-residence, did not have the heart to say so to the older man. After all, he had been at school with Berto's son, and Emilio would not shatter Berto's kindly affection. Emilio kept his dark, young secret and merely observed, sadly, 'After the capitalists have finished with us I doubt if there will be anything left for the Communists to take over. De Renault, for example – '

'Better her money should go to a swindler than to the Communists,' Berto said.

Chapter Fourteen

With the elections and the strawberry festival in the air, and Maggie, so far as Hubert had ascertained, on a trip to Switzerland, and with Lauro away on his honeymoon, Hubert felt it wise to call a rally of his followers and prepare for battle with any such apocalyptic events and trials as are bound to befall the leaders of light and enlightened movements, anywhere, in any age.

Maggie, he hoped, had gone to Switzerland to arrange for the surreptitious payment of his claim for the fake Gauguin, and maybe to raise funds to meet the demands of Lauro's bride and the eventual claims of the other owners of the properties she had thought were hers; she would do this, he reckoned wrongly, without breathing a word to her pig of a husband. He was wrong not only in this reckoning, but also in the assumption that Maggie had received her lawyer's letter about his demand to be compensated for the fake Gauguin. The letter had indeed been sent to her by registered post, but the mails from Rome were fairly disordered, and the letter had not in fact reached Maggie at the Veneto before she had left the villa. Guillaume had signed for it and put it aside, on the tray in the hall, where it innocently awaited the most peculiar circumstances of her return. Hubert did not know this, and in fact he had got into a habit of false assumptions by the imperceptible encroachment of his new cult; so ardently had he been preaching the efficacy of prayer that he now, without thinking, silently invoked the name of Diana for every desire that passed through his head, wildly believing that her will not only existed but would certainly come to pass. Thus, like ministers of any other religion, he was estranged from reality in proportion as he mistook the nature of prayer, offering up his words of praise, of gratitude, penitence, intercession and urgent petition in the satisfaction that his god would reply in kind, hear, smile, and wave a wand. So that, merely because he had known in the past that the unforeseen stroke of luck can happen, and that events which are nothing short of a miracle can take place, Hubert had come secretly to take it with a super-stitious literalness that the miraculous may happen in front of your eyes; speak the word, Diana, and my wish will be fulfilled. Whereas, in reality, no farmer prays for rain unless the rain is long overdue; and if a miracle of good fortune occurs it is always at the moment of grace unthought-of and when everybody is looking the other way. However, Hubert, largely through his isolation at Nemi and from not having seen Maggie in person for a number of years, believed that Diana of the Woods could somehow enter Maggie's mind, twist a kind of screw there, and force her to do something she would not otherwise have done.

Moreover, he had not allowed for a change in Maggie, a hardening. In the carefree past she had been more or less a docile pushover where money was concerned, and Hubert miscal-culated the effect upon her of being married to steady-minded Berto, of having had her suspicions aroused to the point of almost-justified paranoia by various threats to her moneyed peace, and, most of all, by the new economic crisis which Hubert had mentally absorbed in those months from what he read and heard, but which had not closely touched him.

Maggie would come back from Switzerland, he felt sure, and make a settlement for the Gauguin. Indeed, he could hardly think of Maggie without the word settlement coming to his mind.

Lauro and his buxom horror-beauty of a wife would also return and, should it please the gods, Lauro might even join the Fellowship of Diana and Apollo, in the same way that the three other boys had returned to him, those secretaries of the first, beautiful summer at Nemi, when the house was newly built, in 1972, that year of joy and of outrage, when Hubert was free to leave his doors unlocked, could come and go as he pleased, but when Maggie began to desert him, searching as he did after strange gods and getting married to Tullio-Friole. As it happened, the return of the secretaries was a mixed blessing, but Hubert thanked Diana for them all the same.

In the meantime he thought it well to declare a special con-gress of his flock. Pauline Thin, who in kindly moments Hubert called 'Our Mercury', sent messages by telephone and by grape-vine word of mouth to numerous fellow-worshippers who lived within easy travelling distance of Nemi; she also sent out a number of telegrams, cautiously-worded in each case, in order to get together a preliminary meeting of kindred souls, the elect Friends of Diana and Apollo, and so prepare for an even grander gathering which Hubert projected for the following autumn and which he spoke of variously as an 'international synod', a 'world congress' and a 'global convergence'. Hubert was aware that the ecclesiastical authorities as well as the carabinieri already viewed his house with suspicion and that his activities were regarded with a certain amount of local disfavour. 'They can't pin anything on me,' Hubert said, 'not drugs nor orgies nor fraud. We are an honest religious cult. All the same, we have to be careful.' Mostly he feared Lauro and the Radcliffe family, feeling sure they would, if they could, use any eventual excuse to bring trouble on his Fellowship, which was covering expenses by now, very nicely. What Hubert had in mind for his final project was to try and syphon off, in the interests of his ancestors Diana and her twin brother Apollo, some of the great crowds that had converged on Rome as pilgrims for the Holy Year, amongst whom were vast numbers of new adherents to the Charismatic Renewal movement of the Roman Catholic Church. News had also come to Hubert of other Christian movements which described themselves as charismatic, from all parts of Europe and America; a Church of England movement, for instance, and another called the Children of God. Studying their ecstatic forms of worship and their brotherly claims it seemed to him quite plain that the leaders of these multitudes were encroaching on his territory. He felt a burning urge to bring to the notice of these revivalist enthusiasts who proliferated in Italy during the Holy Year that they were nothing but schismatics from the true and original pagan cult of Diana. It infuriated him to think of the crowds of charismatics in St Peter's Square, thumbing their guitars, swinging and singing their frightful hymns while waiting for the Pope to come out on the balcony. Not far from Nemi was the Pope's summer residence in Castelgandolfo. Next month, he fumed, they will crowd into Castelgandolfo, and they should be here with me.

Pauline, meanwhile, was having the time of her life. Men pressed her against the wall and kissed her whether she liked it

or not. She found herself at the centre of Hubert's young following, surrounded by attentive people and to spare. She was determined to keep her privileged position of having been in with
Hubert from the start, holding on to it partly by a habit she had
of reminding Hubert by little hints, privately from time to time,
that some of those records she had been obliged to put in order
over the past three years still puzzled her. Pauline's allusions to
the records inevitably subdued any attempt by Hubert to get rid
of her, as he could now afford to do. He, meanwhile, on these
occasions, finding himself stuck with her in this uneasy relationship, got himself quickly out of his troubled state of mind by
telling himself he was fond of Pauline, very, very fond. When
he told himself this for a few minutes continuously, he believed
it, and did not appear in the least aware of having capitulated to
a piece of blackmail, except that on such occasions he called her
Miss Thin for the rest of the day. Perhaps it was his age; at all
events he associated his pagan cult with his own very survival
and was ready at least to endure Pauline for it; he was prepared
to love her as far as he could and to let her fill the house and
garden with anyone whomsoever, so long as they didn't bring in
forbidden drugs, use up the hot water in the house, and provided
they subscribed to the Fellowship. On these conditions he was
content with the arrangements that Pauline made and especially
with her rule that nobody could approach him except through
her; that suited him very well.

Pauline herself had put a number of young people to work for
the cult. She had roped in Letizia Bernardini as press officer and
Pietro Bernardini as public relations officer. There was an older
man, Pino Tullio-Friole, Berto's son, who also made regular pil-
grimages to the home of Hubert, descendant of Diana, bringing
contributions of money and precious objects and some of his
wealthy friends who liked to attend the religious services and
afterwards sleep with whoever was available. Pino, who was in
his early forties, despised Maggie and resented her marriage to
his father.

Hubert brooded especially over one of the many press cuttings
Letizia had produced for him. It was dated 18 May, and was
taken from the English-speaking paper of Italy, *The Daily
American.*

'Cardinals, bishops meet, dance in Rome,' was the headline. It said:

Rome, 17 May (AP) – Bishops, archbishops and cardinals, struggling to keep their hats in place, sang and danced in ecstasy, embracing one another and raising their arms to heaven.

The Most Rev. Joseph McKinney, auxiliary bishop of Grand Rapids, Mich., joined hands with the Most Rev. James Hayes, archbishop of Halifax, who in turn linked arms with Leo, Cardinal Suenens of Belgium.

The unlikely chorus yesterday opened the Ninth International conference on charismatic Renewal in the Roman Catholic Church.

The conference theme of 'renewal and reconciliation' – the theme of Holy Year – underlines the movement's search for wholehearted approval in the official Church.

A crowd of about 8,000, most of them Americans, gathered at the catacombs of St Callixtus, burial place of the early Christian martyrs, for the opening ceremony. A young band led the congress in song, and delegates from Quebec to Bombay testified to the growth of the movement in all continents.

Cardinal Suenens, archbishop of Malines, urged participants to use the four-day reunion 'to renew your faith, to renew your hope in the future, to love each other like you never did before'.

The Charismatic Movement, a predominantly lay movement claiming more than half a million followers, emerged in main line Protestant churches in the early 1960s and in Roman catholicism in 1967, among students and professors at Duquesne University in Pittsburg.

It is characterized by fervent prayer meetings, gifts of the spirit such as 'speaking in tongues' and efforts to breathe new life into personal religion.

In a recent report, American Catholic bishops credited the movement with 'many positive signs . . . a new sense of spiritual values, a heightened consciousness of the action of the Holy Spirit, the praise of God and a deepening personal commitment to God.'

But they warned of dangers inherent in the revival – divergence from the official Church, fundamentalism, exaggeration of the importance of the gifts of prophecy and speaking in tongues.

'Tongues is not the important thing; the important thing is the change in your life,' said Bob Cavnar, a retired U.S. Air Force colonel who came here for the meeting from Dallas, Tex.

Cavnar, introduced to the movement by his son Jim, was one of

70 congress elite renowned for speaking in tongues and selected to receive messages to the conference from the Holy Spirit.

Hubert kept many such cuttings, read and re-read them, with a sense of having been cheated of his birthright. He had sent Pauline at the beginning of June to one of these meetings and afterwards had locked himself with Pauline into the drawing-room, or rather, locked out the rest of the drifting acolytes and lovers who at present made up his household, to hear her story.

'It started off,' said Pauline, 'with a mass.'

'In church?'

'No, no. It was an altar set up in this flat in the Via Giulia. I don't know whose flat it was. Well, they had a mass, there was a Catholic priest with his vestments, and the congregation, about thirty people.'

'What sort of people? Rich, poor, how did they strike you? All English-speaking? What language was the mass?'

'It was in English, but there were lots of Italians and French, all sorts. All sorts of people and some nuns. Quite a lot of nuns in their habits; and later I found some were nuns and priests in ordinary clothes. They seemed all ages, really, but only one or two really old, and they were nuns.'

'It is from ordinary people that the great revenues come,' said Hubert. 'They are filching the inheritance of the great Diana of Nemi, the mother of nature from time immemorial.'

'I did talk about Diana, don't worry,' Pauline said. 'A number of people were very interested. And do you know who was there? – Those Jesuits, Cuthbert Plaice and his friend Gerard Harvey the nature-study man, were there. Father Gerard, in fact, was urging some of the young men to come to one of our meetings and telling everyone how wonderful Nemi was, how the environment comes right up to the back door and so on. Father Cuthbert was asking me a lot about your personal origins, Hubert, and I told him well, it was a long story. Then – '

'Miss Thin,' said Hubert, 'I want the whole picture of this charismatic meeting and you can tell me afterwards what the Jesuits said. At the same time, my dear, I must say it was most commendable of you to get your word in about the true Fellowship. You're wonderful, Miss Thin, you really are. Tell me about the mass.'

'Well, the mass only preceded the meeting. It was an ordinary mass except for the swinging hymns, and the fact that the Kiss of Peace was real kisses, everyone kissed everyone. That sort of thing. The nuns seemed to like it and there was lots of embracing and singing.'

'We should have nuns in the Fellowship,' Hubert said. 'Diana always had her vestal virgins. We should have vestal virgins watching a flame on the altar day and night.'

'Well, they would have to be part-time,' Pauline said. 'Who is going to come and watch a flame all day?'

'When we have a greater following,' Hubert said, 'all these things will fall into place. Did the Jesuits participate in this orgy?'

'Well, I wouldn't say it was an orgy. The Jesuits were there as observers, anyway. The prayer meeting that followed the mass was more exciting, when they spoke with tongues and made emotional comments on the scriptures. They made a sound like an Eastern language, Hebrew, or Persian maybe, or Greek. I don't know what; but that's speaking with tongues. Then they prophesy. There was a woman there, about thirty-five, she prophesied a lot, and would you believe it, she was a doctor. She proclaimed a passage from the Gospels and closed her eyes and threw up her hands. Everyone said "Amen". Then we sang and clapped hands in syncopation, and sort of danced – '

'What passage from the Gospels?' said Hubert.

'Oh, I don't know. Something about St Paul in his travels.'

'That is not the Gospels. It is probably the Acts of the Apostles. What was the text?'

'Oh, I don't remember. Something about the Lord. It was all so noisy, and everybody was excited, you know. It wasn't so important what the words were, I think.'

'It never is,' Hubert said. 'And what were the Jesuits doing?'

'Well, they didn't join in but they seemed to be enjoying it all. Their eyes were all over the place. Cuthbert Plaice saw me. He said "Hi, Pauline, how do you like it?" I said I liked it tremendously, and I really did as a matter of fact, but the feeling wore off afterwards, you know.'

'We must step up our services in the Fellowship,' Hubert said, 'that's clear.'

It was a hazy hot afternoon towards the end of June. Beyond the ranges of the Alban hills you had to imagine the sea, for indeed it was there, far away, merging invisibly into the heat-blurred sky-line.

Pauline had been busy over the past ten days, putting such a massive amount of energy into the task she had undertaken that in fact she felt she would never again in the course of her life find it in her to repeat the effort, even although Hubert kept reminding her that this was only a preliminary little gathering to the one planned for the autumn.

At the end of ten days Pauline had arranged a fairly big gathering of Hubert's faithful to be held in the large overgrown garden behind the house stretching to the dark, moist woods. She had announced the event as a 'secret meeting', totally avoiding any written messages. Pauline had spent many hours on the telephone and had travelled around in Hubert's car to notify the Friends of Diana and to exhort attendance. The object of this meeting was to form a nucleus around which the future cells of the Fellowship were to collect.

Pauline had not been able to get much done with the garden, but she had cleared enough to put up an altar and a flowery canopy, and to prepare a covered marquee for the fruit juice and sandwiches.

'What will we do if it rains?' she had asked Hubert snappily on one of those frantic ten days of preparation.

'It will not rain,' thundered Hubert.

On the last day she had been to Rome to get her hair cut and set, and also to buy the remarkable outfit which she now, as the expected throng began to accumulate, triumphantly wore. Too late, Hubert had seen her and exclaimed, 'You can't wear that!' This was a khaki cotton trouser-suit with metal-gold buttons on the coat and its four pockets; Pauline had tucked the trouser-legs into a pair of high canvas boots, so that the whole dress looked like a safari suit. The hunting effect was increased by a pale straw cocked hat which perched on her short curled hair.

'What do you mean?' Pauline said when Hubert, already waiting in his leafy bower, bedecked in his silver-green priestly vestments, had exclaimed 'You can't wear that!'

'It's entirely out of keeping, and irreverent. You look like the commandant of a concentration camp or something out of a London brothel.'

'It signifies the hunt,' Pauline said. 'Diana is a huntress, isn't she?'

'She is always portrayed wearing a tunic,' Hubert said, 'and a quiver full of arrows.' It was a hot day, and his vestments were heavy, which made him feel sicker than ever.

'Well, I can't wear a tunic,' said Pauline, 'I haven't the figure.'

'The figure!' shouted Hubert from under his greenery and his robes. 'The figure . . . ' he shouted across the garden. 'If you think your figure fits into that outfit, with your haunches like a buffalo's –'

Pauline started to cry, pulling from her satchel-bag a large red handkerchief with white spots which it would seem was designed, even the handkerchief, to enrage Hubert. Pauline's skinny boy-friend Walter came out of the house, and stopped in some astonishment at the scene. He had not seen Hubert before in his robes nor Pauline in her new outfit, although he had seen her cry at various times.

Hubert, who had taken some care to pose himself under the bower, was unwilling to disarrange the effect. He stood motionless with his arm raised to receive in benediction the people whom he could already hear arriving at the front of the house. Motionless as he was, he screamed in his heat and fury, 'That woman has no sense of stage management. Tell her to go and remove those objectionable clothes. She's supposed to be the chief of Diana's vestals and she looks like Puss-in-Boots at the pantomime. Don't forget I've had experience with the theatre, I've had a lot of success, and when I ran my play in Paris, *Ce Soir Mon Frère*, I took responsibility for all the costumes.'

Walter, unable to make sense of the quarrel, said to Pauline, 'What's the matter with him?'

'I have to wear something to symbolize my authority in the Fellowship,' Pauline wailed from behind her red handkerchief. 'Otherwise I'll just be taken for one of the rest. I know what I'm doing and I've worked myself to death for ten days. The running

153

about, the phoning, the fruit juice, the hairdresser, the sandwiches, and choosing my suit and getting it altered, and making the list and typing the order of business for the meeting.'

'Why don't you take off the boots and the hat?' said Walter against the background of more explosive sounds from Hubert at the other end of the garden. 'You'll be too hot in all that stuff. It looks fine, but –'

'Here they come,' said Pauline, as a group of people walked up the side-path, chattering, to reach the back of the house. 'I'm on duty.' She strode to the little gate that divided the pathway from the garden, threw it open and began to receive.

Some had come from enthusiasm, some from curiosity, and a few peasants and trade-workers of the district who had already been initiated into the cult had come because they liked the international and egalitarian atmosphere.

Pauline had put out benches in front of the throne under the leafy bower where Hubert stood. She scrutinized each person, greeting them with an aloof, red-eyed smile, as she waved them to their seats.

'Why, Pauline,' said Father Cuthbert, 'you look very sporty.' Pauline waved him on, while Walter, beside her, in his blue jeans and open-necked shirt, smiled nervously. The priest passed on, accompanied by his fellow-Jesuit Gerard Harvey.

One local woman whispered to another, 'Those Jesuits always come, both of them.'

'The Jesuits always go two together, never alone,' said her friend.

'Like carabinieri,' said the other, 'because one can read and the other can write,' and her laughter crackled in the air like a fire in the grass until Pauline's frown quenched it.

By four o'clock they were all assembled and the gate was locked. Pauline had confiscated a motion-picture camera from Letizia Bernardini who had brought her brother Pietro to take a film of the proceedings. Letizia looked sour but did not challenge the booted leader. Berto's son Pino was also of the party, he having been especially attracted to this meeting because of Maggie's feud with Hubert.

Not long ago, Letizia's friend, the psychiatrist Marino Vesperelli, whom she had brought to dinner to meet Maggie that night at her father's house two years before, had discovered in the big general mental hospital in Rome a Swedish patient who had no relations who bothered with him, no friends, but who was apparently cured of the drug addiction which had landed him in that place two summers ago. In conversation with the patient Marino learned that he had been at Nemi with Hubert, working, he said, as a secretarial aide; and in this way, with Letizia's help, Kurt had been safely restored to Hubert who was horrified but impotent to protest; besides, Pauline had taken the boy's part. Kurt was now an acolyte in the Fellowship. He got up late and went out often in a little *cinque cento* car that Letizia had lent him : Hubert prowled around Kurt's room and searched his pockets while he lay asleep, hoping to find traces of narcotic drugs or a hypodermic needle, and so an excuse for getting rid of him. However, Kurt was so far blameless, only somewhat lazy, and here he was as part of the household to help with the meeting in the wild-grown leafy garden.

Pauline's energies had brought back two other lost sheep, named Damian Runciwell and Ian Mackay, only a little changed in appearance and very happy to come and spend another summer with Hubert as in the idyllic past of 1972 when they had all lazed and lain around together, wearing fantastic jewellery and cooking fantastic food. Pauline had often heard Hubert talk nostalgically of those days before she had come to work for him, and before Maggie's marriage had spoiled everything. Like a good sheep-dog Pauline had rounded up three of those four secretaries, and brought them happily before Hubert. Hubert had much to bear in these days of his new prosperity. 'I would have brought you Lauro, too, if I could have done,' Pauline assured him.

'I'm sure you would,' Hubert had said.

'Well, all I want to do is to make you happy, Hubert,' said Pauline.

'It's the thought that matters, Miss Thin,' Hubert said. 'Diana be praised.'

'Oh, aren't you glad to see these old friends? You know how you always talk about that summer before I came to help you out. Now you can relive it all over again. Except, of course, for Lauro. I'm sorry about Lauro. Only, you know, he's absolutely over there on the Radcliffe side and making a fortune. And getting married, too.'

Hubert would have thrown Pauline out that very evening, the three young men with her, had it not been that she knew too much, she knew too much. And here they were among the crowd of selected followers in the garden.

Hubert smiled on them all benevolently when they were seated. About thirty people, he thought. Pauline Thin must be out of her mind, he thought, to call a secret meeting of thirty-odd people. What sort of secret is that?

He decided to change his plan somewhat, and to refrain from discussing anything that might be deemed illicit by the Italian or ecclesiastical authorities, such as the raising of funds and the missionary work necessary to internationalize the Fellowship. A service of worship and a testimony of faith might equally serve this purpose, together with a deliberate accent on the charismatic features of the old, old religion of nature.

'I am the direct descendant of the goddess Diana,' he announced, 'Diana of Nemi, Diana of the Woods and so, indirectly, of her brother the god Apollo.'

Sitting apart from the congregation the two Jesuit observers gave out charismatic smiles in all directions and made way for a late arrival whom Pauline had sent to sit with them. Another observer, Hubert thought. How many observers do you have at a secret meeting? He glared at Pauline who looked angrily back, with fury on her face under her ridiculous hat. Evidently she was still dwelling on Hubert's insults. As well she might, Hubert thought with desperate resentment of the woman as he looked at her, ordering people around, placing them here, guiding them there, with those boots on her awful legs. Hubert, under the leafy trellis, breathed deeply. He noticed that Pauline now held a black-bound book in the hand that indicated the seats; Hubert thought it looked like his Bible but then he put the thought aside, not seeing what she could possibly want to do with it. As she also held the confiscated camera at this moment, Hubert assumed she had also, probably quite needlessly, taken charge of someone's book : bossy little nobody.

Walter, the weak fool, was beside her, holding a list and ticking off names. Who were all these people? Pauline had told Hubert from time to time of new people who could be trusted. But he had no idea they amounted to so many. Two American art historians, very cultured, very rich, Pauline had said. A girl from Rome, 'my best friend there', Pauline had said. Then she had said on one occasion, 'a girl-friend of my friend and she happens to be Michael Radcliffe's mistress'. Hubert had felt satisfaction at this. Yes, but how did they add up to so many? Hubert did not know most of these people who sat before him.

From the house stepped another robed figure. He was dressed in a toga-like garment which bunched and bundled about his tubby body. It was the lawyer Massimo de Vita; he had come to stand by Hubert's throne and give a simultaneous translation for the benefit of the Italians present. 'Friends,' said Hubert, holding out his arms in benediction, while Massimo announced, *'Amici'*.

'Friends,' Hubert said. 'Brothers and Sisters of Nature. As I have said, I am the descendant of Diana and Apollo, the gods of the old religion that goes back beyond the dawn of history, into the far and timeless regions of mythology where centuries and aeons do not count.'

Massimo de Vita kept even pace behind Hubert, who spoke slowly, somehow without his usual energetic conviction; he was still ruffled by Pauline Thin; she had put him off his stroke. 'Diana,' he went on, 'Goddess of Wildlife, is older than man. She fought on the field of Troy and was humiliated by her jealous step-mother who, as it is written in Homer, took the quiver of arrows from Diana's shoulders and whacked her with it. But such was the charisma of Diana, the virgin goddess, protectress of nature, that she took no revenge, but rather decided to come to Italy, change her name, and dwell amongst us at Nemi. You must know that her name in Greece was Artemis and not far away from the hill upon which we are gathered here in this garden is Monte Artemisio; and down below us lies the sanctuary of Diana, my ancestress, ravished and pillaged . . . ' And with worthy self-effacement Massimo de Vita recited, *'Diana, la mia antenata, rapita e saccheggiata . . . '*

Meanwhile the sudden voice of a woman cried out the determined statement, 'I'm going to testify.' Hubert, startled, looked towards the voice, while the toga'd advocate, also surprised, instantly pulled himself together, and, believing this to be part of the show, since the voice was Pauline's, continued his dutiful translation ' . . . *adesso vengo testimoniare* . . . '

'What is this interruption?' said Hubert, as everyone turned to look at Pauline.

'*Cos'è questo disturbo?*' translated Massimo into his loud-speaker, although his eyes looked desperately about him for some guidance. He got none whatsoever. He looked towards Pauline, seeing her for the first time that day in her strange sporty outfit and immediately presumed that this interruption was a prearranged affair : a sort of dialogue, all part of that sense of theatre Hubert had so often said was necessary for the success of the Fellowship.

'Miss Thin,' Hubert bellowed into his amplifier, 'do you realize you are in Church in every important sense?'

Massimo continued translating.

Pauline bounded up to the leafy bower and stood beside Hubert, grabbing the loudspeaker. 'I have a right to testify and prophesy,' she proclaimed, 'and I want to testify from the New Testament.'

Father Cuthbert jumped up and down in his seat while his companion, Gerard, smiled eagerly. The rest of the congregation stirred and asked of each other what was it all about, and then fell silent as Pauline's voice boomed out, 'The First Epistle to Timothy, Chapter 1, verses 3 and 4:

As I besought thee to abide still at Ephesus, when I went into Macedonia, that thou mightest charge some that they teach no other doctrine,

Neither give heed to fables and endless genealogies, which minister questions, rather than godly edifying which is in faith . . . '

The congregation remained silent, waiting for further enlightenment which it was clear Pauline, adjusting the loud-speaker, was preparing to give. Only Cuthbert Plaice moved to whisper something with gleaming eyes into his fellow-Jesuit's ear. Hubert, immediately sensing sabotage, attempted first to possess himself of the microphone. But Pauline hung on to it. Hubert therefore, in terror of what she might say next, all in one gesture made as if he were adjusting the instrument for her better to speak and then stretched his left arm at right angles to his body so that it rested across her shoulders in a protective attitude. Thus he made it appear that Pauline's interruption was part of the service, and even his first exclamation – 'What is this interruption?' – might have been part of a dramatic litany. Pauline looked amazed, and turned to Hubert as if to ask if he really meant it.

Massimo, meanwhile, was still catching up with the Italian translation of Pauline's text, which he found difficult.

'Proceed,' said Hubert, grandly.

Two young men in the congregation who had been drawn to the meeting by the rumour that Maggie, whom they both knew slightly, was to be present, sat near the front. One was a former chauffeur of Maggie's and the other was that portrait-painter who had been recommended by Coco de Renault, and for whom she and Mary had somewhat disastrously and very expensively sat. Before setting out for Nemi they had pepped themselves up with trial injections of a new amphetamine drug. The scene before them gave the two young men to believe that the new drug was a very great advance on any previous drug they had sampled, and, as Massimo's garbled version wobbled over his loudspeaker, the two young men began to clap their hands in rhythm.

Pauline pulled herself together to proceed with her testimony under the surprise of Hubert's bidding. With Hubert's arm fondly resting on her shoulders she changed her tone of fury to one of breathless timidity. 'I only wanted to point out,' she told the congregation, 'that the words of the Apostle Paul refer to Diana of Ephesus, where there was a cult of Diana, and that's what inspired me. If you remember in The Acts, and I could find the place, I think – ' She started to look through the Bible in her hand, while the loud rhythmic clapping increased, others of the congregation being encouraged to join in. As she floundered, Father Gerard, perceiving her difficulty, charismatically rose and called out, 'Chapter 19.'

'The Acts, Chapter 19,' said Pauline, turning to the place, while Hubert stood loathing her, imprisoned with his arm in its draped and silvery-green sleeve resting consolingly on her shoulder. 'Read,' he commanded his jailer; whereupon the

Jesuits exchanged joy-laden glances. 'He's being very broad-minded, isn't he?' whispered Cuthbert Plaice. The hand-clapping increased and some of the congregation began to sway. Pauline visibly cheered up and now read aloud to this rhythm, with her finger on the place,

'For a certain man named Demetrius, a silversmith, which made silver shrines for Diana, brought no small gain unto the craftsmen;
Whom he called together with the workmen of like occupation, and said, Sirs, ye know that by this craft we have our wealth . . . '

'Piano, piano,' pleaded Massimo. 'Read slowly, Miss, I can't keep up.' Pauline began to change her rhythm, stumbling along until she was reading in a kind of syncopated time to the loud hand-clapping, allowing two beats of theirs to one of hers. 'Courage!' bawled Hubert grimly. 'Read to the end.'

' . . . Moreover ye see and hear, that not alone at Ephesus, but almost throughout all Asia, this Paul hath persuaded and turned away much people, saying that they be no gods, which are made with hands:
So that not only this our craft is in danger to be set at nought; but also that the temple of the great goddess Diana should be despised, and her magnificence should be destroyed, whom all Asia and the world worshippeth.
And when they heard these sayings, they were full of wrath, and cried out, saying, Great is Diana of the Ephesians.'

'Enough, enough,' said Hubert, drawing the microphone away from her. Massimo had by no means caught up, but he skipped a good part, few people present being any the wiser, and ended up, 'Basta, basta! Evviva la Diana d'Efeso.'

Hubert turned to Pauline, who was now thoroughly bewildered by his actions, and embraced her on both cheeks, with the ritualistic gesture of the kiss of peace. He then made a sweeping indication that she was dismissed, and, to the ever-louder clapping of the crowd she descended amongst them. They were making other noises too, now, and standing on the benches.

'And I say unto you,' crooned Hubert into the microphone, 'that Diana of Ephesus was brought to Nemi to become the great earth mother. Great is Diana of Nemi!'

'Diana of Nemi!' yelled someone in the crowd, which inspired Pauline's boy-friend Walter to strike up his guitar. Soon everyone was chanting, 'Diana of Nemi! Diana of Nemi!' The seats were empty, the congregation in raptures all over the place, dancing, clapping, shouting. Hubert gazed on the scene with benevolent satisfaction, relieved that nobody seemed to have taken in the true meaning of the passage. He smiled indulgently, there under the leaves. Then he sat down on his throne, gathering his robes about him, smiling even upon Pauline who was dancing and singing ecstatically with the others and looking such an absolute mess, believing herself once more in Hubert's favour and not caring in the least that he had turned her treachery to his own account.

'I want to testify!'

Hubert turned from his musing, annoyed to find a thin girl standing before the microphone at his side. He recognized Nancy Cowan, the former English tutor to Letizia and Pietro Bernardini who was now simply part of their household, waiting for Bernardini to marry her in the course of time. Hubert rose, uncertain what to do, since the people who were jumping about the garden had come to a standstill at the sound of her voice, and Walter, the damned fool, stopped strumming his guitar.

'I want to say,' said Nancy, 'that the biblical passage you h‑ve heard is a condemnation of the pagan goddess Diana. It implies that the cult of Diana was only a silversmith's lobby and pure commercialism. Christianity was supposed to put an end to all that, but it hasn't. It –'

'Well said,' Hubert boomed into the microphone. He had taken over, edging her out of place, and he now put a hand on her shoulder as he continued. 'Our Sister Nancy tells us that Diana of Ephesus was betrayed. Christianity was betrayed, and now we have the great mother of nature again, Diana of the Woods, Diana of Nemi. Great is Diana of Nemi!'

Massimo, who had joined the crowd, returned to his place in time to translate a portion of this speech, but meanwhile something was going wrong with the ritualistic side under Hubert's leafy bower, for, as he had spoken, Nancy had thrown his hand off her shoulder and was now tugging and tearing violently at his robes.

The clapping recommenced, everyone crowding round to see the new event taking place before Hubert's throne. It looked like a fight, and the bemused congregation turned into an audience. Walter, assuming that this affair, too, was part of a previous plan, strummed up once more. 'Great is Diana of Nemi! Long live Diana of Nemi!' Nancy was fairly strong, but Hubert now had her by the hair. His sleeve was half torn off. Presently Letizia excitedly came to help Nancy in whatever role it was she was playing; she was probably drawn to the girl's assistance by the fact that she felt in conflict about Hubert, disliking him personally but fascinated by his nature cult. The sound of hand-clapping mounted again, all round the fighters; Letizia was fairly carried away, so that, in passing, having drawn blood from Hubert's cheeks with her nails she frenziedly tore off her own blouse under which she wore nothing. She fought on, topless, while Nancy concentrated on tearing the green and shining robes piece by piece from Hubert's back.

The noise in the garden was louder than ever. The two priests stood some way from that throne and scene of battle, exhorting frantically. Cuthbert came a little too close and received a casual swipe from Hubert which sent him to the ground. Soon the clothes were torn from the Jesuits, and in fact everyone in the garden was involved in the riot within a very short time.

Mr Stuyvesant and his young friend George Falk did a tour of the house, meantime, to see if there was anything worthwhile. They puzzled for a long time over the good fake Gauguin, then passed on, touching nothing and apparently just breathing as they walked. They noted several valuable objects and the lack of any burglar alarm, unaware as they were that the house would very shortly be emptied of its contents even before they had time to inform their friends what the contents were.

In their self-contained way, they walked back through the ecstatically distressed crowd in the garden, got into their car and drove off.

The party in the garden did not end abruptly, but piece by piece, stagger by stagger. Marino Vesperelli, the psychiatrist who had steadily wooed Letizia for the past three years, lay naked and very fat under a mulberry tree, repeating fragmentary phrases with his eyes staring at the twinkly-blue of the sky between the leaves. 'Exhausted. Group therapy,' he said. 'Letizia. The group.' She, meanwhile, lay on her back across him, gazing up likewise at the branches wherefrom was hanging, for some reason, the twisted and bashed-in skeleton of Walter's guitar. Letizia looked down at her breasts and turned over to comfort her plump suitor.

Pauline wandered in the overgrown and now overwrought garden, looking vainly for her hat while Walter waited for her in the road, his car already packed with some of their possessions. Hubert had in fact thrown her out. He gave her twenty minutes in which to leave, refusing absolutely her offer to bathe a wound on his hand. 'I'll kill you,' Hubert said.

'I thought you were charismatic,' said Pauline. 'At the reading of my testimony from the Bible you showed charisma.'

'Look at my head, Miss Thin,' said Hubert.

'I didn't do it,' Pauline shrieked.

'To all intents and purposes,' Hubert said, 'you did.'

Massimo de Vita came to Pauline's room shortly afterwards and told her she was in trouble, she must pack and go. 'Italian prisons are not very nice. You brought drugs to this house. You created the orgy. People have been hurt and disturbed greatly. Soon it will be all over the countryside and the carabinieri will inquire.' She packed a few things, but not all, unwilling to make such a clean break. To give Hubert a last chance she returned to look for her hat in the garden, as she explained to the waiting Walter. Under Hubert's window Pauline called up, 'Hubert!'

His bloody head appeared. 'I'll wish you good afternoon,' he said. This was followed by one of the heavy metal taps that had been wrenched from every bathroom and washbasin in the house. It hit her on the head and blood spurted down her face. She ran, then, out to Walter and the car, and set off with him towards Paris.

The young portrait-painter had lost a tooth but he felt that the trip which his new amphetamine-based drug had induced was well worth it; and he said as much to his friend, Maggie's former chauffeur, as they sat indoors, squeezed together on the draining-board of the kitchen sink with their feet dabbling in the basin which was filled with cold water.

'It's all over,' Hubert moaned. 'My hopes . . . my . . . I'll kill that woman Pauline Thin if I see her again. I shall have to leave Nemi, but I'll see Miss Thin shall die.'

He was lying on his bed with Massimo hovering over him. His cheeks and hands were scarred and swollen with scratches from the fight, but the most visible wound, a cut on his forehead stretching from the eyebrow to his fairly receded hairline, had come about from his precipitate flight into the house, when he simply banged his head on the lintel of the door.

Massimo, who had early taken refuge from the riot in the garden, was trembling but unharmed. He wrung out a towel in a basin of water beside Hubert's bed, and applied it to the wounded head. He said, 'What do we say when come the journalists? If arrive the police . . . ?'

'I will kill her. She has to die,' Hubert said. 'I shall make her die wherever she is, because I will it. I will send emissaries to kill her.'

The door opened then, and Hubert's three restored secretaries appeared. Kurt Hakens, his red hair now short-cut, with his arms looking like legs and his legs all uncontrolled. Ian Mackay, squat and tough, looking far more like a swarthy Sicilian than a Scotsman, and Damian Runciwell, the big-boned Armenian who had once been the best of the secretaries as secretary. This Damian looked at Massimo and said, 'Get out.'

There was something in the secretaries' attitude that made Massimo place the bowl of water on the floor, drop the damp towel into it and stand up, ready to go.

'Boys, boys!' said Hubert. 'This is no time to be rude. Go and kill Pauline Thin. She must be hovering around somewhere. She'll never leave.'

'Out,' said Damian to Massimo, who went.

'Boys, I've been wounded severely,' said Hubert. 'Look at my head.'

'We've come to kill you,' said Ian, producing an ugly, long and old-fashioned revolver from his trousers pocket.

'Put that silly toy away and bathe my head,' Hubert said. 'Do you want me to have to go to hospital? As it is, I wouldn't be surprised if the carabinieri arrived at any moment.'

Kurt had taken out a revolver, too. His was shiny and modern-looking. 'For God's sake, what are you doing? It might go off,' Hubert said.

Damian now turned nervously to the others and said something that Hubert couldn't hear. He jerked his head towards the door, perhaps indicating that they should leave, or perhaps referring in some way to Massimo, who had been the last to depart.

Ian, with his revolver pointed at Hubert said, 'Who was he?'

'Who? Massimo de Vita? He's my lawyer,' Hubert said, sitting up in some alarm, with his hand to his wounded head.

Damian walked to the door, opened it and stood half in and half out of the bedroom. He said to the other two men, 'Come here a second.' They followed, Ian still keeping a watch on Hubert, and started arguing in whispers which presently began to sound like the spits and hisses of recrimination.

Hubert screamed, 'What the hell's going on?' and started to get out of bed. Whereupon the three surrounded him and pressed him back. Damian was crying all over his broad face.

'Hubert,' he said, 'can you give us a drink? It's all too unnerving, my dearie. It's all too much.'

Ian put his revolver back into his trousers pocket where it bulged unbecomingly. Kurt rather coyly went over to the bed and placed his smart little gun upon it.

'Have you boys been taking drugs?' said Hubert.

'My word of honour,' said Kurt. 'I'm cured. My psychiatrist will tell you.'

'Drugs,' said Ian. 'All he can think of is drugs when there's a threat on his life. He doesn't think that certain people might have a certain reason to pay us to kill him.'

'We never meant to do it, Hubert,' said Damian, weeping still. 'Not really.'

'Bathe my wound,' said Hubert, 'and tell me who sent you to scare me.'

Damian started washing Hubert's wound at the point that Massimo had left off. 'We need a drink,' said Ian.

'Well, go and fetch a drink. Fetch some disinfectant and a dressing of some sort,' Hubert said. 'I don't want to get stitches in my head. I shall bear the scar of Pauline Thin all my life.

When you've had a drink you can go and find her, shoot her, and hide her body in the woods.'

'Hubert, the Marchesa de Tullio-Friole sent us to kill you. Really she did,' said Damian.

'Maggie? She offered you money?'

They were silent then, and obviously embarrassed. Hubert said, 'Then you'd have done so if you hadn't bungled it, if you hadn't come in when my friend Massimo was here?'

'No, Hubert, it was all a pretence. We would have hid you and shared the money with you.'

'Would you go to court and swear that Maggie bribed you to murder me?' Hubert said.

'No,' said Ian.

'No,' said Damian, 'I wouldn't like to go into the horrible criminal atmosphere of a law court, Hubert.'

'No, I wouldn't go near the police ever again,' said Kurt.

'I might force you to testify,' said Hubert. Ian's hand went to his bulgy pocket. 'But I won't,' said Hubert. 'Descendant as I am of the great Diana of Nemi, I have been struck by disaster after disaster all in one afternoon. Such is the fate of the gods. Have you ever read Homer? Has any one of you read Homer? Worse things than this occurred to the gods and their descendants in those days, and so it isn't surprising if they happen to me in times like these. In fact, it proves my rights and titles. *Rex Nemorensis*, the King of Nemi, king of the woods, favoured son of Diana the mother of nature.'

Ian came back with a bottle of brandy, four glasses, a bottle of kitchen alcohol and a wad of cotton wool. 'It's all I could find,' he said. 'This house is not at all as well equipped as it was in the old days when we were running it.'

'Tell me,' said Hubert, 'did you really come here to kill me?'

'Of course not,' said Damian, crying again. 'Don't remind me,' he said.

'Ian, I want that revolver, please. Give it to me.'

Ian handed it over. Hubert examined it well. Then he examined the gun that Kurt had placed on his bed. 'Who gave you these?' he said.

'Maggie. She got them out of her husband's armoury. Mary was with her,' Ian said.

'Yes, Mary was there,' said Kurt.

'How much did she offer you?'

'She didn't specify. She said she'd pay a fortune but month by month in instalments, in case we talked. She said Mary was her witness as an alibi that she was somewhere else with Mary that day, so if we got into trouble it was useless to try to incriminate them. She meant it, Hubert.'

'You tell me you had nothing in advance? She paid you nothing?'

'Not a dollar, not one little dime,' said Ian, very quickly and definitely, and the other two murmured agreement.

'Then you are imbeciles,' Hubert said. 'I know that woman. She once said to me, "Faggots are things that you put on the fire." Very amusing. She thinks you're expendable. I will never know for sure whether you three boys meant it, either.' He locked the two guns and, placing them under the sheet beside him, lay back. 'Give me some brandy,' he said. 'I don't think you would have had the nerve to go through with it, anyway. Maggie has always been utterly foolish. She never consults the experts.'

Early next morning, Massimo returned to the house ostentatiously with a removal van, waving a file of documents that might have contained anything. To establish himself well as an outsider he stopped at the post office to ask the way to Hubert's house, volubly explaining that he had come on behalf of his client, the Marchesa Tullio-Friole to order the house to be vacated.

One by one the contents were stacked into the van and taken away to a safe place. Hubert was left with a bed, a stove, his everyday clothes, the television, the refrigerator, four kitchen chairs and four deck chairs. His tattered green robes as well as the good ones went with the van. His documents, so neatly arranged by Pauline in their boxes, went too. The pictures, fake and real, were stacked carefully and so was the furniture, expertly packed in the movers' cartons. Off went all these goods, under the tutelage of Massimo de Vita, and Hubert sat in the kitchen with his boys. 'It's like that previous summer before Maggie got married,' he said. 'Darlings, find something to cook.'

After lunch Hubert telephoned to Massimo de Vita 'Just to check,' he said, 'that the goods are in a safe place.'

'They are safe, don't worry,' said Massimo.

'When will they be leaving the country?'

'Be careful on the telephone,' said Massimo softly and then, in a louder voice, he said, 'With valuable stuff you have to be careful of thieves listening in, you know. Your possessions, Mr Mallindaine, will be leaving Italy within a few days. I have an export permit and all the documents. As a foreigner, you are easier to export than many other clients.'

Chapter Fifteen

Maggie was being driven by car from Geneva to Lausanne when she remembered the hired assassins she had sent to Hubert. Seen in the light of the greater outrage perpetrated upon her by Coco de Renault, the arrangements she had made with these frightful people now seemed foolish. She hoped they had been too weak or had lacked the opportunity to carry out her orders. She had made no advance payments, only a gold watch apiece, each one slightly different to show good taste; and Mary would have to stand by her if there were any accusations. When she reached Lausanne Maggie put a call through to Mary from her hotel.

'Mary,' said Maggie, lying on the bed wrapped in towels, for the call had come through while she was in her bath, 'I've drawn the ace of spades in the game of life.'

'Excuse me?' said Mary.

'I say I've met with disaster.'

'Oh, have you had an accident?'

'Coco de Renault has completely disappeared with all my money.'

'That's impossible,' Mary said.

'I have to find him,' said Maggie, 'and I have to get back home. My cheques here are bouncing and my bank managers are not in the office when I want to see them; they are all otherwise occupied to a theatrical degree. I've never felt so humiliated in my life. Tell Berto to send me some money.'

'All right, Maggie. But there must be something wrong.'

'Don't tell Berto about Coco's disappearance. I don't want to give him a shock. He'd be furious.'

'Berto's in trouble,' said Mary. 'He had a burglary.'

'But I thought he warned the police about those two men who came to case the joint.'

'I know. Two detectives went along, and they said the burglar alarm was O.K., then the next day, it was only on Tuesday, Guillaume let in a couple of carabinieri, only they weren't carabinieri, they were people dressed up like carabinieri. They tied up the servants and they took the Veronese and all the silver, and they also took that portrait, school of Titian. Berto says they will hold the paintings for ransom as they're no use on the market, but Berto won't pay ransom. He says his hairs have gone grey overnight, but he already had grey hair. I like Berto so much, Maggie.'

'What about my jewellery?' Maggie said.

'They took that too, Maggie.'

'Guillaume!' shrieked Maggie. 'I don't trust that Guillaume. He must have been in with it. It was an inside job. Guillaume has to go. I'll tell Berto. It's either Guillaume or me. Berto must choose.'

'Maggie, the police questioned all the servants and the police believe the servants. Guillaume got hurt in the struggle, too. Didn't you read the papers? It happened Tuesday and it was all in the papers yesterday. Berto says – '

'My jewellery,' Maggie said, 'is the important thing to me at this moment, and Guillaume has it.'

'Maggie, there's an echo on the line; it's an awfully bad line.'

'It wasn't in the papers here,' Maggie said.

'It was in the Italian newspapers. Maybe it isn't a big enough robbery to make the international headlines,' said Mary. 'There have been an awful lot of robberies.'

'A Veronese is an international robbery,' Maggie shouted frantically.

'Well, some art thieves took a Rembrandt from Vienna the same day. Did you read about that?'

'No, I didn't. The press is hushing it all up,' said Maggie.

'I guess there are too many to report,' Mary said.

'Look,' said Maggie, 'I'm coming home. Tell Berto to get me some money here by tomorrow morning. I have to get out my best jewellery from the bank and sell it, and Berto has to sell some of his land. We're paupers. Guillaume has to go to jail and I have to get the contents of my house from Hubert. I hope nothing has happened to him, Mary; it was silly of us to – '

'Not on the phone,' Mary said. 'I told Michael what we'd done. He was so furious. He said not to mention it on the phone. Anyway those boys are staying over there in that house with Hubert and all the furniture's been taken away by your lawyer. They had an orgy, couple of weeks ago, but I wasn't there, myself. Everyone else was.'

'Which lawyer took my stuff?' Maggie said.

'Massimo something. The one in Rome.'

'He's a crook,' said Maggie. 'He's a Communist and he's working for Hubert. I gave Hubert's boys each a gold watch and all they can do is have an orgy. Did the police break it up? Why didn't you call the police?'

'I wasn't there. Nobody denounced them to the police. Everyone was afraid and they got away. The police went round last week to have a look but all they found was Hubert and the boys in the empty house.'

'Berto will never believe it,' Maggie said, 'and I'm going to fight every inch of – '

'Berto doesn't know a thing,' Mary said. 'We can't hurt Berto. He's too nice.'

'And what about me?' Maggie said. 'Doesn't anyone have any feelings for me?'

'Oh, yes, we do, Maggie,' Mary said. 'Oh, yes, we do. We love you and we care for you a lot.'

The first thing Maggie did when she put down the telephone was to order as many Italian newspapers as possible. Maggie was still, so far as was known, one of the hotel's wealthiest clients, but the best the night porter could do at that hour, well after midnight, was to send to the station for the early morning edition of *Il Tempo* which he delivered to Maggie at about one-thirty. She was still awake, putting her disasters in order of priority. There was no word of the robbery at Berto's villa; it had evidently become old news. But the headline in the Roman crime section caused her to put another call through to Mary.

'Oh, can't you sleep, Maggie?' said Mary anxiously. 'Michael said I shouldn't have told you all those things, I should have waited. Berto is going to call his bank in Geneva tomorrow morning. He tried to call you but he couldn't get through. It's terribly difficult from the villa. Can't you sleep? Berto says I shouldn't have told you about your jewellery because he should have liked to be with you when you heard.'

'Well, I want to know about your jewellery,' Maggie said. 'You said you were putting it in an out-of-the-way bank for safety.'

'Oh, goodness, yes. It's all in a bank, I don't know, Michael's trying to get to sleep. It's on the Via Appia.'

'Banco di Santo Spirito?' said Maggie.

'Yes, that's it. If you need money that bad, Maggie, I can get you a loan without pawning my jewellery. You just talk to Michael when you come home; I can talk to Daddy, and – '

'Number 836 Via Appia?' said Maggie.

'Well, I don't know. I guess there's only one Santo Spirito on the Via Appia.'

'Get up and look,' Maggie said. 'I must know the exact bank and the exact number of the exact street. There has been a robbery at the Santo Spirito. It says here in this morning's *Tempo*, Wednesday, 16 July, that there was a robbery over the week-end and they found on Monday that the gang ransacked the strong-boxes. Get up and see if that's your bank.'

'Oh, no! Oh, no!' Mary said. 'It can't be. I haven't heard anything. Maybe they tried to get me. We just got back this morning from the villa . . . ' Maggie then heard her say, 'Michael, wake up, my jewellery's been robbed. What is the address of my bank?'

It was indeed Mary's bank which the belated report referred to. Mary also informed Maggie that she hadn't insured this jewellery, believing it to be safe in its vault. Her voice was strange; she spoke with awe as if she was in church. 'What an experience for you!' Maggie said. 'You poor child, what an ordeal to have to wait till the bank opens in the morning before you can find out whether your box was one of the unlucky ones or not.' She spoke with genuine concern, thinking mainly of a special diamond brooch and an emerald ring of great value that she herself had given to Mary. But Michael came on the telephone, unreasonable with anxiety and short-tempered. 'What sort of a woman,' he said, 'would ring us up in the middle of the night, twice, with the very worst news? You could have let us sleep till the morning. Now Mary's crying. She wants me to call the bank manager. How can I call him in the middle of the night, what good will it do? I don't know him. Mary isn't a bit materialistic, that's what you don't realize, Mother. There's an economic crisis and you've got to face it. It's what – '

'We're ruined!' Maggie shrieked back. 'We've all become paupers overnight, and the first thing that happens when a family is ruined is always a quarrel unless they are very rare people, very exceptional. And I'm just so sorry to see that you are very, very ordinary, and also common from the Radcliffe side. The whole family quarrelled over their trusts and their wills, and what's more, it was only an hour ago that Mary told me you all cared for me and loved me. It isn't my fault if Mary's lost her jewellery. Maybe she hasn't. I hope not. I'm going to speak to Berto.' Maggie hung up at this point, looked at herself in the glass and was amazed to find herself still glowing and handsome. She took a bath, telephoned for a bottle of champagne, asked to be wakened at eight, and went to bed where she slowly sipped three glasses before she went to sleep.

It made Lauro very happy indeed to be summoned from his honeymoon cruise by Maggie, although he was putting on a great air to the effect that she had done something outrageous in putting through a call to the captain of the *Panorama di Nozze*, that cruise ship with twenty-one newly-wedded couples on board on which he and Betty had been spending their honeymoon. Lauro had already, in times past, visited the Greek islands with Maggie's entourage, he had seen the labyrinthine home of the Minotaur and he had been to the Acropolis. The tone of the honeymoon company appalled him. Twenty-one pairs of newlyweds; every morning a round of sniggery remarks; dancing until three in the morning with uproarious jokes about exchanging partners and which is the way to *your* cabin? The awful brides whispering together over cocktails, and Betty no better than the rest.

He sat with Betty now in the comfortable lobby of the hotel in Lausanne, while Maggie, reassuringly radiant, heard out his outraged complaints with an obligingly penitent expression that meant only that she had more important things on her mind than to waste words in defending herself.

'You're so right, Lauro,' she said. 'I should have realized . . . I should have been more thoughtful . . . Your honeymoon. It happens once in a lifetime, doesn't it?' She turned to plump, bridal Betty who had clearly been to the hairdresser and had dressed very carefully for this meeting. 'I do apologize,' Maggie said, 'if I may call you Betty?'

Betty drooped her lids and shrugged, as if not prepared to show any lack of support for her husband's complaint. 'We nearly didn't come,' she said. 'But then the captain made out it was so urgent, and the transport being all arranged, Lauro thought maybe you were ill and so we came ashore that day.'

'Lauro could easily have come alone,' said Maggie, 'and left you to finish the cruise.'

'What a suggestion,' said Lauro. 'How could I leave my wife alone on a honeymoon cruise, Maggie, are you crazy?'

'Well, now that you're here, Lauro, may I have a word with you?' Maggie said.

'Go ahead,' said Lauro, refilling all three glasses with the champagne that Maggie had ordered for the party.

'Well, it's business, Lauro. Betty must, of course, get used to business practice, and as you are my confidant and secretary I must speak to you alone. If Betty will give us half an hour. I'm sure there's some shopping she wants to do. The boutiques of Lausanne are charming; she can get some ideas for her boutique in Rome, don't you think?'

Betty said, 'Just what I was thinking myself,' and put down her glass with a sharp tinkle.

Lauro considered the matter importantly, with his lips pouted together. Then he said, 'Yes, I think Maggie is in the right. Come back in half an hour, Betty, all right?'

'Fine,' she said brightly, 'lovely.'

They watched her as she passed through the lane of little tables to the vestibule, and out of the swing doors, in her cream and brown linen suit.

'Are you happy?' said Maggie to Lauro.

'Of course,' said Lauro. 'Betty is a wonderful wife. She's beautiful and also intelligent. We Italians, you know, like women to be women, and to be shapely.'

'I often think Italian girls are very mature in their appearance,' Maggie said, 'a little over-full, but it's a matter of taste.'

'I won't hear a word against Italian girls,' said Lauro, 'and especially my wife.'

'You're perfectly right,' Maggie said in hasty conciliation. 'I only meant that maybe the trouble is that they have their Confirmation too early. In the Anglo-Saxon countries they aren't confirmed till they're fourteen.' She waved the subject vaguely aside. 'It's a matter of national custom, that's all. I'm sure I'm not bigoted. Well, Lauro, I've got something really serious to discuss with you. It's serious and it's private, and I can't thank you enough for breaking off your mass-honeymoon for me, Lauro.'

'It was a very lovely and very expensive, exclusive honeymoon cruise,' said Lauro. 'Today we were to go on donkey-back into the mountains.'

'All on donkeys together, twenty-one *sposi*!' marvelled Maggie.

Lauro looked sour.

'But Lauro, I'm in trouble, darling,' Maggie said. 'I really am.'

Lauro cheered up. 'What's your problem?' he said.

'I see in the newspapers,' said Maggie, 'that a lot of people are getting kidnapped. In Italy it's becoming a national sport. Every day there's someone new. Where are all the millions going to?'

'It's a criminal affair,' Lauro said, 'mainly run by the Mafia but there are independent gangs, maybe political. I don't know. Why don't you keep your bodyguard? What happened to your gorilla?'

'I can't afford a bodyguard. I'm broke,' said Maggie.

Lauro laughed. 'If that were true why would you be afraid of being kidnapped?'

'When it's known that Coco de Renault has disappeared completely with all my holdings, all my real estate, all my trusts, all my capital, I won't have to fear being kidnapped.'

'What are you talking about, Maggie?' Lauro said. 'You ask about kidnaps, then you tell me this story of de Renault. I think you try to make out you're poor because you're afraid. But no one will believe you, Maggie. You have to take care. It's not nice to be kidnapped. Sometimes the victim never comes home. Remember how they cut off young Getty's ear. They keep you in a dungeon for weeks.'

'Coco has disappeared. I've tried to trace him. I've had private detectives and my lawyers trying to trace him. They say he's somewhere in the Argentine; that's all the news I can get. I'm not sure if they're right or wrong. Maybe the investigators can't be bothered any more. In the meantime the detectives have to be paid, lawyers' fees have to be paid.'

'And the police?'

'Which police? He belongs to no country. Then if I make a scandal, the tax people will start nosing into my affairs, that's all. I want to kidnap Coco, that's what I want to do. I want to extort my money out of him. At least I might get a part of it, something. I want to kidnap Coco de Renault.'

Lauro said, 'It's a criminal offence, kidnapping.'

'Oh, I know,' Maggie said. 'I know. Why shouldn't I be a criminal? Everyone else is.'

'Maggie, your husband –'

'He'll never know,' said Maggie.

Lauro sat back in a worldly way with an unworldly expression. 'You're a wonderful woman, Maggie. What's in it for me?'

'Ten per cent,' said Maggie.

'Twenty,' said Lauro.

'Including the expenses and the pay-offs, though,' Maggie said.

'No, no,' said Lauro. 'There's a big risk for those poor people who do the actual work. They risk a life's imprisonment if they don't get shot by the police. Then they have to find the people to do the first part, take the prisoner; then they have to find the good hiding places; they have to find the family and make the telephone calls, and they have to feed the man.'

'All right, thirty per cent inclusive,' Maggie said.

'Who is the family?'

'An American wife, rather ancient-looking, living here in Lausanne. I've seen her at a distance, poor dreary soul. The investigators say she swears she hasn't seen him for five months, but they don't believe her; neither do I.'

'You think he'll visit her one day?'

'I don't know. I think he's probably changed his appearance by plastic surgery. The reason I think so is that he's done it twice before.'

'He'll never come back to Switzerland,' Lauro said. 'If he's now a millionaire in the Argentine, why should he want to see an old wife?'

'There's a daughter at college in America,' said Maggie. 'She'll be home with her mother this summer. I think he might want to see the daughter.'

'You would have to demand a very large ransom,' said Lauro, 'to make it worth your while.'

'I'll demand a large ransom,' Maggie said. 'After all, it's my money, isn't it?'

'My contacts don't run to the Mafia,' Lauro said. 'I'm not in touch with the underworld at all.'

'Oh, come,' said Maggie, 'don't exaggerate, Lauro.'

'I know very few,' Lauro said.

'If I sell my big ruby pendant,' said Maggie, 'I can offer to those very few friends of yours a good sum in advance. My ruby is one of the few things that haven't yet been stolen. I've had some jewellery stolen from the villa and I think Mary has probably lost hers in that job at the Banco di Santo Spirito the other day.' She was crying now.

'I don't know what to believe,' said Lauro, 'but somehow I believe you, or you wouldn't have torn me away from my bride and my honeymoon.' He, too, had tears in his eyes at the thought of his lost paradise as it now existed in his head, if not in fact.

'Betty will be back soon. Can you get rid of her for the afternoon? She can use my car,' Maggie said.

'I suppose so,' Lauro said. 'I get rid of her and I take you up to bed. Isn't that your idea?'

'It's usually your idea,' said Maggie, 'isn't it?'

'I suppose so,' Lauro said.

Dusk had fallen when Maggie arrived two days later at the Villa Tullio. Berto was not expecting her; he had heard no word from her and had been unable to find her at any of the Swiss hotels she usually stayed at. Berto was worried; he could not quite understand why she had needed money. He made arrangements for the money to reach her, but afterwards, when he had tried to reach her by telephone at Lausanne, she had just left the hotel.

Mary also had tried to reach her, overjoyed that her safety-box, being one of those set high in the wall of the bank-vault, had escaped the gang's frenzied operation. Mary had telephoned to Berto in the Veneto. 'I'm worried about Maggie. Where is she?'

'I don't know,' Berto said. 'She's left Lausanne, and I can't find her anywhere else. I'm worried, too. Have you seen this morning's paper? Another kidnapping.'

'Oh, Berto, darling, don't worry,' Mary said. 'Would you like me to come and keep you company?'

'No, my dear, don't think of it.'

The chauffeur who drove Maggie home to the Villa Tullio that night was thoroughly puzzled. The Marchesa had dressed herself up so peculiarly. She had gone to a flea-market in a small town on the way home, all on an impulse while he waited in the car-park. This chauffeur had long been in Berto's service and had very few original thoughts about Maggie. He respected her considerably because she was Berto's wife and hence the Marchesa, and he felt it natural that she should have illogical impulses. He had taken her all over Switzerland on a mystifying route, not consequentially, not economically planned; first the Zürich area, then the Geneva area, then Zug, then Lausanne. To him, it was all a great *non sequitur* but Maggie was always careful to see that he had good rooms and ate well and was comfortable, as a lady should. It had not caused him to quibble in his thoughts when Lauro and his bride turned up at Lausanne, that Lauro at Maggie's request had then sent him on a trip around the valleys and up the mountains on a sight-seeing tour with Betty for the whole afternoon, from twelve-thirty to six-thirty. The chauffeur had lunched at pretty little Caux, high up on a mountain path, Betty sitting at one table, he at another, despite the girl's invitation to sit at the table with her. Betty had marvelled at the little chalets, and the chauffeur had agreed with a totally unscientific will to please. 'My husband, my poor husband,' Betty had said, 'is busy with that Marchesa all the afternoon and he's on his honeymoon.' The chauffeur merely said that such was life. 'Her houses at Nemi are built on my land,' said Betty. 'They're *abusivo*; she has to pull down those houses or else pay us. That's what they have to discuss, and believe me – '

As she spoke the chauffeur pulled up at a cottage-weave shop and asked Betty if she would like to look round it. Betty spent some time there, buying embroidered placemats and a shawl, then re-entered the car, into the back seat, daintily, with the door held open for her by Berto's chauffeur.

The next day Maggie had gone to Geneva and dropped Betty at the airport to catch a plane for Rome. Then, with Lauro, she had gone to a newly constructed block of flats where there was no concierge but a press-button phone at the entrance. Lauro pressed a button but there was no answer. The big glass-fronted doors were locked. Maggie got back into the car and waited. Lauro walked up and down the little pathway with its tidy new plants on either side; he pressed the button again from time to time; he looked up at the windows; he looked at his watch.

Maggie, who seldom explained anything, had evidently felt it necessary to explain to the chauffeur that they were waiting for a dressmaker, very brilliant and not yet famous, whom she simply had to see. They had an appointment, she explained.

It was too bad, said the chauffeur, to keep the Marchesa waiting. They waited twenty more minutes before a Peugeot drew up. Three youngish men got out, very quickly, and made for the entrance where Lauro was waiting. The chauffeur had not been able to see their faces for they kept them quite averted from him. One of the men, saying something to Lauro, indicated vulgarly with his thumb the car where Maggie sat with the chauffeur and said something in French, which the chauffeur didn't understand, but which sounded disapproving. Maybe the man had not wanted to be seen. At any rate one of the men had opened the door with a key, and Lauro was answering back, looking at his watch. Maggie then got out of the car with her charming smile and followed the four men into the building. That took up the rest of the morning. Maggie emerged without Lauro, and they were off, back to the Veneto, stopping for meals on the way, and then, unaccountably, at a little market-town where Maggie had spent an hour while the chauffeur waited in the car-park.

He had waited, which is to say he had taken an occasional walk around. From what he saw and what he heard, Maggie had no rendezvous with anyone this time. A rendezvous, although its purpose might escape Berto's good chauffeur, might at least have been explicable. What was thoroughly inconsistent was that Maggie had stood there at a stall, innocently buying a heap of dreadful clothes; and they were plainly intended for herself for she held up these rags against her body to get a rough idea if they would fit. A worn-out long skirt of black cotton, a pair of soiled tennis shoes which she actually tried on there in the street, a once-pink head scarf, a cotton blouse, not second-hand but cheap, piped with white, and terrible. The chauffeur wandered back to the car and waited. Maggie appeared before long, with her sunniness intact, and her light-hearted walk, holding in her arms the bundle of these frightful garments, not even wrapped in a piece of paper.

The chauffeur took them from her and placed them carefully in the boot. All he said was, 'The Marchesa should leave her handbag with me when she goes shopping. There are bad people about.' Whereupon Maggie searched in her handbag, quite alarmed; but everything was all right. They drove on.

Towards dusk next day Maggie wanted to stop in Venice for a rest and a drink. She left the chauffeur at the quay and, hiring a water-taxi, directed it to a smart bar. Later she returned in a water-taxi and kept it waiting while she demanded of the chauffeur the old clothes from the back of the car. Wrapping them, for very shame, in a tartan car-rug, the chauffeur handed them over. Maggie redirected the taxi to the bar.

She returned looking so like a tramp that the chauffeur failed to recognize her at first. 'Marchesa!' he then exclaimed.

'I changed in the ladies' room,' Maggie had said. 'Did I give you a fright? I want to play a joke on my husband.'

Onward to the villa. It was dark as they approached. 'The back entrance,' Maggie ordered. 'I have the key.'

The chauffeur, still puzzled, drove round the villa to the firmly locked and heavy back gate in the wall which led into the paddock, the orchard, the kitchen garden, and finally to the great back door.

'Let me accompany the Marchesa,' he said, fetching out his big electric torch. He had in mind those masked balls he had heard of, and felt a little guilty and low-class, lacking that sense of humour of the sophisticated. He decided to try to enter the spirit of the thing.

Maggie attacked the big gate with her key while the chauffeur's torch shone on it. With the first touch, a furious din broke loose. Barking of dogs, the screams of women, male voices roaring out the worst possible obscenities, and above all the words, 'Ladri! Ladri! polizia!' – Thieves, police . . . Maggie screamed, but bells were ringing now, searchlights beamed from the rooftop of the villa and Berto's dalmatian, Pavoncino, came streaking towards the gate, barking only less loudly than the barking in the air.

The pandemonium continued while the chauffeur pulled Maggie back into the car, bundling her into the front seat beside him. He drove off at full speed round to the front of the house and got out to ring the bell.

Here, Pavoncino awaited them, barking. But soon, having recognized Maggie, he was wagging his tail. Maggie sat on and waited. A police car drew up, then another.

In the midst of the turmoil Berto appeared with Guillaume, both armed with guns.

The police had taken Maggie into custody and were holding the chauffeur with his hands behind his back.

'Berto, it's me,' Maggie called out.

'Where are you, Maggie? I can't see you,' Berto called. 'Are you all right?'

'No, I'm not,' Maggie said.

The police could not understand English and had already bundled her, in her rags, into a police car, around which the dog pranced joyfully, barking loudly.

The noises in the air ceased abruptly. Guillaume slowly opened the front gate, still with his gun poised. Then, perceiving the dog's demonstrations of welcome, cautiously approached the police car where Maggie sat meekly, handcuffed to two burly carabinieri.

At first he didn't recognize her, and could hardly believe her voice when she called 'Berto!'

'That's my wife,' Berto said. 'Maggie, what are you doing? You've set off my new burglar alarm and all the loudspeakers and the electronic communication with the police station. What's wrong?'

Maggie was released in due course of time, and brandy administered to the chauffeur. The policemen were invited inside and apologized to, refusing, however, to drink while on duty; they seemed happy enough to have a nice glance round the drawing-room.

'I dressed up as a pauper,' Maggie explained in the best Italian she could manage. 'Because I am a pauper. I'm ruined. I just wanted everyone to know.'

Berto, placing to one side for the moment his bewilderment, translated this with considerable modifications. He explained, in fact, that the Marchesa had only meant it as a joke; she had not known of the burglar alarm.

Many more apologies from Berto. Sincere and profound apologies. The police went away and Berto stood looking at his bedraggled wife, still handsome and gleaming through it all as she was.

Chapter Sixteen

Dear Hubert,

On my return from a business trip to Switzerland I found a letter from my lawyer, Avvocato Massimo de Vita, in which he tells me you are claiming that I gave you my Gauguin, and that moreover my Gauguin is a fake.

As it happens, I did not give you my Gauguin and my Gauguin is not a fake.

I plan, in fact, to sell my Gauguin. In these days of tight money one has to plan one's budget, and Berto plans to take my Gauguin to London to sell it. I plan also to dispose of my Louis XIV furniture. I heard an absurd rumour that my furniture and pictures had already been taken away from the house, but naturally you would have informed me had they been stolen. There are so many rumors!! However, I plan the move for Wednesday. As you know I'm not so very keen on Louis XIV and I don't need it anyway really. I don't use it, do I? We are planning to collect it next week Wednesday August 27. It is such a long time since we met. We are planning to pay you a visit, Hubert, to discuss your future plans, as we are selling the villa to Lauro as it appears the land on which it is built belongs to Lauro's beautiful new bride. Isn't it fortunate that Lauro has been our friend all these years? Would you believe it, but he even cut short his honeymoon to come and discuss my plans with me! What good fortune that the land does not belong to a stranger! In the meantime of course I am taking action against Mr de Lafoucauld who arranged for the purchase of my properties at Nemi as it seems he was most untrustworthy. That is not his real name, of course, but Berto has talked to the police, they have found him in Milan and certainly he will go to prison. Berto has said he no longer cares if his name gets into the papers in connection with a criminal action as we are the innocent party, always have been and always will be.

I hope you can find some other spot in Nemi to continue your plans for your new religion. It sounds very exciting and I would have loved to have been there, too, but I was in Switzerland and besides, Berto is so conventional, he would hate it if I got mixed up with drugs, orgies, etc. etc. Isn't it good that Lauro is willing to make a little arrangement with me for the house, as it is really an illegal house although I didn't know it at the time, of course. I plan to move in as soon as possible. Berto, of course, was angry about the orgy but he would naturally prefer you to go quietly. I mean, we don't want to complain to the authorities as that would be unpleasant. It has been good of you to keep my pictures and my furniture in good condition. I have tried to get in touch with Massimo de Vita to tell him personally what my plans are, but his office telephone number doesn't answer. A few weeks ago I read in the papers that the Lake of Nemi is 'biologically dead' which means it is polluted, but they are building a new sewage system for that clinic, so it doesn't all go into the lake. I am sure your ancestors would turn in their graves and I do feel for you, after those beautiful ships of antiquity sailed so proudly on its tranquil surface. Of course, Nemi is beautiful and Mary will be sorry to leave, but their house is also illegal and I don't know if they can make arrangements with the owners of the land, and in any case Michael says we shouldn't have to pay twice for a house. It is a worry for the Bernardinis also, especially as his wedding to Nancy is to take place soon. She is a very fine young woman and will be a very good housekeeper for him I am quite sure.

If you see Avvocato Massimo de Vita please tell him he has got it all wrong about my Gauguin. I really feel that lawyers these days are very slipshod in their work. Hardly any of them care about their clients any more. I plan to go to another lawyer.

Don't forget Wednesday, 27, the van will be coming, naturally with an armed escort as one can't be too careful these days.

Arrivederci and all my love,

Maggie.

P.S. It is terrible the times we are living in. I just read in the *Herald Tribune* about a dear friend of mine, a financier from the Argentine, Coco de Renault, being kidnaped. Apparently they are asking a fantastic ransom and the poor wife and daughter in Switzerland are absolutely frantic. I put through a call to them immediately but they didn't want to talk so as to keep the line free for the kidnapers to negotiate. The family say they haven't seen Coco for months and they don't know where he is, which is terrible, but the newspapers say he has to send them a power of attorney to release all his money for the kidnapers, and it's possible the banks will not accept his word in which case he could be killed. It is terrible to read about these events and even more frightening when it is someone you know and it reaches your own door. Personally, I think the wife has already got all his money tucked away somewhere in Switzerland, though the talk of powers of attorney is her way of trying to drive a bargain. They usually put their money in the wife's name or in a numbered account so I hope my friend will be released unharmed, but how dreadful to pay it all to criminals!

Hubert read the letter slowly to Pauline Thin who had returned the day after Hubert's three former secretaries had left.

Since the furniture had been taken away there had been quarrels every day amongst them all; the boys simply didn't have the stamina to sit it out for a month all sleeping on camp-beds and eating in the kitchen. A month was all Hubert had asked of them, just for the sake of appearances.

Maggie's furniture and her pictures had already been sold in London. Even those pictures which had been copies, and the set of Louis XIV furniture which had been reconstructed, with an original leg here, an arm there, had fetched quite a fat sum, while those original paintings and articles of furniture which remained had fetched a fortune. After Massimo's half-share had been deducted there still remained a fortune for Hubert, that fortune which he had felt all along that Maggie should have settled on him. It was now only a matter of keeping up an appearance of poverty for a month or maybe a little longer, so there should be no question that he had made off with Maggie's property. Massimo had left for some unknown destination; he had said California, which meant, certainly, elsewhere; evidently he was used to departing speedily for elsewhere from time to time. Hubert's half-share of the sale was safely in that nursery-garden of planted money, Switzerland.

'Miss Thin,' said Hubert when Pauline arrived at the house the day after the departure of his three discontented friends, 'if you have come to collect your remaining goods and chattels you have come in vain. The bailiffs have been. They have taken everything, including your knickers. All they have left me are the bare necessities and I, descendant of the gods, am a pauper. What is more, Miss Thin, you have much to account for.'

Pauline said, 'So have you. Five months' pay for a start.'

'Don't be vulgar,' he said. All the same, he opened the kitchen cupboard and took a bundle of notes out of a tin. He counted out her pay. 'Women,' he said, 'are incredibly materialistic.'

She sat down on a kitchen chair and checked the money. 'Your boy-friends have gone,' she said. 'I dare say they left for idealistic, not materialistic, reasons. That's why they left you all alone here, without any comfortable furniture. Where did you get this money from, Hubert?'

'It's no business of yours and you're no longer my secretary. You wrecked my Fellowship and you wrecked my reputation. I have had an anonymous letter from someone in the village comparing me to some false Catholic prelate who set himself up at Nemi with his gang of acolytes two years ago in a villa, with all his holy pictures and his crucifixes and his apostolic papers in order. He claimed to have a commission from the Holy See to purchase vast stocks of merchandise, and when the police finally surrounded the villa he committed suicide. I have all the details here. The author of the letter enclosed the press cutting.'

He had passed it over to Pauline. 'See what the bloody fool killed himself with,' he said, 'a glass of *vino al tropicida*! It sounds like some speciality in a restaurant, but it's rat-poison in wine. A very low-class suicide, and I wouldn't care to know the author of this anonymous letter who suggests I do the same.'

'The hand-writing's pretty awful,' said Pauline.

'So is the spelling. Some village woman. What does it matter?'

'Oh, Hubert! You would never think of suicide, would you?' Pauline said. 'I don't want this money, really. Take it back. Here it is.'

'Suicide is not remotely in my mind,' Hubert said. 'But I'll put my money back in the tin for safe-keeping. I hope you've learnt your lesson, Miss Thin.'

'I'll go shopping and I'll cook for you,' Pauline said.

'I had another letter,' Hubert had said, and he then had proceeded to read aloud to her Maggie's letter.

'That woman is dangerous,' Pauline said. 'Where's her furniture at the moment?'

'How do I know? Her lawyer took it away.'

'And your manuscripts, Hubert, where are your documents?'

'In Rome,' Hubert said. 'Transferred to Rome, as was the cult of Diana which, for political and very democratic reasons, spread to Rome in the fourth century B.C.'

'I saw Father Cuthbert in Rome,' Pauline said.

'I dare say you spoke about me. What else would you have to talk about, my dear?'

'Well, Hubert, I think he's got a good idea that you should take up the Charismatic Movement in the Church and run the prayer meetings. You do the murmuring rite so well and Cuthbert said it wouldn't be in conflict with Diana as the preserver of nature, not at all.'

'It is a long time,' Hubert said, 'since Homer sang the wonders of Artemis who came to be Diana. He called her the Lady of Wildlife. There's much to be said for charisma and wildlife.'

'They're the new idea,' Pauline said, meekly. 'You have to make a living somehow, Hubert. You can't stay here with these kitchen chairs.'

'One way and another, Miss Thin,' Hubert said, 'I haven't done so badly.'

'We leave tonight at midnight,' Hubert informed Pauline. It was Tuesday, 26 August, thirteen days after the Feast of Diana and one day before the date fixed by Maggie for the removal of her furniture which wasn't there. That morning, when Pauline returned from her trip to the village to buy provisions, he had taken the newspapers out of her hand, as usual, waiting for her to serve the coffee. 'We leave at midnight,' he said.

Over coffee he handed her a newspaper, folded back to reveal a picture of a decapitated statue. 'This is a sign,' said Hubert. Two statues flanking a fountain in Palermo had been mutilated by vandals; the newspaper had printed the one which had suffered most. The headline read, 'Diana Decapitated', and the picture showed a sturdy and headless nude Diana with her hound and her stag. 'It's a definite sign,' Hubert said, 'for us, don't you think so, Miss Thin?'

'One good thing,' said Hubert, 'about having nothing left to protect is that I can go for a walk.'

He left before sunset, while Pauline set about putting their few household possessions in the back of the station-wagon ready for their transfer to Rome. Bobby Lester, her previous employer so long ago, and a friend of Father Cuthbert, had lent them his flat overlooking the Piazza del Popolo. She placed the tin box with Hubert's money on the kitchen table to keep an eye on it and sat down beside it dutifully and happily doing nothing but reading small paragraphs in the newspaper and listening to the transistor radio. She wore a black cotton blouse and a red skirt that made her hips seem wider than ever; they spilt over the kitchen chair in a proprietary way, and she knew she was indispensable to Hubert's future.

Hubert, meantime, had decided to take his last look at beautiful Nemi, where from every point appeared a different view, every view a picture postcard except that it was real. Down the old Roman road he went, past the old town-council building and into the village. All during July and August Nemi had been crowded with holidaymakers; even a few foreign tourists and some of the pilgrim crowds of Holy Year, lately coveted by Hubert, had brimmed over from near-by Castelgandolfo where the Pope held court in his summer residence. But now, as the road grew darker, there were few newcomers to be seen; most of them had returned to the lodgings which had been provided with great efficiency by the neighbouring convents. After dark, a few local people grouped around the bars and various courting couples leaned over the wall beside the castle, looking at the moon.

Outside the church a mosaic plaque had been put up to commemorate the Pope's visit to Nemi in 1969. Hubert paused on his way to look at it and saw by the road lamp how it bore on the left the crest of Nemi, blue, white, yellow, rich red and gold, surrounded by the motto *Diane Nemus* : the Woods of Diana; on the right was a gleaming emblem of a local Christian order of monks, and above them the Montini papal coat of arms, that of Paul VI, crossed by the gold and silver keys of St Peter. Hubert's walks in Nemi had been few. 'Nemi is mine,' he murmured, 'but I must move on to Rome.' In fact, he felt carefree and rather glad to be leaving, seeing that he was now in funds and how his future prospects, in collaboration with the Jesuits, seemed full of hope and drama, the two things Hubert valued most in life, all things being equal on the material side.

Down he went to the garden walk on the steep cliffs by the lake, across the bridge, towards Diana's temple. The moon was almost three-quarters full and on the wane. 'Always cut wood when the moon is on the wane,' an old countryman had told him during his first years at Nemi when he had gone out to gather firewood. He smiled at the moon, with no one to see him, and felt very deeply that he was descended from Diana the moon goddess.

The spot where Diana's temple had been located was not accessible to the public, and even the local people never went to the thickly overgrown alcoves that remained of her cult. But Hubert knew the way to that area which had been named, in more historic times, the Devil's Grottoes. Not only were the relics of antiquity to be found there, but also numerous caves leading deep into the heart of the cliff under the castle, where vagrants, in the days of lesser prosperity, could take refuge. These caves were now abandoned and overgrown, some of them totally concealed by dense greenery. He plodded through the thick undergrowth, over uneven ground, stopping to hack off a stout branch to help him to beat his path. 'Always cut wood when the moon is on the wane.' The branch broke easily from the low tree.

Suddenly Hubert saw a shape approaching, an old woman, it seemed, probably a gipsy, picking her way towards him. She lit her steps with the aid of a flashlamp. Behind her, but much further into the dark thickness of the wooded cliff, he thought he heard an exchange of voices, but then, stopping still, he heard nothing. The crone, dressed drably with a scarf round her head, came closer and was about to pass him with the usual 'Buona sera' of the countryside. 'Maggie!' said Hubert. She stopped and shone the torch on him, and started to laugh.

They sat together looking at the lake and the bashed-in circle of the moon for only a little space. Maggie, of course, had taken up almost from where she had left off, and, without any explanation for her appearance or her presence in that deserted spot, said first that she was fine thank you, how was he? 'Fine,' said Hubert.

So they found a place to sit and Maggie said, 'You would never believe it, Hubert, but my daughter-in-law, Mary, has fallen desperately in love with Berto and he's awfully embarrassed because he loves me exclusively, as you can imagine. He's trying to pass her off to a journalist friend of his, rather elderly, as he feels that Mary really wants an older man, a sort of father figure.

It's rather pathetic, but it's all Michael's fault; although he's my own son I know he's neglected Mary and is altogether inadequate, between you and me.'

'It will sort itself out,' Hubert said. 'You look wonderful, Maggie, in spite of all these clothes and things.'

'Hubert, you're always so charming! My clothes are a symbol of my new poverty, of course. And then, dressed like this, one hopes to avoid being kidnapped. It's such a danger, these days. One is in peril.'

'Oh, I know. You told me in your letter about poor Coco de Renault. Any news of him?'

'Well, I wouldn't say *poor* Coco. But maybe he's going to be poor after he pays the ransom. What about you, Hubert? Are you prospering?'

'Mildly,' said Hubert.

'Of course,' said Maggie, 'I happen to know that you've sold all my furniture and pictures. My letter was just to satisfy Berto, and be above-board, you know. Where is Massimo de Vita?'

'Honestly I don't know, Maggie. There isn't a thing you can do about it.'

'I know,' she said, cheerfully.

'I'm sorry to hear that Renault made off with all your fortune,' Hubert said.

'I'm getting it back. In fact it has already been arranged,' Maggie said. 'Less thirty per cent.'

'That would be the kidnappers' share,' Hubert said.

'That's right,' said Maggie.

'Where have they got him?' Hubert said. 'The papers seem to have dropped the story, so I suppose he isn't in Italy.'

'Well, some say California and some say Brazil,' Maggie said. 'But in fact he's right here in a cave in this cliff, well guarded. I've just been to visit. Hubert, I simply had to go and gloat.'

'I can well understand that,' said Hubert. 'Is he to be released soon?'

'Some time tonight or early tomorrow morning. The wife delayed a lot and that made Coco very angry. But in the end she had to make over everything to me in Switzerland, all of it. I wouldn't settle for less.'

'Can he be trusted not to report you?' Hubert said.

'Well, naturally, he couldn't índict me. He's too indictable himself. There are times when one can trust a crook.'

'There's something in that,' Hubert said.

She said good night very sweetly and, lifting her dingy skirts, picked her way along the leafy path, hardly needing her flashlamp, so bright was the moon, three-quarters full, illuminating the lush lakeside and, in the fields beyond, the kindly fruits of the earth.

More about Penguins and Pelicans